A Wicked Pack of Cards

ROSEMARY HARRIS

A Wicked Pack of Cards

Walker and Company • New York

Copyright © 1969 by ROSEMARY HARRIS

All rights reserved. No part of this book may be reproduced or transmitted in any form or by any means, electronic or mechanical, including photocopying, recording, or by any information storage and retrieval system, without permission in writing from the Publisher.

All the characters and events portrayed in this story are fictitious.

First published in the United States of America in 1970 by the Walker Publishing Company, Inc.

Published simultaneously in Canada by The Ryerson Press, Toronto.

Library of Congress Catalog Card Number: 72-108617

Printed in the United States of America from type set in the United Kingdom.

Chapter One

That was the foggiest year I can remember. A year when from April onwards the spring mists came rolling in continually from the sea to wrap the town in their damp, all-penetrating embrace. Later on, in the summer, there must have been good days, wet days or colder ones I suppose, but whenever I think back it's the foggy ones I remember: the veiled horizon, and the foghorns mooing out at sea.

When the fog withdrew a little I was always conscious of it waiting to come back again, like some strayed animal trying to enforce its presence. It lay out on the evening tide simulating a long gold sandbar, banked itself purple towards nightfall, rolled itself smotheringly round the fishing boats as they left for the fishing grounds at dawn. It had a presence, that fog, one impossible to ignore. And I remember it lurked in some dun-coloured disguise or other near the distant rocks at low tide, on that morning when I emerged from my small bow-fronted house with the letter in my hand.

They were all three waiting on the esplanade. I could see them there down the steep stretch of Mariota Street which separated us; but I walked slowly, reluctantly, all too conscious of how unwelcome was the news I had to bring.

Nicola was dressed in faded jeans topped by a fisherman jersey. As I approached she was doing hand turns over the rail, while her dark plaits flailed the air. Neither of the other Hallifords made a move to copy her. Stewart's seventeen-year-old frame was unadapted to such manoeuvres. Even in the sea he tended to look like a floundering stick insect, or as if some medical student had assembled him roughly from a bag of old bones. He wore glasses, had a face that resembled the young Aldous Huxley's, was unusually good at mathematics, and could suddenly surprise everyone by jumping higher or running faster than anyone else.

Culbertson just stood there dreamily staring out to sea. She had an ice cream cornet in each hand and she licked first one, then the other, with the thoroughness that characterized her. She was a pale fawn-coloured child from top to toe. Everything about her was rounded, fawn, and firm. She had a round head, with straight fawnish hair clipped short all over like a boy's, the same colour as her lightly browned face. Her limbs were firm and rounded, so was her torso. She was browned evenly like a biscuit that has been in the oven just the right length of time. Because of her compact solidity she looked on the verge of being stolid, but when she danced it was easy to remember *The Winter's Tale*: "When you do dance I wish you a wave of the sea; that you might ever do nothing but that . . .".

The only colour about Culbertson was her eyes, large dark seal's eyes which held a formidable if placid stare. She appeared a Donatello child, biddable too, but I dreaded ever coming up against her will. It was like granite, or a stone pier set in the sea. Her true name was Caroline, but since her parents had taken her in a carrycot to bridge parties she had been known as Culbertson. She seemed acclimatized to it, and so were the rest of us, but now and then she would say: "It won't do later, at the Garden." And Stewart would reply with his usual chant of: "Headline—Culbertson Slays them in Giselle: Assoluta Relinquishes Crown", to which she would reply quite seriously: "You see? It wouldn't do." We all agreed. I knew she would end at Covent Garden, in the centre of the stage. There was not only her amazing talent, there was her character as well. She was nine and a half years old, had been training for two of them, and this morning wore nothing but a beige kilt which reached from below her rounded navel to the top of her plump thighs.

Nicola completed a circle on the rail and came upright to face me, just as Stewart said: "Here's Jane. Hi-ya, Auntie."

Neither of the others greeted me. Culbertson smiled lovingly and continued to lick. Nicola's eyes were fierce on the letter in my hand, with its foreign stamp.

"Well—is she coming?"

"Yes."

"Oh hell—ruddy, ruddy damnation hell," said Nicola despairingly. And added her favourite sick comedian's sickest word, while staring defiantly into my eyes.

Not so were the twenty-five-year-old aunts of Victoria's age addressed. I tried to look quelling but failed, while Stewart gazed at me with his slow bony smile.

"There are no words Culbertson doesn't know. She won't use them, anyway."

"That's not the point, Stewart, it's——" I broke off. "Nicola, why do you mind Gabriella coming so much?" But I knew. It was complicated, being fourteen in that household.

"The summer holidays will be ruined, that's all. The sulkings there'll be—you wait and see. Cooked up rows, and ears to the keyholes, and floods of tears every time Daddy puts himself out to be pleasant to her. Can't Susie see that the way she goes on is enough to drive him into other women's beds? Not that anyone with a grain of sense would expect him to bed down with what's practically his own stepchild."

"*Nicola.*" I felt my aunt's whalebone stays creak where my brief bather actually was.

"Pas devant Culbertson," said Culbertson equably with her good accent, as she continued to lick.

"—and in any case, can't you try not to dislike your stepmother so much? It only makes things worse, it——"

"Nicola doesn't dislike Susie." Stewart lounged against the rail, his bones outlined sharp against the sky. "You can't dislike someone who doesn't exist."

"That's even more unkind."

"Darling Jane, calm yourself. When you spring hotly to Susie's defence we all notice the hollowness. You're being a very heavy relative this morning, aren't you? Protecting Culbertson from the facts of life, and all. You needn't bother, she's precocious, aren't you, Culbertson?" They both stared at her with some pride, and raising her sticky mouth for one second from the cones she responded briefly, "Yes."

"So I should just marry old Roger straight away, if I were

you," advised Stewart, "since you're starting to go Jane Austen on us. It's a very bad sign."

"You're an impertinent gang," I said helplessly; and crumpled Gabriella's letter into a ball, and tossed it towards the nearest litter bin. "I can't imagine why I put up with you at all."

"Because you love us, and we love you; but madly." Nicola put her arm round my waist and urged me nearer the beach steps. "Come on, Janey. Let's go bathe—that fog's lurking out there waiting to roll up again, the beast."

"When's she coming?" Stewart was following us down.

"Gabriella? In two days."

At these words one of Culbertson's ice cream cones came hurtling high over my head, rocket-direct, and landed on a middle-aged woman's sun hat. What happened then seemed a poor omen for Gabriella's visit: as bad as the perpetual bank of fog, which was beginning to move in softly across the sea.

I parted from my Hallifords at half-past twelve. We had walked up steep Mariota Street together, and turned right into the terrace where we all lived. Some eight doors up, on the left, facing south, was my small double-bowfronted house. The children were bound for my brother's house, at the far end. A large lime, unusual in this town, grew out of the pavement in front of it, and gave it the obvious name of The Lime Tree House. Mine was simply Number 16.

Now I stood in front of it and watched them go, Culbertson trailing behind her two elders and lost in some private dream which certainly included the Garden, and probably the Firebird. My hair, wet from sea and incoming fog, curled damply against my neck. I shook my head irritably, and——

"Zo charming a family," hissed a voice in my ear.

I jumped, and turned. Madame Sosostris stood there, snuffling with pleasure at having caused surprise. On her arm was a basket packed with *pâtisserie* from the nearby bakery.

"Yes—they are nice children."

"Nice children!" Madame's wooden little face gave a derisive grin. "Very English. Very noncommittal, Jane."

I was still feeling so Austen that I almost told her my name was Miss Halliford. How much better Emma could have dealt with a Madame Sosostris than I. Emma, who did not scruple to tell her dearest friend Harriet that a Miss Woodhouse could not visit her if she fell so low as to become a Mrs. Martin. I would have liked a few lessons from Emma this morning.

"You must have zome nice nice children of your own," Madame crowed, before I could think of anything to say. "And you had better hurry, too. Life—it go poof! And vile you vait—gone! Vy you not marry that sveet dear man of yours and have done vith it? Time vill not go backvard for either of you. It is utmost stupidity to vait, or you vill lose him. I tell you this because you are not vise, and my cards they vould tell you just the same." She fixed me with an unforgivable crocodile eye in which I recognized a Tarot stare.

To my humiliation no searing reply would come. All I could think of to say, as though excusing myself for not marrying at once to suit her convenience, was: "I—I'm soon off to the States. My books have been doing so well out there that my publishers have suggested one with an American historical background."

"A book. The vorld is full of books. Too full. You marry, dear."

"It's far too full of people as well," I said angrily, "and I don't know that I particularly want to increase them."

"This is cowardice. Listen, books for ven you are fifty-five, sixty, seventy, no? But earlier—love and common sense; yes, love." She gave me a lewd Middle-European poke in the stomach, and nipped smartly across the road, leaving me in full fume and somehow sure that Emma was watching me from a cloud with disapprobation. Everyone I knew was too much for me this morning, and I retreated sullenly into Number 16. Immediately the telephone in my sitting room began to ring.

"Hello?"

"I couldn't get you earlier, Jane darling, were you on the beach? Look, I'd like to come over and lunch, you idle woman—rather taken it for granted, I'm afraid. My secretary's putting any patients through to you, that all right?"

I drew a deep breath. Here was a third chance to be firm.

"No, Roger, it's not all right. I've only just come off the beach, you were right there, anyway. The house isn't done, and nor am I, and there's no lunch. You tell your Pamela to catch those patients redhanded before they can block my telephone."

"Janey, what's the matter, you sound thoroughly upset? Got a touch of the sun? Or the fog? I'm bringing lunch, so you needn't fuss—mortadello, and French bread, and fruit. See you in ten minutes. If old Mrs. Hamly rings up and starts about her gall bladder just deal out some bland reassurance and say I'll get round to her after six. Be seeing you, my love." Before I could get in a single word of firmness he had rung off.

I swore sicker words than the sickest comedian. Then I dialled Roger's number but he was not, cannily, answering. No doubt his Pamela, secure in knowledge that the patients had been passed over to me, was on her way out to lunch. In no sweet frame of mind I walked upstairs to rid myself of sand and sea and fog. The house looked disgraceful, undusted and unkempt. There were crumbs in the dining room, glasses in the sitting room, mouse droppings in the hall, and my bed was still unmade. But if people had to behave like this with me, I thought, on a long wave of mutiny, they could definitely put up with the result. But definitely, as Nicola would have said.

Chapter Two

As I came downstairs again Roger was just getting out of his car. I glanced round me at the household chaos, and opened the front door. On the opposite side of the road, several doors towards Mariota, Madame Sosostris was peering out at us with approbation. It made my greeting of Roger rather chill.

"Hello there."

"Hello, darling. Could you come and take the wine? I bought a bottle on the way because you sounded as though you really need it. Feeling more gruntled?"

"Not very."

"How unlike you. I'll have to take a look at your gall bladder. This mortadello smells high, what do you think? Oh damnation——" For behind us the telephone had begun to ring. Roger took my arm and propelled me gently in its direction. "The doctor is having a well-earned lunch. Tell them, bicarbonate. If it's a fit, keep lying down. Death, I'll be round to sign the certificate later."

"I'm glad you're not my doctor. Hello?"

"Oh Jane, is that you?" There was a note of tearful self-commiseration in Susie's voice. "I rang up because the children say you've heard from Gabriella, and she's coming. Is it true?"

"Yes, of course."

"Well, I only wondered. They do like teasing, and they aren't always truthful, you know. I can't think why she didn't write to me. It's a bit casual, isn't it?"

"Because Erik asked me to write to her, Susie," I managed firmness for the first time that morning, "since you wouldn't."

"Yes, well, I must say I think it's unnecessary to have a twenty-two-year-old girl about the house. The children don't need her, they're so self-sufficient and they have so many friends already, and——"

"It's because Erik thinks Ingrid would have wanted it." Perhaps this was tactless, but like everyone else I had loved the Swedish Ingrid—my first sister-in-law and the children's mother—dearly.

"But it's not even as though she were Ingrid's child, I keep telling him!" Susie's voice rose on a wail. "It's ridiculous that because Ingrid had that first marriage to her middle-aged Frenchman who went and died that we should have to put up with *his* child, till kingdom come! Why—she's not even Erik's stepchild—she's, she's nothing."

"No, I don't think she does come under the forbidden degrees." I knew this was really the trouble; and Gabriella, in her own way, was almost as beautiful as Ingrid. I opened my mouth to say so, and then shut it again. For if I did say so there would be a storm of jealousy about Ingrid, and more trouble for the children. "She's coming in two days, Susie. I must go now—sorry, but I've got someone to lunch."

"Oh——" there was a quickening of interest in Susie's voice, "the children didn't say—It's Roger, I suppose? I can't think why you don't marry him, Jane, and have done with it, and——"

"And get out of all our lives," I finished mentally for her, as I said good-bye and put down the receiver.

"That's what I came round to talk about," said Roger, who had been listening.

"Susie—or Gabriella?"

"Marriage."

"Oh Roger, please not today. It's—it's so foggy."

"After lunch, not before." His mouth shut in a grim line. Usually Roger seemed so deceptively mild and benign. He had a wide mouth, the square shortish nose that denotes courage and a pugnacious temper, thick black eyebrows and, at the age of thirty-seven, rapidly greying hair. I had been caught originally by his charm—a quality I really mistrust—combined with a certain pathos which he often used mercilessly on his patients, particularly when he wanted to rid himself of the more hypochondriacal ones. And beneath all this was concealed a will second only to Culbertson's. I have seen them clash head on, and if ever the irresistible force met the immovable object——

One look at the line of his mouth, and I went hastily into the dining room to lay the table for two.

The mortadello was high. In the end we made do with cheese, fruit and wine. I talked non-stop, determined to put off the moment of confrontation. Roger leaned back in his chair and sipped at the burgundy and sardonically watched me. He was waiting until I had talked myself to a halt; but this morning, I told myself, straightening my spine and reaching for the burgundy bottle, I had plenty to keep us going. "To crown everything, Madame Sosostris caught up with me. She's always lying in wait, since she came to live in the terrace. I can't think why—it's not as though I ever go near her and those cards. If only the Hamiltons had never sold her their house. You wouldn't think she'd have had enough money to buy."

"I don't suppose she declares her sessions for tax."

"She told me once that they insist she keeps an appointment book."

"Then she certainly keeps two. One she shows them, and one she doesn't."

"You're probably right."

Silence. Roger shifted his weight on to his elbows and leant towards me.

I said feverishly: "No—she horrifies me. I can't explain. That wooden little face, like a carved Indian mask with that alive little nose in the middle of it, wiggling about for news. I had a dream one night about that nose, did I tell you? It grew immensely long, and crossed the road, and peered in at my window. It was looking for something. Blindly. I woke up shaking all over."

"Very old-fashioned of you, Janey. Pure Freud."

"You can laugh—I tell you, it was a horrible dream. Sinister. And her stories are sinister, too, all that about being a refugee, and the DP camps she was in, from the East to Northern France, and the things she's seen. I feel she enjoyed seeing them," I said horridly, "if she ever really did. 'There is nothing you can tell me, that I cannot tell you vorse,' that's what she always says to anyone; and then out she trots another horror."

"Aren't you taking it a bit seriously? I suppose she wants to make herself important, the way we all of us do, and that's her method. She can't have many others left."

"She's got her inquisitiveness to keep her warm. And her Tarot too. She seems to have fascinated everyone in the street with it. You see them slip into her house sideways, hoping no one has seen them. She won't be happy till she's got me in there, and seen the Hanged Man and the Struck Tower, or whatever it is. But I'm not going."

I glared at Roger as though he were trying to make me. He merely grinned, and moved the burgundy bottle out of reach.

"You aren't eating enough food for all you're drinking," he explained kindly.

"Well, give me a pear then—— And I don't like Culbertson going over there so much. Susie's such a fool, you'd think she might keep an eye out occasionally, whether she cares or not."

"Culbertson?" Roger frowned. "I've not seen her there. Why, does Madame S. ask her?"

"Oh no." I looked at the table, and muttered: "Well—I don't know, but——"

"Is Culbertson spying again?" Roger gave an exasperated sigh. "Something will have to be done about her, Janey. I'll speak to Erik. You and Susie are too soft about it."

"Is that so? Well, you have a try. It's like dealing with a young mule. In fact I thought you had had a try, and the result was——"

"Deadlock," he admitted, leaning back in his chair. "But honourable deadlock is better than retreat. She's more like a Humboldt's woolly monkey than a mule, that child."

"She's fair about her findings, anyway. She doesn't tell tales. She just has to know. She has a passion to know."

"That is a Humboldt's woolly monkey."

I laughed, and agreed.

Once, when we had all been sitting round my brother's dining table, Stewart had asked: "Cully, if you break both your legs, both, and can never be a dancer, what will you be instead?" And without a second's hesitation she had replied: "Oh, I'm going to be the first woman head of Scotland Yard."

"Why?"

She had just looked at him with her round dark eyes, and slowly shaken her head. Yet we all understood. I don't know if it was the result of Susie's upbringing—say, rather, Susie's attempt at upbringing—but Culbertson had to know. And it was soon after this that I noticed she had methodically put herself in training for her second choice. When Culbertson wasn't at her classes, or working at the *barre*, she was Watching. I often felt like a bird being televised on its nest. It was impossible to read a letter in front of her, for she had trained herself to read almost any fist backwards at a distance of two yards. Looking up from some private missive you would find those huge eyes concentratedly boring a hole in the paper. She got hold of all our letters somehow, even if she had to piece them together from the dustbin. Her ears were permanently and openly at keyholes. If you held a private conversation with anyone it was essential to frisk the room for Culbertson first. She could be found flattened under sofas, laid out in the bottom drawer of a chest, wrapped in a coat in a cupboard, behind the kitchen stove.

No amount of retribution made any difference. My brother Erik once outraged all our consciences and modern psychiatry by an old-fashioned beating; but even while he was telling me of it with tears in his eyes, Culbertson was discovered curled up behind Stewart's cello. She was incorrigible. The only thing to be said in her favour was that she never used her private knowledge for gain, blackmail, or revenge. She simply enjoyed it, like a stamp collector.

I could never forget what must have been the penny black of her collection. It was one evening when Roger and I had agreed to dine at my brother's, since everyone else but Culbertson was out. At half-past nine we saw our charge to bed and then after a tour of the garden eventually settled to intimate conversation on the drawing room sofa. I was lying happily extended when I grew suddenly aware, staring over Roger's shoulder, of something not quite right.

"Roger—what's wrong with the grandfather clock? It's stopped."

He had given an exclamation of annoyance. "I know women are supposed always to think of several things at once——"

But I had struggled out of his arms, and was standing before the clock. It breathed, instead of ticking. A large velvet eye gazed back at me piercingly through the glass panel where the pendulum should have been visible swinging to and fro. I pulled open the little door.

"Culbertson, come out at once."

She looked at me without batting an eyelid. She had nothing on, and her brown body blended very well with the light wood of the clock's interior. If I had not been sensitized to her ways we would never have discovered her. Behind me on the sofa Roger had given snorts of mingled fury and amusement.

"It's been disappointing," said Culbertson, fixing me with her severe reproachful eye, "and not at all like voles."

"*Now* Jane——"

I came back to the present. Roger was fixing me with a reproachful eye too. He put his hand over mine. "Are you going to marry me, or not?"

I sat there, looking at our joined hands. I loved Roger, and yet I didn't want to decide anything until after America.

"Well? If it takes so much thinking about by this time, I take it the chances aren't very good. I don't think we can go on this way."

I gave him a quick glance. He wore a look I had seen before. "I don't see why not," I said feebly, "for a bit, anyway."

"Well, I do. I'm old-fashioned. I don't like us hanging on like this. Nor will the town, quite soon; I'll end by having to give up my practice here. There's nothing to stop us marrying, is there, except America? And marriage would get you out of Susie's hair. You're far too emotionally bound up with those children. In a way, I'm not sure it's fair to her, she's hopeless, but she might do better without you: considerably better, I think."

"Roger," I said rapidly, "I do love you, really. But think a little, darling. I'm fairly well known already. Oh—I've had some luck before, but now I've a chance of being better known.

Don't you see what it could mean to us? Look, if we marry now, that's that, so far as my work's concerned. No, don't interrupt—it's perfectly true. I'll be far too busy as your wife to keep up with it. I couldn't go off on these leisurely trips which after all are important to it—even the English ones. And if I'm earning too we can have a different way of life, we——"

"I haven't the slightest desire for a different way of life," said Roger obstinately, and withdrew his hand.

"Well, I have!" My temper flared. "One can be romantic as one likes, but you need a lot of cash these days not to spend all your time in the kitchen sink or changing nappies——"

"So you'd sooner spend it signing copies in a drugstore."

He spoke curtly.

"Roger darling, there's no need to choose. In a year or two we could have it both."

"You could, Janey. You could have it both—with someone else; not me."

We were staring with hostility at each other, on the verge of quarrelling. Then Roger said: "Or—am I just being slightly foolish, and is it Cosway?"

"It's not Cosway. I'm fond of Cosway, but—— Oh, why can't you understand?" I said bitterly.

"I do understand, that's just the trouble. It's you who don't understand, Janey, because you're deliberately blinkering yourself. Life doesn't have these built-in guarantees you want. It can end any time, as it ended for a girl I saw today in hospital after an accident. And if you love somebody, you put them before the sort of unreality you're craving for, that's all. And that's what I'm asking you to do."

I stared into his eyes. He had gone rather pale. "No," I said wretchedly. "I'm sorry, Roger. It's—no. I couldn't. Not yet."

"I shan't ask you again."

"That's up to you."

There was an awkward silence. Then Roger stood up and began clumsily putting the things together.

"Don't bother about those. Please. I'll do them later." My mouth was dry. "I've a lot to do around the house."

"Then I'd better get on. There are one or two patients up

this end; another reason for lunching with you." He gave a faint unamused smile. "Your unpopular Madame S. amongst them."

"I didn't know you were her doctor. That's something entirely new, isn't it?" I tried to keep the conversation going.

"Newish." He was not to be drawn. He stood and looked at me. I felt compunction, and half a desire to take back my words. He came over to me, put his arms round me, and kissed the side of my head. "Good-bye, Janey."

"Aren't we going to see each other again?" I had hardly expected to feel so stunned. "Why—in this place—we're bound to meet."

"Of course; constantly. That was just symbolic. Now I'd better hurry." There was a droop to his shoulders which had not been there before.

"Roger," I said hastily, "I'm not entirely sure——"

The telephone began its intrusive ring. Had he even heard me? He went through to the sitting room, and held a conversation with one of his patients. After it finished he looked at his watch and said: "Running latish. I won't say it's been nice. It hasn't—very."

"I'm sorry. I'm really sorry, perhaps we could just——"

"No, Janey, we couldn't. Good-bye." He looked at me soberly. "If you marry Cosway——" he gave a very faint smile, "I'll find a way of murdering him; by injection, perhaps——"

"Don't say things like that. And I shan't marry Cosway."

"Don't tell me he hasn't asked you?"

"Several times, but——"

"Oh, I see—— Another of us. Poor old Cosway. Not so desirable as the call of America, either."

"Roger, don't. You're taking this quite wrong, you——"

Whatever way he was taking it, he had gone.

Chapter Three

It had been an effort to prevent myself from following Roger, and calling him back. We had had this sort of argument often enough before; never with such bitter finality. As I cleaned up the house I was trying to fool myself it wasn't final, and I was upstairs by the time my mind had calmed enough to let me be conscious of outer things: then I found myself staring at my own books on the shelf beside my bed. I touched one of them lovingly. I was not particularly proud of them, yet they had done so much for me. History had been my best subject at school; later, as a student, I had taken a course in archaeology—and both interests had paid off handsomely when I began writing historical novels to help pay my household bills.

It had all started by chance years before, one dreadful summer when Stewart and Nicola had mumps and were constantly, querulously demanding entertainment. For their benefit I had written a long, intensely high-coloured effort set in seventeenth century Sussex at the time of the Civil War. At Nicola's instigation I had typed it out and sent it to a publisher. To my surprise it had not only been selling ever since but had settled my career as well. I did a book a year, and was half-way through one with a Cornish setting now. Before I went to America—I ought to leave in November—it would be necessary to visit Cornwall again and finish my researches first hand. I had already rented, blind, a small house on Bodmin for three weeks. It was in the heart of country where I could enjoy myself poking and prodding at such intriguing antiquities as the Hurlers, those fascinating stone circles on the moor itself—as well as acquiring some background of local history.

Now I was depressed at the prospect, since my row—argument—with Roger. Surely he would come round again, he always had before. . . . But within was a doubt; a cold suspicion that I was behaving none too well.

Outside the window that interminable fog had turned the sunshine to a peculiar apricot glow. I hardly saw it. I was thinking that one day I might take a land rover and go to Ur of the Chaldees, or board a small cheap Spanish boat for South America, and climb to Macchu Picchu the Inca city; or see Cuzco, and the silver mines of Potosí. Unless I was washing the behinds of Roger's babies, and their nappies, in a Seaminster Regis sink.

No—even if my wilder dreams failed to materialize there was at least going to be enough cash to pay the nappy service elsewhere. Roger had had an appalling time with that unfortunate first wife of his, and I was not going to let him in for living with another cross and thwarted one. She had died only eighteen months ago, after a protracted illness, and while she lived I had almost given up all thoughts of marriage. Surely Roger and I could now be understanding enough to allow each other a little leeway? Surely most men would be thankful for a spell of freedom. I was forgetting that the proposed leeway was mostly for my own benefit.

All this time I had been energetically clearing up my house. Owning it still delighted me. It had reached the market just when Erik had bought me out of the family firm, ours jointly since our father died. I had no feeling for the business, and since Erik was eighteen years older than I, had been in it since he left school, and had frequently told me I was a drag on the Board, it had seemed sensible to let him take over entirely. With my share of the capital I had bought and furnished Number 16, and the remaining money had given me a small income which my writing augmented. The fact that since Erik acquired my shares the firm's value had tripled, then quadrupled, did not worry me at all. It was all due to his own skill. He might look indolent, he might be indolent, so far as his resistance to women in general and Susie in particular was concerned, but in his business—and perhaps to get away from Susie—he worked.

Thoughts of Susie increased a niggling sense of guilt towards her. Roger had hinted I was interfering in her life, and he was right. It was the children, really, for whom I interfered. . . . Although people who interfered always could trot out a reason, it was always love of someone or other that drove them on, never a passion for power and a desire to prove other people small. Perhaps it was just as well I was soon off to Cornwall. In the meantime I would visit Susie for tea, and try to soothe her down. With Roger on call this week end, because his partner was off duty, I had nothing else to do.

It was Saturday, which was why the children had been at large. They were not due to break up till the middle of next week. Fortunately for Culbertson there was a very good small ballet school near the downs, which was already providing child dancers for shows up and down the country. Stewart was a weekly boarder at Keeperston, some miles off. Nicola attended a day school, one that had had its beginnings when a Mrs. Aylmers instructed select pupils, while the Regent and his poor suffering Papa had turn and turn about patronized Seaminster Regis, before Brighton's more attractive claims had dashed the townspeople's hopes of continual and thriving royal trade.

I didn't find Brighton more attractive. I loved Seaminster for itself. And its self was unique. At one time it had been a small fishing village, nothing but a few houses and a stone quay making an artificial harbour off the south-east shore. Then, with the first tentative royal paddlings and dippings, it had expanded inland, up the sloping cliffs so that every north-by-south-running Seaminster street led sharply up or down. To celebrate a return to sanity George III had built here, not an Englishman's oriental dream of a pavilion, but a strapping, hideous near-cathedral, which had been known colloquially as Sea Minster, and had eventually lent the place its name.

Everything that Brighton had was here, on a far smaller scale. We had our legends, and our Lanes. We had enchanted Mrs. Fitzherbert, bored Lady Jersey stiff. We had one tiny pier, which looked as though an iron spider had spun it out of filigree on a May morning. I was sure that Roger had dug himself into Seaminster like a mole, and if I married him—— Very deliberately I switched my mind to the Incas, collected a carrier bag from the kitchen, and went out into the street. After shopping I could walk back along the esplanade, and pay my penitential visit to The Lime Tree House.

The shopping was soon done, for I kept forgetting it was Saturday—what a doctor's wife I should make—and, since no delicatessen was open up this end of the town, I could look forward to a semi-fasting Sunday. If Roger and I had not quarrelled we could have shared his Sunday joint, but now my pride saw starvation day ahead, unless Susie asked me to lunch, which was unlikely. She hated cooking, and there would have been endless moans about how fast a joint vanished and how boring it would be to start cooking again on Tuesday. Sadly I took my almost empty carrier to the esplanade, and sank down in a deckchair while I waited for the twenty minutes or so to pass that would make it reasonable to appear at Susie's door.

The fog had rolled itself out to sea again, and the tide was high. It was still a generally hazy day, though, and the sun weak enough for a faint chill to bring up goosepimples on naked skin. I began to wish that my dress was more than a linen shift, yet was too lazy to go back home and change. So I sat pretending I was warm enough, and thinking that I preferred the sea wild and blue, or flat and translucent green, to this treacly oily no-colour swell which constantly rose up and dissipated itself without energy on the pebbled shore. It looked hand in glove with the fog, that swell, as though one were the result of the other.

Now Madame Sosostris came into my mind. It may have been because her house was straight behind me, and if I turned my head I could have seen it, for on this sea front there was only a long row of single-storey cottages, and then behind them the steeply sloping gardens of houses on the south side of my street. Madame Sosostris. Naturally it was not her true name. I had—we all had—almost forgotten what that was. Someone had nicknamed her after Eliot's clairvoyante, the wisest woman in Europe with a wicked pack of cards; and it had stuck, so that now, we even heard, she enjoyed the name herself. That her cards were wicked I was prepared to bet. She could cause consternation, pleasure, or anxiety, at will. There was a match on between us. She was determined to tell mine, while I had never let myself be drawn. "I am sure there is zomething very extraordinary, very rare, to come out of your cards, Jane," she would say to me, that entity of a nose seeming to eye me uncannily from her face. "I feel you are only at the start of happenings."

"I like to live my happenings as they come," I had told her, "not dread them in advance."

"Vy, do you think then they vould necessarily be of dread?"

"Not really. But I do know that kind of thing worries me. I don't like to see things being done in front of me which I can't understand. It's like not knowing if a doctor has given you a year to live."

"Then you should tell them for yourself."

"I wouldn't know how."

"You could learn." Suddenly her nose seemed to advance a foot. "You have the gift. Yes—I am sure you have the gift. In the occult, I am never wrong."

"You tell that to my family, and watch them laugh." I hurriedly walked away. It was hard to bear the thought of sharing a gift with Madame Sosostris across the road. We might start to share that nose as well.

If only my close friends, the Hamiltons, had not moved away. Once I had loved the house where Madame lived, almost more than my own; now I never willingly set foot there. It was small and white, with one delicate turret in front, and another to match it on the south side, which lent it a strangely unreal air. Two of the downstairs windows were in opposite walls, so that you could see straight through them to the glittering Channel beyond.

These were not in the room where Madame entertained her clients, and laid out their futures on a fumed oak table. How well I knew that room—I could sit and remember it at will. The front door was set at a curious angle on the right, and knocked, so to speak, the corner off the house; and it led straight into this room: sitting room or whatever you liked to call it—card room, perhaps. In the side wall was a small round window, like a porthole. Side, because here the house was detached where a narrow unmade-up track led down towards the sea. There was another porthole-like window, high up in the back wall, which looked out on a combined balcony-landing of an open stairway in white wrought iron that the Hamiltons had erected at the house's rear.

This led at one end into the narrow track, and at the other formed a second balcony outside one turret bedroom. It had been an admirable arrangement for the Hamilton children who never had to bother their elders by trooping in and out of downstairs rooms on their way to and from the sea. And it added to the house's general charm, giving something of a stage set appearance to what was already a house faintly marked with the aura of eeriness, and now plainly the gingerbread home of an authentic witch.

Since the fog had come to stay, this aura had had an enhanced effect: an insubstantial house afloat in a fog, fog seen through the windows, fog drifting round the apple trees in the garden, fog turning the turret eyes to a milky blindness reminiscent of the eyes of dead cooked mackerel. Sometimes I felt that the house emanated fog; that Madame Sosostris manufactured it within, and sent it oozing out of keyholes and through and round the window frames, until it built up in the street and then the town as though someone were spinning it endlessly on an invisible loom. Madame Sosostris had come with the fogs; and was it over-imaginative to believe that the fog had come with Madame Sosostris? They had both, at any rate, invaded our small town together.

"What a pleasant surprise," said Cosway's voice just above my head.

I barely started. Cosway was not the sort of person to make you start. His voice was soft and sleepy, attractive if a bit monotonous, and not suddenly distracting as a birdlike or harsh voice can be. Cosway had a pleasing personality too, even if it were slightly limp. People were always delighted to see him. His nervous friendliness, his habit of blinking through his spectacles, his shabby and uncared-for air, made everyone feel good-natured towards him. I smiled at him now, as I turned my head. I was delighted to see him, after my lowering scene with Roger.

"Dear Cosway, I didn't know you were back."

"Of course I'm back. It's your birthday tomorrow, isn't it? And then there's Culbertson's show on Monday. How could I miss either event? You look very elegant, Jane. But you always do. I like that black linen."

He smiled very kindly at me. He was sensitive, and probably guessed how I was feeling. Cosway had a singularly attractive face when he smiled, although it was a bit shapeless, as faces go. It was a face with no great definition, but it emanated Cosway's feelings better than some more decisive features could have done. I was always amused by the way his face went into folds when he was talking or thinking: not crinkles, or wrinkles, but folds. There is a certain kind of flesh which does this, and I cannot describe it any other way. He was peering at me now with the surprising shrewdness he possessed, which was often disconcerting from such a vague personality.

"Jane, you're depressed."

"I'm twenty-five tomorrow. Enough to make any woman depressed."

"Nonsense. You've never worried about age in your life. Not that sort of girl. You'll look lean and elegant and curly-haired till you're ninety at least."

"If I live till ninety I'll be scraggy as an old hen, with a National Health wig."

Cosway didn't reply. After a moment he said: "Is it Roger?"

"Is what Roger?"

"This general fog surrounding you."

I gave a slight gasp. If only he hadn't said that, it was like telepathy.

"What did you say?" This time he was peering at me in concern.

"Nothing. I—I—— No, it's not Roger, I think." There was no need to discuss the row; not even with Cosway. "Perhaps it is the fog. I wish it would go away."

"They say it will clear tomorrow, in time for your birthday," he said comfortingly.

"For weeks they've said it will clear. But it's never really gone —not far—since those first thick mists in March. I remember the day it began, because it was the day that woman fell off the esplanade—— Why, it must have been about here." I looked down at the beach some feet below us, and wondered how I could have forgotten; how I could unfeelingly have sat myself just by the steep steps where that unfortunate stranger had walked into air, and fallen, and——

Cosway was frowning, at sea.

"What woman?"

"Surely you remember, but—— Oh, I forgot: you weren't here then. She didn't make much of a stir, poor creature. I don't know if they ever found out where she came from, or who she was. Only, they thought she was a total stranger here, or she would have been more careful—— It was this time of thick mist, you see, coming and going in patches, like it does; one moment you can see quite a long way, and the next you're blinded. She just walked over the edge. She'd hit her head, falling—— And then, it was full moon, and very high tide—the tide came in—— They asked Madame Sosostris if she saw anything from her house, but she hadn't." I got up quickly. The treacly oily swell looked like a smug menace, a wolf in sheep's clothing.

"Come on, Cosway, I'm getting cold."

He gave a sympathetic shudder. "So am I. But come on to where?"

"Susie's."

"Oh—home. Susie's overwrought. That's why I came out."

I smiled. Trust Cosway to make himself scarce when his elder sister was 'overwrought'.

"Did she penetrate to your flat, then?"

"She did." He took my carrier bag from me, and put his other arm in mine. "I gave her coffee and comfort, and some advice; and then I escaped."

"What sort of advice?"

"Any sort. Susie loves advice but she never listens to it, so I usually say the first thing that enters my head. This time, that if she wouldn't cry again for a whole year, and not be cross, and make herself pretty, and never ask Erik if he loves her, then he will. He's too indolent to do anything else."

"Did you tell her that too?"

"Yes. I flatter myself it was sound."

"It was. Very. As a matter of fact I used almost the same words three months back."

"With what result?"

"She went straight down and made a scene about me, and couldn't speak to me for six whole days."

Cosway gave his gentle laugh.

"Poor Erik. Was he indolent about loving Ingrid?"

"No. He didn't love Ingrid—he adored her. Which is why Susie won't have so much as a piece of Swedish furniture in the house. Not even our mother's—Erik's and mine, I mean."

"It's odd, how dark you and Erik are, with all this Swedish blood."

"Not dark: brown. It's a fallacy, anyway, that all Swedes are fair."

"I suppose you both feel very much at home in Sweden."

"Yes. Very. Particularly with Ingrid's relatives. And with Ingrid herself, of course——" I stopped, and looked out across the oily sea—"when Erik brought her back from a business trip I was only seven. She was like one of the family."

"Well, she was a sort of cousin, wasn't she? I wish I'd met her. Everyone says she had this wonderful quality of sympathy——"

"You'd have liked her. It was frightful when she died. The children——"

Cosway put his arm round me. "I'm sure I would. All the same, Janey dear, and please don't mind my interfering like this, I sometimes wonder if——"

"I know what you're going to say, and I've come to the same conclusion myself. At least Roger had, and perhaps he and you are right. If I see too much of the children, and that makes it more difficult for Susie. Do you remember Aunt Aggie, Cosway —my father's sister? Well, if she were living near them, I wouldn't worry half so much. Even Culbertson likes her, but she never will leave London." I sighed, and Cosway tightened his grip.

"I don't mean it's bad for you or the children, my dear, but bad perhaps for their relationship with Susie."

"Have they one?"

"Yes—sometimes they have. She can be goodhearted, you know."

It was comfortable to talk it over with Cosway, who was so

kind. I felt glad suddenly that Roger was not there to see us walking so intimately together; glad, too, he had been up this end earlier, was now safely over on the west side of the town. At that moment Cosway said: "Hello, isn't this Roger's car?"

It was Roger's car, parked by the side of the road. We stood and looked at it. I wanted to remove Cosway's arm from my shoulders and hurry on, before Roger, closing the front door of the cottage where he was visiting, came with his quick steps across the road, his black case swinging in his hand. Even as I thought of it the whole sequence happened; and there was Roger, four feet away, regarding Cosway and me with eyes that, alarmingly, held no expression at all.

"Hello, Cosway," he said genially. "Nice to see you. London all right?"

"So-so. Very overcrowded."

"We're overcrowded here, these days."

Well, you could make what you liked of that. But Cosway who, as I've said, was intuitive, looked at him sharply. He was not provocative by nature, yet his encircling hand very surely and absently stroked my arm.

"You look cold, Jane." Roger stared at my goosepimples which had risen again from my chill dismay. "I mustn't keep you both hanging about or you'll have pneumonia like the poor old woman I've just visited. It's this fog—makes the day colder than you think. Be seeing you some time." He got into his car and drove away.

"Oh Jane dear," Cosway sounded distressed, "I do hope Roger wasn't——"

"Did you need to stroke my arm at that precise moment?" I burst out irritably.

"My dear, I didn't think—— Well, damn it, yes, I did think, and I'm glad I did. Roger doesn't own you, after all. I'm his rival, and he knows it," said Cosway, pompous and faintly ridiculous; but he took his arm away and peered at me with his normal nervous blink.

"Are you cross?"

"It's stupid to ask people if they're cross," I said vehemently. "A stupid, stupid habit."

What with the cold, and the fog, and Cosway's depressed silence, we reached The Lime Tree House in no fit state for Susie's umbrage to begin.

Chapter Four

I often felt that Umbrage must be Susie's middle name; that some repressed fairy godmother with an angry complex, hovering over the font, had slipped it in for good measure and seen that her protégée lived up to it. She could not accept that people do talk about each other, and not always kindly, and so was constantly suspicious to see two people whom she knew together. It made things difficult for the children, who were often accused of hiding things from her; and since everyone hides things Susie was triumphantly able to prove her belief that they were not so open as she would have liked them to be. Really she wanted to be told she was the best, most attractive person in the world, and far, far more attractive than poor Ingrid had ever been. I was sorry for Susie, in a way, and thankful for her sake that nearly everyone round her was very sensibly not open, but shut.

When Cosway rang the doorbell of The Lime Tree House—his upper flat had a side entrance of its own—I could already visualize the look we should see when Susie opened. And when she did, the look was there: Jane and Cosway. Together. Talking about me.

"Oh, come in."

"I found Jane on the esplanade," Cosway said too heartily.

"Yes? In this fog?"

She really was outstandingly pretty—pink and white and *cendrée* fair—when she could get that hostile self-pitying look off her face. The trouble was that Ingrid had been so much more than pretty, with bone structure of a type to make men gasp. All the same, Erik might have been quite comfortably relaxed with his Susie, if only——

Cosway followed me into the hall, and I followed silently in Susie's footsteps. We were in for cold umbrage, not wet umbrage. On the whole I didn't know which I disliked more. Wet umbrage was embarrassing but quickly over, cold umbrage tended to linger. Occasionally cold umbrage dissolved into wet umbrage, which was unfair. Now I wished myself at home.

"Would you like some tea, Jane?" She sounded as though I were expecting a seven course dinner with champagne. I said hastily: "Oh—thank you, Susie; not unless you're having some."

"I've just put on the kettle. I'll send one of the children to take it off, and put on the larger one."

"Put on both," said heartless Cosway. "Jane's cold, poor girl. We must warm her up."

"That's not a very sensible dress for this weather, is it? Attractive, but not sensible." She gave us an inclusive glance in which I read the words, "Sitting about undressed on the esplanade to attract Cosway."

"How's Roger, Jane? As you're so devoted to each other I always say you ought to marry and get it over."

"Everyone always says it. Perhaps that's why we don't."

"So amusing of you both."

We were in the large panelled drawing room. I looked round it appreciatively. Erik had refused to have it altered, and it was the only place in the house except the kitchen where I still felt at home. I liked its faded green panels which made an unobtrusive background for every season's flowers.

"I'll tell Erik you're here."

"Don't bother him, Susie, if he's working. We'll meet at tea."

"I must just see about that kettle."

"Let's go to the kitchen, if the children are there."

"No—do be comfortable. I'll be back."

She went out, ostentatiously shutting the door after her. I heard her go upstairs to Erik.

"We're in for it." I sat down on the sofa.

"I wonder if I'll be getting back to the flat, Jane? You'll make my excuses for me, and——"

"You'll stay here to pour oil on troubled waters. Deserter. Coward."

"Yes, I suppose I am a coward. I'd do anything to avoid a

scene." Cosway sighed, took off his glasses and polished them. His eyes looked like two nervous fish trying to escape from a glass bowl.

"It won't be a scene. Only a little mild hysteria and repressed aggression, ending in tears."

"I'm wondering if I left my electric fire on." He escaped, just before Susie returned, looking suspicious.

"Cosway thought his electric fire was on."

"How like him. And he does forget to pay his bills———" Susie plumped herself down on a nearby stool and proceeded to embark on the sort of conversation she deprecated so much in other people.

"Yes, well—poor Cosway," I defended him, and added a banal phrase, "he really needs someone to look after him." One often did, regrettably, talk down to Susie.

"He and Roger." She gave me a meaning look that made me regret having spoken. "See here, Jane, forget about Cosway for the moment. Erik's busy, which is really a godsend, because I want to talk about Gabriella."

"Please Susie, do let me give you some———"

"I know what you're going to say, and it's not the least use your saying it," her voice rose slightly, "because you never can see anything from my point of view. Nor can Erik. That's the whole trouble."

"Then if it's no good our talking about it———"

"I didn't say that, I want you to listen for once. Just to listen."

"Oh, very well." I sat back and clasped my hands behind my head.

"It's that tone of voice—'Oh, very well.' Can't you see, can't you begin to see what I have to put up with in this house already? It's not as though the children were mine—— Of course I worship them, simply, but even you must admit Nicola uses appalling words, and Culbertson never obeys anyone, and Stewart will be amused in that annoying way all day long———" Her tone of voice was not one normally associated with worship. "The fact is, they don't care about anyone but themselves. And you know Erik, so long as I cook and cook and cook for them all, and never bother him about anything, that's all right. Well, is it fair? Is it fair on me to introduce someone of Gabriella's age when I don't want her here at all, simply adding to the work, and probably encouraging the children?"

"Are those your only objections, Susie?"

"Of course they are. And pretty big objections too." But her eyes fell before mine, and she flushed.

"Why are you so unsure of Erik?" I asked softly. "He's never unkind. If you'd only stop fussing him so much he wouldn't bother to look at anyone else. He's far too lazy. And too fond of you," I added hastily.

"Oh, you are intolerable! They're the very words Cosway's just been saying, of course he's told you all about it, you never do anything but get together behind my back." Her face went red and began to pucker. Overhead I heard Erik's footsteps, he was coming down. I glanced at the clock. Four forty-five—oh, thank God. I got up and awkwardly patted Susie's shoulder. "Don't cry, Susie. Really, if you want to keep Erik, do stop crying. He won't be interested in Gabriella. He's tired, and she's young and puppyish. Be tolerant with him and Gabriella too— you be your nicest, kindest self," I made an unseen wry face, and continued without hope, "It will all work out, you'll see."

She gave me a sudden upward look. "Yes—but would you like her round with Roger? Or—Cosway?"

"Today she could have both with pleasure." It was without much thought I said it, and she answered, submissive but triumphant, "You can be sweet sometimes, Jane. Then I'll send her round to you quite a bit, if I may."

"Of course. Don't forget I'll be in Cornwall some of the time."

"Still, I'm sure we can work something out together." She rose, quite elated. "Erik's gone down to the kitchen. Let's go through and have family tea, to warm you up."

I followed her, thankful that tears had been averted. Sometimes I wondered if there was anything the matter with Susie's tear ducts. Erik was once so troubled about what he took to be her continual depression that he had sent her to a psychiatrist recommended by Roger, who was optimistic about the possibilities of cure. Susie herself had returned from her third visit optimistic too. "He's pleased I can cry so much," she told us all, "he's says it's a catharsis. I cry all the time with him. He thinks I was very rejected in childhood, but couldn't cry about it."

"Didn't you cry in childhood, Susie?" Cosway had blinked in a puzzled way. "I seem to remember torrents of tears, like Rachmaninov's 'Spring Waters'."

"Oh yes, but I was redirecting it. I didn't cry about the right thing. Not about my rejection." She looked round us triumphantly; we, who had all rejected her. "Dr. Fosborough thinks I've never been able to accept my mother's rejection of me."

"Mother doted on you," said Cosway disapprovingly.

"That was the trouble, wasn't it? Not sincere. They call it the 'double bind'. It's worse than outright rejection, any day. You were only outwardly rejected, Cosway, so you had a better chance."

"That's why I blink instead of cry. Still, so long as Dr. Fosborough thinks he can cure you."

Dr. Fosborough did think so. He thought so for six months, after which he inexplicably went to South America, saying he thought a break in treatment would do Susie good, and help her to apply new attitudes to living; but Susie, confirmed unaccountably in rejection, had continued to shed tears. The whole thing had made Erik and Cosway suspicious of Roger, sorry for Dr. Fosborough, who was generally considered excellent at his job, and resigned in a fearful way to a future of Susie's crying.

We came into the kitchen. Erik kissed me, while the children greeted me in enthusiastic chorus. Luckily Susie was quite buoyant since I had given her *carte blanche* to palm Gabriella off on me, and remained complaisant. Culbertson came across to lean against me like a young and solid steer supporting itself by a tree stump. She wore jeans, with a sweater full of holes. By the withdrawn look in her eyes I knew her concentrated on choreography; or a letter which might be read with profit.

"It's Jane's birthday tomorrow," Nicola told the table unnecessarily, as we all seated ourselves, "and we've got her two presents that she'll never, never guess what."

"Your grammar is so graphic," murmured Stewart, helping himself to three scones.

"I hope it's an exciting present?"

"You'll see." Culbertson began to munch near my right ear. "It's probably the most o-rig-in-al present since the world began."

"It will make your name in the terrace." Stewart started to laugh.

Nicola shook back her plaits and looked doubtfully at the food. "You'll be famous, I should think. Make lots of money, too."

"I can't wait to see it."

"You've overexcited your poor aunt," said my brother. "Better give it to her now, or she won't sleep all night."

"Do you know what it is, Susie?"

"They haven't confided in me." She shook her head tolerantly, "But I never think surprise presents are safe."

"Coming to lunch tomorrow, Janey?" Culbertson tempted me.

"You know she and Roger always lunch together on their birthdays."

Culbertson gave first her stepmother and then me an unfathomable look. For an uneasy moment I wondered if she could have been hidden away in my dining room during the argument. I was too proud to tell Susie that I wasn't lunching with Roger.

"Then we might give you our present tonight."

"But she mustn't open it tonight."

"Oh, I want to *see*——" mourned Culbertson.

"All right. I'll open it today," I promised them, just as Cosway rejoined us. He avoided my reproachful eye, glanced like Nicola at the cakes, and limited himself to a cup of tea. It was not that Susie couldn't cook. She did, lavishly, but nothing would restrain her to classic simplicity, which was one reason she was always tired. She was greatly given to what I called tarted-up things named, revoltingly, Anchovy Regattas, or Cheese Dreams; while, with Chaucer's Cook, of blancmange, she made it with the best.

When the children stayed with me we followed a simple diet

of steak and apples, boiled eggs and bananas, until Stewart or Nicola rebelled—and then I would cook some meals so overwhelming that our metabolisms would be shocked into hysteria; and next day we would have steak and bananas for lunch, boiled eggs and apples for supper. It was simpler, and more convenient.

This meal time passed in unusual peace. Susie was quite gay, and presently surprised me by extending a hesitant invitation to supper as well as birthday tea. Erik was visibly happier than for some while. If he would only exert himself more, I thought sadly, he might eventually have altered Susie's mood changes for some real change of heart. His usual lazy optimism was not enough. I noticed that Cosway had lapsed into a kind of withdrawal. He often dealt with potentially disruptive situations by becoming part of the landscape, and this attitude of his always amused me: I could never decide whether it stemmed from weakness, or strength.

The children were plainly concentrated on this unusual present they had found for me. I hoped it was neither alive nor obscene. It would be just like Stewart and Nicola to see framed pornographic etchings from some back shop in the Lanes as a huge, Susie-tormenting joke. This certainly was a fair-weather meal we were enjoying, and it might not last. . . .

"I ought to be going now, Erik. Thank you for tea, Susie. When Gabriella comes on Monday, send her along to say hello. Oh, of course—I'll be seeing you tomorrow."

I stood up, and glanced out of the window. You would never have thought we were in the second half of July. The fog had sucked its way back into the town as though it had followed me and Cosway here from the beach. It was so fine, it was like a veil. There were minute drops of moisture on the window panes——

"Now!" said Culbertson triumphantly.

"I'll get them." Nicola went out of the room with her light and certain step.

Silence fell. It was as if all our spirits—with the exception of Culbertson's, who was jumping up and down—had sunk a degree on some emotional barometer. An unreasonable anxiety oppressed me. Cosway let out a heavy sigh.

Nicola reappeared. She carried the two promised parcels.

"I'm going to explain to Janey, from us all. You can guess this one's a book, can't you? Don't open it first, because it tells you about the other which is the real surprise. So—here." She triumphantly dumped the second packet into my outstretched hands. Culbertson's breathing sounded apoplectic.

"Well?" said Stewart impatiently. "Aren't you going to open it? We promise it's not alive——"

This may sound ludicrous now, but the moment Nicola gave me the parcel I knew that I couldn't bear to open it: my spine literally crawled with apprehension. In that second I vividly recalled Madame Sosostris' face when she told me I "had the gift". "In the occult," she had said, "I am never wrong." What exactly had she meant? Did a "gift" for the cards entail also what could be termed second sight?

"Oh go on, go on," begged Culbertson, "you are slow, Janey, do hurry up."

"Can't I really keep it for tomorrow?" My laugh was forced. I wanted to drop the parcel on the floor.

"They'll never let you get away with that." Susie was watching me with amusement. "You're almost frozen, aren't you, Jane? You've gone quite blue—I'll lend you a sweater to go home in."

Culbertson put out a finger to touch the parcel, which was squarish, and hard, like a box. "You undo it here, with this bit of string," she coaxed, and guided my reluctant fingers to the knot.

The wrapping paper fell apart. The present was a box: unimpressive, mahogany, plainly old. There was nothing whatever about it to cause the strange discomfort I had felt—still felt. I put it down hastily on the tea table, and stood back as though to admire it.

"There's nothing at all to see." Stewart's voice was deliberately patient.

"It's a fine box," I said weakly. "Thank you all very much."

"The box isn't the point at all. It's just a box. You open it, Jane. Goodness—anyone would think we'd given you a toad."

Three eager figures pressed forward round me. Three eager faces alight with anticipatory laughter watched me. They knew

I would be as thoroughly amused and pleased as they were. They couldn't for the life of them understand my drawing back. How could I explain that I would almost sooner die than open it?

"She's pretending," said Nicola suddenly. "She's having a joke—aren't you? Great—you're some actress, Jane."

There was nothing for it but to open the box. I grasped it firmly, and in my imagination heard the irritating scale of chipped notes that was Madame Sosostris' laugh. I was again struck by a wave of senseless apprehension. The box's lid flew up, and I was staring down at something very ordinary—or: was it so ordinary, after all? These were playing cards, but cards with a difference; and not just the difference of age, either——

In my hands I held the Tarot pack.

"Aren't they marvellous?" said Nicola's voice in my ear. Her face was pressed against my shoulder. She put out a finger and touched one of the two visible top cards lovingly. "They're desperately old, the man said. He wanted to put it over us they came from Ancient Egypt, but of course we knew better than that. Eighteenth century, that other antique man thought—the one Stewart knows in the town. We took them to him. Who do you think owned them?"

"The book tells you how to use them," joined in Culbertson. "It's not old, of course. Stewart wrote to Foyle's for it, so it's bound to work."

"We thought you could set up in opposition to old Madame; drive her mad. Didn't you say she told you you could do it? That's what gave us the idea. But it was a terrible bit of luck, finding these."

"She's so amazed she can't speak," put in Stewart.

"You are a set of silly children," Susie's matter-of-fact voice was indulgent behind us. "Let me see, Jane. They're not exactly pretty, are they? Ugh—and that man hanging upside down. I should have chosen a better top card for a birthday, if I'd been you, Nicola."

"I didn't choose it," said Nicola crossly. "It was there. Anyway, he's not all that sinister—means sacrifice or something. This other one opposite him, with the moon and horns on her head, is the Priestess. She's rather fine, isn't she?"

"Let's all have a look at them," Cosway suggested. "Pass them round."

"But that book says people mustn't casually handle them, unless the cards are being told, or the influences get mixed."

"A lot of medieval nonsense," said my brother.

"Well, anyway, only Jane's to hold them. Go on, Jane, take them out one by one and show us."

The box and its contents still affected me with this inexplicable and oppressive dismay. Automatically I obeyed, automatically I made a show of pleasure which appeared to satisfy the children.

"Let's count the first five cards down each side as your birthday fortune, Jane." Susie entered into the spirit of the thing in a way I resented. "Without that hung up creature, I mean. We can look up the meanings."

"That's the Juggler, or the Fool," said Culbertson suddenly, as my fingers touched the second card down. "He's sometimes good, I think, and sometimes bad, but often you can't trust that person though he's near you. He's fool's luck, too. Luck that looks good, but's not."

"Evidently Culbertson's already learnt the book by heart," Stewart began to unwrap the second package. "You've not looked at it yet, Jane. The illustrations are nice, just like the cards."

But catching sight of Culbertson's unfathomable and guarded eye, I guessed she had not learnt from any book.

Chapter Five

I woke to my birthday with a certain reluctance, a feeling that it would be good to hibernate. The black quarrel with Roger re-entered my mind, and even the edge of excitement had been taken from America. As for those cards the children had given me, it would have been pleasant to relieve my feelings by dumping them in the sea, which would have made me unpopular for life.

I got up. The weather forecast was correct; the fog had cleared, and the day was brilliantly sunny and already hot. I considered doing penance in church for a misspent year, and dressed hurriedly and went down to the kitchen at the rear of the house for a closer look at my sole egg. Propped up on the window sill in a conspicuous position was a paper parcel marked "fragile" in Roger's hand.

That was a clever move, I thought. To give me nothing at all would look too deliberate. This way, by coming round to the kitchen window when I was still asleep, Roger had been certain of avoiding me. As I went out to collect my present I wondered how early he had come, and it was with almost as much reluctance as I'd undone the Tarot, though without the horror, that I unwrapped his gift.

And it was beautiful. An exquisite ivory representation of the Chinese goddess Kwan Yin. Her hands were extended compassionately towards me, which gave me an invigorating hope that she would offset any ill luck one superstitious side of me was convinced the cards would bring.

I was still admiring her when the telephone rang. As I went to answer it I was trying not to recognize my eager haste. Cosway, or—Roger?

"Janey? Will you lunch with me? Unless I'm being tactless, and are you——"

"I'm not lunching with Roger."

"Well, then—I really would be delighted if you'd come out with me, to celebrate your birthday?"

"Thank you, Cosway." I hesitated.

"We could go to that new place along the coast. Where they're supposed to do crab and lobster so well."

"It's probably booked, at the week end."

"I'll ring at once and ask, if you'll come?"

I stared unenthusiastically at the mouthpiece of the telephone. "That's very sweet of you."

"Right. I'll ring back later and tell you if I've been able to book." He rang off—and I had forgotten to tell him I would be in church. Still, I could always telephone him later. I went into the kitchen again, and fiddled about with the breakfast things. The goddess Kwan Yin surveyed me serenely from the table, her feet still shrouded in wrapping paper.

"You needn't pretend to be so compassionate," I complained, "if that's all you can do." I was unwrapping her feet when the telephone rang again.

"Jane? As it's your birthday, would you care to come out and lunch with me somewhere today?"

I was still trying to find words when Roger's voice continued with careful formality: "I've provisionally booked a table for two at that new place along the coast."

Formality . . . no suggestion we should lunch at his place. . . "Where they do crab and lobster so well?"

"Ah, you've heard about it then. Well?" His tone was more frigid: I was being misconstrued. My mouth was open to say: "Sorry, but I'm lunching there with Cosway," yet it came out as: "Thank you very much, Roger, I'd like—yes, I'd love that."

"Good. How's Madame Kwan Yin?"

"Enchanting, and most beautiful. Many, many thanks. She's looking exquisite on my kitchen table. Where did you find her?" It was a long while since I had been nervous with Roger.

"My secret, but I'm glad she's satisfactory. I'll come along at twelve thirty, if that suits you?"

"I'll be waiting."

"Good-bye, then."

"Good-bye."

I stood staring at the silent telephone. What had I done? Stood up poor Cosway, who really did not deserve it. The telephone rang again. I approached it as though it were a cobra. "Hello?"

"Hello, Janey, you sound most suspicious. Well, that's that, I'm afraid—couldn't get a table. You were right. However, not to be downhearted. Where else would you like to lunch?"

"That is a blow." I turned my head, and through the doorway my eyes met the serene ivory gaze of Kwan Yin. "Cosway, I really would love to try that place with you some other day."

"We can do that too. This is your birthday lunch, remember?"

Evidently no goddess of compassion could be entirely counted on. "But Cosway," I stumbled, "we're all meeting at tea, and—that is——"

"That is, it was Roger who was on the line when I tried to ring you back just now?"

"Oh Cosway, I do feel mean, I——"

"He's coming round to you, I suppose?" Cosway sounded faintly masochistic, rubbing salt into the wound.

"No, no—as a matter of fact, he wanted me to go out with him."

"Lobster and crab?" asked Cosway too acutely.

"Well yes, but——"

"Anyway, he won't be able to get a table." There was a certain satisfaction in Cosway's voice. Then it faded. "Or—did he happen to get the last one for two which the proprietor so sadly assured me had just gone?"

"Cosway, I'm feeling meaner and meaner."

"So you should, woman. I shall probably go out and have tea somewhere entirely alone, while you're blowing out your candles. And brood. One day you'll get yourself murdered, Jane. If not by Roger, by me. Good-bye."

An emotional relationship that is in the doldrums appears to have one of two effects on people: either they stop eating altogether and take to black coffee, or they eat too much and have indigestion. Both Roger and I belonged to the latter group. Whatever else that lunch did or did not make clear, it confirmed that we both have good appetites, particularly in distress: by the time coffee was reached we had vicariously assuaged emotion and were both calm, reasonable, adult, and politely estranged in sympathy.

"You're looking particularly elegant today, Jane." In the past there had been more love in Roger's voice when he told me there was a boil coming on my nose.

"Thank you very much. I often wish people wouldn't say that to me."

"Cosway, I suppose." He gave a sardonic smile, and stirred his coffee fiercely.

"Well yes, he said it yesterday, as a matter of fact."

"You appeared not to be disliking it."

"Because I didn't hit him when he put his arm round me? Wouldn't that have been rather unnecessary? We only met on the esplanade, we——" I stopped. I owed Roger no explanations. Why should he be so prepared to think the worst of me?

"It's a sign of love," said Roger, as though reading my thoughts.

"It's nothing of the sort. It's possessiveness."

"We seem to be riling each other just lately."

"And what's that a sign of?"

"Frustration, perhaps. Anyway, you don't like being told you're elegant. Why, Jane?"

"Well—when people always use the same adjective, you feel they're making mental reservations. It sounds as though I know how to fold and unfold my legs, but my features one by one wouldn't knock anybody flat."

Roger looked amused. "Wouldn't you sooner have it that way than be clumsy? Not that I agree with your low opinion of your features."

"I'd love to have every single attribute there is, most women would. So I'm a bit more like Susie than I thought."

The conversation, the lunch, seemed unproductive. Felt it, anyway. On the surface there would have been nothing wrong to people who knew us both, but underneath I was aware of flatness, like stale sodawater. This is the way a marriage ends, I thought, when someone is about to leave; both parties are deliberately kind to each other, and neither side has yet mentioned divorce. It was better for this to happen now, my friends would have said. Or was it? Might not the whole thing, and a great deal of effective marriage counselling, add up to the fact that a lot more determination is needed to make most relationships work than is usually shown?

Suddenly I wanted very much to get away from Roger, to think things out. "I've—I've a lot to do at home, Roger, before going up to have birthday tea with the children. If I can eat any. Thank you for an enormous, and most heavenly meal."

"A lot to do." He eyed me closely, jealously.

"Yes—you'll think it incredibly funny, but the wretched children have given me the Tarot——" And I went on to say that I ought to put in some study on my present, or permanent offence could be given, particularly to Culbertson who was quick to spot a fraud. At the time I wondered uneasily why I had fixed on that excuse: a moral obligation to study what appalled me.

I don't think Roger believed my curious explanation. Half his mind was fixated on thoughts of Cosway. He had reached the point when he was annoyed with me himself, but wanted no one else to muscle in. Like a dog that keeps an old bone under the carpet for a rainy day.

"There's a patient I ought to look in on again, once I've dropped back home to see if there are any recorded messages. After that I might tell the operator to call me at Susie's and join the tea myself."

"Why don't you? They'd love that."

"And would you? I'll come along and pick you up, when I'm free."

"You'll find Madame Sosostris the Second in full spread."

"Then you can tell me my unsettled future. Leave the door ajar, and I'll just walk in."

So we arranged it between us; and Roger dropped me at Number 16 on his way down town.

Chapter Six

I took the Tarot box and accompanying book down to the dining-room table, and carefully lifted out the cards. Seen on this sunny day they had a curious vivid beauty. They had come down through the years with their glow of colour intact. I laid them out in two large semicircles, and my respect for Madame Sosostris grew. How could she remember all these? For some while I sat and considered them. The Priestess and the Hanged Man I already knew, and Culbertson's Fool. Some of the others were curious and fascinating: the Hierophant, the Chariot, the Wheel of Life, Temperance; and a skeleton—the Reaper—which gave me a momentary shudder. But the Enchantress, shown with an engaging lion, had charm, and even the Hanged Man, after closer study, was disclosed as hanging head downwards with a calm and debonair expression. All the same, handling them made me uneasy; it didn't—they didn't—give me a pleasant sensation. I turned my attention to the book.

Even the cards' crudest meanings would take long to master. This book, anyway, didn't agree with Culbertson's interpretation of the Fool, and I found myself wondering how much she had gleaned, and had an uneasy suspicion of how she had done it. Roger was right: she should be prevented from her semi-criminal activities.

Suddenly a touch of yesterday's cold horror returned. "I'll be firm with the children," I thought. "I'll tell them their presents are wonderful, but if they want any fortune-telling done they can read up the art themselves." Yet even as I was thinking this my eyes were drawn to the page which told of the simplest practice spreads. My hands went out and gathered up the cards. I reversed, I cut, I shuffled; I put the pack together, and laid seven cards face downwards in the rough shape of an inverted horseshoe.

I sat and stared at them, and it was as though the fog had come down again, on me at least, whatever the day was like outside. Hesitantly I turned up the nearest cards, then, with increasing speed, the others. My hands hovered over them: the Lovers, the Black Magician, the Empress, the Lightning-Struck Tower; then a court card—the Page of Swords; and finally, following each other out, the Seven of Swords, the Seven of Pentacles. Somehow I didn't like the look of them at all . . . yet whatever cards my hands had picked on could mean nothing—I was no seer. In any case, perhaps I had only to pick up the book and translate my random choice into the most attractive future——

"Zo," said an all too familiar voice in the doorway. "Many excusings, Jane, but hoping to borrow your milk is. . . . Vy, ah-hah!" A finger wagged remonstratively at me. I sat there glaring at her, feeling both furious and foolish. Damn the children. Damn Roger, for making me leave the door on the latch. Damn that artful nose wiggling ecstatically in the doorway.

"Our Jane is sly, eh? She take my advice and set up in opposition, but does not tell her old friend." Madame skipped across to the table and put her little wooden-feeling arm round me. It weighed like a yoke. Accompanying her came a wave of onions, and the stuffy smell of her dirty woollen cardigan.

"I know nothing about them." I spoke as haughtily as possible, inescapably pinned down as I was in my chair. "The children gave them to me on my birthday, wretched brats, but I don't understand the Tarot at all. I don't even like it. Did you say you were out of milk? I'll get you some." There was only one bottle in the fridge, but I would thankfully drink my breakfast coffee black if it would rid me of her.

"Zo kind, always zo good." Madame's arm felt less like wood than an iron bar. It was impossible to get up without a graceless struggle. She was eagerly studying the spread. I heard her make a strange sound like "Her-ump" beneath her breath. "Your birthday is, eh? Zo. You give me milk, I give you birthday present, I give you insight, hah. Here ve have excellent simple cut.

Easy interpret—but books, no." Her rheumatic fingers were more agile than they looked. She flipped the book shut, as an accomplished pianist might close a book of exercises. "Must interpret alvays vith heart, not head."

"Please, Madame, I don't want to hurt you, but I look on telling cards purely as a joke, and so——"

"Then as a joke ve tell them. You have here zome interesting cards, Jane. Very strange. I am not sure vot these portents of are—to tell, ve must look and look, vith other cuts." She released me suddenly and sat down at my side, sliding my chosen cards towards her. "And I tell you, Jane, it is just as vell you think it joke. For now I see these cards clear, I see they are not nice at all. This English vord, nice! Nothing too good is. Zome fog——" I started—"zome danger. Much bravery needed." There was a distinct gloat in her face, a tremor of eagerness about those little wooden, dirty hands.

"I'll get the milk," I said, rising.

Madame shot me a derisive glance.

"Much bravery, I say, Jane. And already you are not brave at all. This does not do."

Nettled, I sat down again. "All right. Tell me the vo-worst."

"Is not necessarily vorse. Life is school, no? Zometimes the vorse that happen is also best, for development. Now. Here ve have past. The Lovers. Zome rivalry, not decided. Is maybe two men. Is maybe man—and rival interest. Vork." She shot me a heavy-lidded glance, and I knew she was thinking of America. "You remember my advice, Jane? Next ve have Black Magician in present. Zomething not to trust, is underhand. Flow under everything, like snake. Or zo I feel: in this cut."

"Is this the man, or me, or the rival interest?"

"Vait. Vait. Is not yet clear." She closed her eyes, and concentrated. "I think this come from past, and vill affect future—vich draw here——" she opened her eyes—"as Empress. Ordinary, ve take as good card, meaning marriage or good ambition."

"I'm so glad something's pleasant."

"But here Empress much affected by cards either side. Undermined Black Magician, and facing——" she held up the

next card with sinister glee—"Lightning-Struck Tower."
"Oh."
"How do you see this card, Jane? Lightning-Struck Tower?"
"It looks as though something happens," I said feebly.
"Hah, yes! Quite right. Zomething happen. Like bolt from blue zvervishhh." She made an indescribable sound which vividly conjured up lightning in action. "Aftervards, nothing the same."
"It's my birthday. I'd sooner not be depressed on my birthday. Why should I be?"
"That is feeble. And it vill happen." Madame was enjoying herself hugely. "I do not say this necessarily outvard event is, although I think zo. Could be disillusionment. Could be marriage or ambition revealed suddenly as disaster."
"Thanks very much."
"Ve consider now next card: how others behave. Or other person."
"Vot—what other person?"
Madame threw up her hands, showing dirty yellowish palms. "This very small spread. Is not detailed—is general. But von thing clear is—since card is Page, then is von young person, and since Page is of Swords, then is person very stubborn, like mule."
"Or Humboldt's woolly monkey." The thought of Culbertson flashed instantly across my mind.
"Pardon?"
"Nothing. I hope this mule won't cause the bolt from the blue."
"Ah. You take already zo important point, Jane. Is: all card affect card on either side. Zo—is lightning, is stubborn young person—is followed by——" she swept the last two cards into her hands and peered at them, "varning of accidents, and journey. That is all, here."
"And quite enough too. That milk—I'll fetch it."
"Vot do ve mean by varning, vot do ve mean by accident, vot do ve mean by journey?"
"They seem clear enough words to me."
"In occult, is nothing clear. Accident can be intention, no?"

"Yes—I mean, I suppose so."

"And journey—can be voyage, can be no more than step to fetch milk, for example," she grinned, "or can even be—to die. Ve all die. This von thing for all of us to be told, vithout cards. Yet in cards, is alvays how cards lie, and in heart," she clutched her chest, "how person feel. And I do not hesitate to tell you, Jane, that here is von big threat to happiness. Perhaps even to life. But whose life, from zo little cards, I cannot tell. Sit down." Her voice had taken on an alarming authority. "Is your birthday, and I give you free sitting, because you are young and foolish, and in need. I tell you more. And you are von silly girl if you do not pay attention to vot I say."

I sat again, propping my chin on my hands. Was it my imagination, or had the room taken on a misty appearance, as though Madame Sosostris had begun to spin fog in my house as well as hers? It was like looking out at everything from inside a misty blue glass. Perhaps this was my occult ability gaining ground, I told myself derisively, in an effort to make light of her grave pronouncements which, in spite of myself, I half believed.

I had to cling hard to this attitude. For the next half hour Madame cut and spread and counted and shuffled, and compelled me to cut and spread and count and shuffle too: and the cards were set to run all one way, to dark delineation of disaster. By contrast, Madame became ever more jovial and excited, as though my fate were at one end of a seesaw and she at the other, and as my prospects sank her spirits rose higher to balance their descent.

"You see," she cried, "is alvays the same. No vay to escape vot fate vill give you. Here ve have quite different spread, and vot have ve? Black Magician, Page of Swords—and accident, alvays accident."

"And Lightning-Struck Tower." I resignedly recognized the old friend.

"And Tower. It quite remarkable is. Now just von more little spread, hey? Von shorty, Nicola vould say."

"Oh, very well." She had sapped my will power.

"Take six cards, please."

Under her sorceress's stare I did my best to concentrate on

51

extracting the cards. In ordinary fortune-telling hearts were cheering cards, weren't they? In the Tarot, hearts were cups. I concentrated ferociously on a good spread of cups.

"Zo. I turn up. And first is——" she slapped it down with relish—"Black Magician."

"And second, no doubt, is Tower." I shut my eyes.

I heard Madame's little fingers scrabble on the table.

"No—second is six of Swords. A varning——"

"Against accident," I repeated mechanically.

"Against recklessness. And here ve have third quite new card—is King."

"Of Cups?" I asked hopefully.

"Of Swords. Very obstinate, thinking man."

"He would be. It's that mule again."

"No—is not mule. Is grown man. But obstinate and—vith other cards—unprincipled. And next card say: tears."

"I see. Not even one little laugh—not even a smirk?"

"Jane, you do not take this seriously."

"Oh yes, I do."

"Fifth—ah." There was almost a note of disappointment in her voice. "Is better. Is Emperor."

"What does he do?"

"Depend on last card." She took a long time picking it up, and I felt she was concentrating on Swords just as I had concentrated on Cups. Then she pondered.

"The Hanged Man?" I prodded her on, at last.

"No. Is the Sun." She nodded glumly, as though she had pronounced final sentence on me.

"Is that bad?"

"Is alvays good. Ven comes vith Emperor, is very, very good."

"What does it mean?"

"Is vish granted. Is like paradise."

"Paradise—for me? In spite of all those Black Magicians?"

She shrugged. "Is here. Is in your cards. This is all I can say. Good comes vith Emperor. And Emperor is man. And all the rest comes——" she swept them together—"vith other man. Take two more cards, Jane. Now. Here is your card: Queen.

52

And here other Queen. Other woman. And this is all I say to end it. You must take care."

"But——" I gazed at her uneasily, "—of the other woman? Or the man? And which man? And who gets the better bit, her or me? And what does the Emperor himself stand for?"

"Is new beginning, is completion. Is perhaps marriage. Is perhaps just understanding. No more, Jane. In veek, ve try again. Perhaps meaning show clearer then."

"This good could be all for that other woman?" I persisted. In spite of determined scepticism I wanted unreasonably to retain that little good for myself.

"This I cannot say. But von thing clear as daylight, Jane: for you there is varning of keep eyes open. If is good or bad, if you have not open eyes, you not see."

It was just as I had always expected, everything about the occult was fog. Everything could be twisted any way you chose. Even my two poor little good cards in the end could be twisted towards someone else.

"I don't want any more of the Tarot at any time," I said explosively, "but thank you very much, Madame. Now I'll get your milk."

She went at last, carrying the bottle. I shut the Tarot box, viciously. One of my friends maintained that fortune-telling was always monstrous because, she said, when you're told something firmly enough, then your subconscious mind sets out to make it true; which was where any truth in prophesying entered. I hoped she wasn't right. It would have been preferable to think that part of Madame's mind had already a slant on my own future than that her authoritative words driven home with such insistence on Black Magician, Lightning-Struck Tower, and accident, could so stimulate the primitive depths of my own consciousness to work against me. Besides, how could I be responsible for 'stubborn young person'? It was not quite——

The latch of the front door clicked again.

"Roger!" I called out gladly. "I'm thankful you've come, I've had an atrocious time with our tame witch. Oh." I had reached the hall. It was not Roger who stood there smiling at me, but Gabriella.

"Jane! You look so very much surprised! Though white—are you quite well, yes? Look, I hope it is not difficult for you, but——" She broke off, and eyed me warily. Then: "But Susie——" and she put out a hand as though trying to explain the inexplicable. It was easy to guess what had happened.

"Susie wasn't expecting you? No—she thought you were coming tomorrow. She sent you on to me?"

"Is that all right?" Gabriella's huge eyes, which used to hold continual laughter, stared at me gravely.

"Of course it's all right. I love to have you here, you know that."

Her eyes lightened. Bloody Susie, I thought. No doubt she made the hurried dusting of one small spare room on a Sunday afternoon seem like all the seven labours of Hercules. Now, as Gabriella moved forward, I saw how she had altered. In the two years since we'd seen her last her puppy fat had gone, and her beauty, formerly veiled, was now apparent. The light from the sitting room doorway fell on her face, revealing her sombre, dark, heavy-lidded eyes, the perfect matt skin, the cast of head and neck which had the grace and poise of Nefertiti's. (Oh Susie, no wonder you sent her on to me! Could the most virtuously married man not be captivated, by such grace alone?)

I led her into the sitting room. She sat down sideways and childishly in an armchair, her long legs dangling over its arm. She wore the simplest of brown sailcloth dresses, very short, which could probably be bought in any cheap store, but on her it looked terrific. I felt a wave of primitive female jealousy, comparable to what a man might feel for another born with a million already in the bank. Nature can be unfair.

She was watching me, a little on the defensive. How unlike the old Gabriella that was, who had been outgoing, expansive, continuously gay and sure of everyone's pleasure in seeing her. What has happened to her? I wondered.

"There was a chance of coming a day earlier, so I changed my ticket." She sighed. "But I thought, family."

"And of course." I made an effort to make up for what I was sure had been a cold water douche from Susie. "We are your family, Gabriella, related or not. And don't pay attention to Susie's moods. She's irritable lately, I'm afraid. We all just have to put up with it."

"That is true?" She frowned. "Why is Susie irritable? Something is wrong with her?"

"Nothing. She just is."

"I would so much sooner be here, then, with you." She gave another small sigh. "Or would this be a trouble, too?"

"No trouble for me. I'd be delighted. But trouble with Susie, yes."

"Why? She does not want me there. It is not simply my early coming."

This new Gabriella was a bit too acute. The old one would not have noticed, or would have laughed.

"Dear Gabriella, whatever happens, for Susie, is the wrong thing. She'd think I had turned you against her." Well, she had to know. . . .

"I see." Then she said unexpectedly, "Poor Erik. My stepmother would have liked him to be happy, she was so generous, but how can he be happy with someone like that?"

"Oh, Erik glides. He's a natural glider."

"Glides?"

"Over the surface." I made a skating motion with my hand. "Like that. One day, when the surface breaks, we may see a different Erik emerge."

For the first time, she laughed. "I hope the surface holds, then. And you, Jane? How is—Roger, was it not?"

"Healthy." It was my turn to feel defensive.

Gabriella narrowed her eyes at me. "You do not want to talk about it?"

"So far as I know everyone in the town talks about it."

"But not you. He wanted to marry you, anyway. Yet no ring——" She was looking at my hand. Then she remembered, obviously, about Roger's wife. "All right, Jane, I did not mean to question you, but we know each other so long, yes?"

"I'm not being cagey. His wife died, and he still wants to marry me. But nothing's settled, yet." Was it?

"Poor Roger. I liked him. I liked him very, very much. Perhaps I will shake you together." She raised her chin and subjected me to a Nefertiti stare.

I went over to the attack. "But what about you, Gabby—no eligible *partis* on the horizon?"

"Oh, me." She looked away. I was aware of some deep undercurrent of hurt. "You know there are always *partis* on the continent, when families arrange things well."

"Yet obviously none to your taste?"

"No." I was sure there had been. She raised her eyes again. "Jane, do not talk to anyone about it, will you?"

"No—why should I? It's not much fun to be too discussed, is it?" I said lightly, and saw it was too near the truth. I got up. "Look, love, would you like to come upstairs and unpack your things for the night? I'm expecting Roger along any time, your first chance to shake us both together. Then we'll all go up to Susie's and have my birthday cake."

"I hope there's a slice for me," she said with a flash of laughter, and pulled herself to her feet. I picked up her case, and motioned her to go ahead up the small flight of stairs. She was half way to the landing when we both heard the hall door open again, and turned.

"I'm late, Jane. Sorry," said Roger. "The patients held me up, I——" Over my head he stared at Gabriella.

She smiled briefly, uncertainly, nodded, and went on up.

"Roger, I've had the most extraordinary——"

He wasn't listening. He was still staring over my head at the now empty stairs. "That wasn't—Gabriella?"

"Yes, a day early." I stopped, sympathetically. "It is staggering, isn't it? Hits you right between the eyes. You'll come round soon." Even as I spoke, I wondered. A small, dry wonder. Susie's remembered voice spoke venomously in my ear: "You wouldn't like her round with Roger, or Cosway, would you?" I refused to hear it.

"She's beautiful, isn't she?" I said inadequately.

"More. Beauty hasn't always quite that quality."

56

"Which one do you mean?"
"Isolde," he said in a wondering voice. "Guinevere. Deirdre."
"Of the sorrows," I completed automatically.
And two of them queens.

Chapter Seven

I would not ask myself outright if Roger had been knocked sideways by Gabriella, but underneath I suspected that he had. I could hardly blame him, though—I, who had hesitated to commit myself until after seeing what America had to offer. Anyway, he had to meet her again some time, yet I must admit that when Cosway merely blinked at her, and promptly gave me all his attention, I felt relief from an unaccountable, unlocatable pain.

The birthday tea, and even the birthday supper, to which both Roger and Gabriella were eventually invited, went off smoothly enough, although the children were wild with disappointment when they found the Tarot had been left behind, and were considerable nuisances until Erik roused himself at last from his habitual indolence to shut them up. He was just in time, for Culbertson, greatly given to nudity that summer, was already at the door wearing only a bikini on her way to burgle Number 16.

"*Culbertson*——" he thundered, "you're not to bother Jane about those cards. A birthday's for pleasure, not penance."

Culbertson swung on the door, her chin tilted mutinously upward. Yea or nay, obedience hung in the balance. Gabriella's soft voice broke the silence. "These cards—they are something to do with that tame witch you spoke of, Jane? The one you had such an atrocious time with this afternoon?"

Culbertson's eye rolled sideways consideringly at me, like a horse's. She was deciding where immediate interest lay. She released the doorhandle to make her way gravely to my side, and leaned heavily and stoutly against my shoulder in a listening pose. Sometimes her grace as dancer was a complete mystery to me.

I dismissed my "atrocious time" as lightly as possible, but

Stewart and Nicola were thrilled by the thought of Madame Sosostris' professional touch applied to their cards, and in a ruthless inquisition drew her prognostications from me.

"Darling Jane!" By the end of the recital Nicola was pop-eyed. "What a future. All those disastrous men. I can't wait to see if she's right."

"Two men," I said repressively. "And thank you very much, Nicola, but I can wait; easily."

"Lightning-Struck Tower," savoured Culbertson, swinging dreamily to and fro on her toes. Cosway, who had not fulfilled his threat of boycotting my birthday, had turned a little pale. He was looking at me anxiously, and out of sight of the others put a protective hand on mine. His nervousness seemed exaggerated but endearing. Roger appeared wholly preoccupied by Gabriella. Susie gave me an unwanted second helping of chicken and said she always felt there was something in these things, which was why she would never have her fortune told; it was often the worst things that came out true, wasn't it? "So I shouldn't buy yourself a car as you were thinking, Jane dear, not if the old psychic saw an accident for you."

"Is Jane buying a car?" Roger's face wore a thunderous frown. He had momentarily detached himself from Gabriella, and I could read in his expression the unfavourable reaction which any reference to my expanding prospects conjured up these days.

"For Cornwall," I admitted. "The house is rather isolated, I believe. My experience of hired cars makes me feel one wouldn't need the cards to predict a sudden end."

"And what sort of a car are you treating yourself to, Jane? A Silver Cloud Rolls?" Roger speared a potato as though it were my American publisher.

"You can spare me the heavy sarcasm. It's a fairly modest Fiat, and a bargain—second-hand but only been run in. The owner is a flash young man with a restless eye for cars. No sooner had he fallen for this than something more suitable for a roving bachelor with a string of birds caught his eye."

"A second-hand car is bound to cause accidents," argued Susie.

"It's no good trying to curb Jane. She's so independent these days."

Gabriella glanced at Roger, then at me with what I thought was compassion; and then her gaze travelled on to Susie. "I would love to see Cornwall. I have so often read of it, and of its legends. It is the country of Isolde, no?"

I experienced a slight sense of shock. Now Roger was looking at me too, but it was hard to interpret his expression.

"Why, yes," I answered. "It's from Lerryn on the river Fowey that Tristan is said to have sailed when he was sent by Mark to fetch the king's bride to Cornwall."

"I wonder why tragedies are so attractive in legend, when they're such unpleasant things in real life." Erik spoke without thoughts of his own past tragedy, I felt sure, but I saw the veins stand out on Susie's hands as her fingers tensed. An expression I knew too well came into her eyes, and it was no sweet look she turned in Gabriella's direction.

"It's a pity we can't take you there, Erik and I, but the summer is such an exhausting time when the children start their holidays; the house seems abnormally full, and then Erik's working so hard himself. I'm afraid, if we went away at all, it would be just the two of us together. Only that's impossible."

"I have come at an awkward time of year?"

"Good heavens, no, I didn't mean that in the least." Susie gave an artificial laugh and crumbled her bread with fingers that shook a little.

("She really is very hysterical," I thought.)

"Gabriella, come to Cornwall with me? If Susie can spare you? It may be dull when I'm out working, but you could get on a bus, and bathe somewhere, couldn't you? If there are any buses."

"Oh, I would love to—may I?" Gabriella's face lighted with the old happiness. "And in return I will act as your secretary; I promise. I will write up all your notes for you."

This failed to please Susie, too. "I'm sure Jane won't want to turn you into a secretary. And the children have been so looking forward to your coming." Possibly she was remembering the advantage that a young and lively Gabriella could be in dealing with Culbertson, and the children's friends. Susie herself was extremely lazy; and thirty-four—a year older than Cosway. I was amused to watch the struggle in her face. "Jane getting a free secretary and ally; or Erik in temptation's path." Perhaps I had a slight desire to remove temptation from Roger's path in the same pathetic way.

"We won't fight about it, Susie. Let's wait and see whose plans fit in with whose. Someone else might like to come as well."

"I almost think that I might come to Cornwall." Roger sat back in his chair, and his dark glance strayed from Gabriella to me as though he had read my thoughts.

"You haven't got a holiday coming up, have you? What will your partner say?"

"I could always make one for your sake, my sweet Janey." Roger's voice was honied, but he was studying Gabriella.

"Let's all have a holiday in Cornwall with Jane." Why did I say Cosway was not by nature provocative? His tone was full of dulcet provocation.

"You've just had one, you can't possibly need another," said Susie scathingly. "Anyway, you're always complaining that you've got to work harder because no money's coming in."

"What do sisters know of a brother's needs? Will you have me, Janey—before Roger settles into your spare room to take Gabriella bathing?"

It was a revelation to see Cosway so ruthlessly tactless, no matter who got hurt in the process.

"Janey, you're going to have your hands full," said Erik.

"So far I've only seen a small photograph of this place, and I can't remember offhand how many rooms it has."

"It will have a Cornish garden, anyway," said Cosway dreamily. "Fuchsia hedges. I'll pitch my tent there. Distant views of wine dark sea. King Mark's horns at twilight——"

"Hunting or cuckold's?" put in Roger.

"It will have a disused tin mine and constant rain. And the nearest you'll get to the Legend will be something called King Mark's Pasty Shop. I'm going there to work, remember? How can I work if I'm shopping and cooking all day long for a load of layabouts?"

"I wonder if Tristan got called a layabout?" murmured Erik.

"Stewart and I will come and shop and cook for you," offered Nicola. "He does very good pancakes, and I can manage stew, bread sauce and waffles if you've got the right irons. Stewart will chauffeur you about, Jane, he hardly ever hits anything unless it's foggy or raining."

"In Cornwall that will be a lot of help. And what's Culbertson going to do?" I had a wistful thought of cancelling the let at once and altogether.

"I'll sleep with dear Cosway in his tent," said Culbertson. "And I'll look after the dog. The one that goes with the house."

Just then Susie, who was liking the conversation less and less, and now showed a marked disinclination for the solitude she had formerly desired for herself and Erik, changed the conversation adroitly by asking how many of us would need transport for Culbertson's end of term do on the next day.

As it turned out, the arrangement was simply managed. For next day I acquired my Fiat, and the afternoon saw me driving Gabriella and Nicola towards Culbertson's school, while Erik, Cosway, Susie and Stewart followed in my brother's Rover. Even Roger, who viewed Culbertson's serious gyrations with some amusement, meant to put in an appearance later on; but his work made him too uncertain a starter for his car to be counted transport for anyone. He had annoyed Culbertson the evening before by asking if she was going to dance the part of a Humboldt's woolly monkey; and I could see she had veered to favouring a match between Cosway and me. This was almost alarming, like having my affairs in the hands of a marriage bureau, for what Culbertson favoured she usually got.

It was another lovely day, as I drove off towards the downs. It seemed as though the fog had really gone at last. As we pulled up out of the town the sea lay spread behind us in a great sheet of sapphire silk, and the horizon was just indistinct enough to hold out promise of further fine weather—a haze lay over the far west. When I stopped the car for a moment on a shoulder of down, so that Gabriella could enjoy the view, the air was alive with lark song.

"Golly," said Nicola from the back seat, winding down a window and snuffling the air like a carthorse, "doesn't it smell good? Downs or moorland, once you smell them you never want to stop. Do you have smells as good as this in your part of the world, Gabby?"

"The same," said Gabriella on a muted note. "And yet, you know—different."

I looked at her, sideways. I wasn't wrong. There was something altogether muted about her on this visit. There were shadows under her eyes, and small lines at the corners of her lips as though she made a habit of compressing them.

Nicola was rattling on: "It's a pity they can't bottle the downs in one great gorgeous bottle of scent, isn't it? And then even on those foul foggy days you'd know what it smelt like——" She leant forward, thrusting her head with its dark plaits of hair between us. "We've a super country, in bits, still, haven't we, Gabriella? Which would you sooner live in—England, or France? France can't be half so spoilt as we are here, with people." She gave a long exaggerated sigh. "I've never been there."

"You stay here, Nicola." Gabriella stared upwards at the larks. "I'm going to, this time."

"Gabby? You are? For good?" I saw the dismayed question, "Near Susie and Father?" shape itself on her tactless lips, and hastened to intervene with a silly joke: "Perhaps Gabby's on the run—a sort of peace-time refugee."

I heard a small gasp beside me, and then Gabriella's too-hasty reply: "Who or what from, I wonder?"

"Oh, as to that——" and, "But are you really staying, Gabriella?" we said together.

"Yes, I think so. Sometimes it is good to be with strangers, who do not know you."

"Not strangers, Gabby," said Nicola, hurt.

"Not you people, stupid one. Just all the people who know everything in one's own town, and who talk, talk, talk— louder than those larks are singing." Suddenly she looked carefree again, like Nicola. "Let us sing with them—yes? You both know 'L'alouette'?——"

She began to sing defiantly in her high soprano. I let in the clutch, and took a second slightly but correctly like Mr. Frank Churchill, with Nicola bellowing loud as a young bull in my ear. When we came round to the last: "Je te plumerai le dos," she broke off bellowing to say: "Really, Gabby, the French can be savage sometimes; poor little larks."

"Oh yes," said Gabriella, quiet again as we drove up a gravel sweep to Culbertson's school. "They can—we can. We can mark each other with our claws till we look like *cuir sauvage*. Look—isn't that Roger getting out of that car, Jane? I do not know that Culbertson will be so pleased to see him here today as you and I." She laughed, and waved at him. I blamed myself for being a Susie and finding her attitude too proprietorial. Perhaps she was merely being part of the family, and everyone in it had the habit of coupling Roger and me together.

He hadn't seen our arrival yet. He was helping someone out of his car, someone like a small dark bundle, who wore a wide straw hat, drop earrings, and a thick woollen cardigan even on this shimmeringly hot July day. I gave an exclamation of annoyance. "Really—it's—it's just not possible of Roger——"

"Cor luv us," Nicola got out of the car and shook herself, "your boyfriend's deserted you for Madame Sosostris, Jane. I said the cards would bring you into competition, didn't I? It's the witch, Gabby, do you see?" Her clear tones must have carried, but Madame didn't seem to care. She tittuped towards me, beaming as much of a beam as her wooden features could assemble.

"Zo unexpected a lift," she began to shout at me, while we were still ten yards apart. "Your dear friend found me by the bus stop, on my vay to see our small Culbertson dance, and vould not take refusal, zo here I come in time to sit vith you all and enjoy ourselves."

Garlic and some cheap scent fought for possession of her person. The smell of the downs was obliterated by it. I quelled my shudder at the idea of sitting with her, and merely looked reproachfully at Roger, who looked back with a bland stare. In spite of his blandness, however, there was still something thunderous about him. I was glad when Erik drove up beside us, causing a diversion. The Rover disgorged its passengers, and we all proceeded into the hall.

Here the Principal met us in a flutter. She was talking to everyone, parents and children, as they passed, while at the same time she was apparently shaping some apology for Erik.

"I do feel I must explain to you about your Caroline——" she began. "Oh—Mrs. Margerison, how are you? Yes, Dodo has gone to change already.... Has Caroline explained? I feel very badly about it because she is quite one of our best pupils, but you will understand, won't you—— Good afternoon, Mr. Keith, lovely weather—that to know when to punish and when not to punish is our most difficult task——"

Erik was looking bewildered. It was obvious he had almost forgotten Culbertson's true name was Caroline.

"... I'm afraid I simply cannot have her investigating other people's letters...."

A small figure in white, which had been coming forward to greet us, backed hastily through a door on the left at these words, and faded discreetly away.

"Admirable woman," hissed Roger's voice in my ear. "Investigating is exactly the word I should have chosen."

"Has Caroline been making a beast of herself again?" asked Susie fretfully. "She would."

Once we had extracted a kernel of truth from the Principal's general greetings we learnt sadly that Culbertson's disgrace had demoted her to the *corps de ballet* for the afternoon, and her two solos had been given to another child.

Chastened by our favourite's public fall we made our way through a passage, and out on to a stretch of lawn. The house was small and Elizabethan. The former sloping rose garden at the lawn's end had been converted to an auditorium, with a stage built in a cup-shaped bowl of ground. In front of the stage an orchestra of young musicians from Seaminster Regis Academy was tuning up. I felt for poor Culbertson. It was a day for shining, not for black disgrace. Even Madame Sosostris was quietened to a smell of garlic at my side.

Someone handed me a programme. I looked round for Culbertson, but she must have been already in the wings. Our party sorted itself out and seated itself. Stewart and Nicola had managed to place Madame Sosostris by Susie, who looked as though someone had laid a drain under her nose. I found myself between Cosway and Roger, with Gabriella beyond us on his other side. Erik, as usual, looked comfortably half asleep. News of his daughter's disgrace had not visibly perturbed him. Nicola had already acquired a large Dairy Raspberry Lick from somewhere, and was sucking it audibly in a way that made a correct woman beyond her look sideways in hauteur.

The Principal fluttered down the central gangway in a swirl of purple chiffon pleats, flashed a general smile, seated herself on a sort of throne at the foot of the aisle, and bowed to the conductor, a handsome young man whose face was already burstingly plum-coloured from nervous tension. The orchestra launched itself unevenly into the Overture to *Swan Lake*. The larks were silenced by competition from the first violins.

That afternoon's memories are all of pink and white to me, as though Nicola's Raspberry Lick had melted together in a swirling mass of swans and princesses, dolls and skaters. A number of portly little swans trod heavily through their dance with creaking knees and rapt expressions. A child with flaxen curls danced a shaky Adagio, the first of Culbertson's missed solos. A small boy made a too-spectacular leap, grazed his knee, and hobbled swearing offstage to the sound of scolding in the wings. And throughout the afternoon Culbertson, stoically dissembling her inner feelings, danced in the *corps de ballet* with an insolent authority that made everyone else look like the amateurs they would probably turn out to be. In the audience a hawknosed man with a pale intelligent face pointed her out surreptitiously to the Principal, who smiled and nodded and set her determined features into an expression of mingled triumph and despair.

"I wonder if they mind their private papers investigated at the Garden," murmured Roger in my ear.

In the interval everyone walked about the lawns, ate strawberries and cream, and cloyingly—and, in our case, insincerely—praised each other's dancers. "How your Celia has come on!" gushed a large woman with bright red gums to a small woman in patterned Tricel, who responded bravely: "But, my dear—your Dodo!"

Both women, whom I knew vaguely, considered me; and spoke with one voice: "I see little Caroline is not even dancing a solo this year. I thought she was so promising. I'm sure the Principal always thought her quite promising."

"Obviously not so promising as little Celia and tiny Dodo," I responded with a tiger grin.

"What's that?" asked Erik's placid voice behind us. "Oh Caroline—yes, she was dancing, but I fear my child has disgraced herself. Can I get anyone some strawberries and cream?"

Culbertson emerged from a nearby bush. Stewart and Nicola converged on her smoothly and inevitably like gangsters. She was taken behind the bush again, and re-emerged ten minutes later in tears and fled towards the house.

"That's that," said Stewart, rejoining us. "First woman head of S.Y. is one thing, but she must learn not to disgrace her family."

Roger gazed at him with admiration. "I can't think how you do it."

"Oh, Nicola and I have decided to take Culbertson in hand, since you've all failed. Mrs. Margerison, can I get you an ice?" With old-fashioned courtesy he bore the red-gummed woman away towards the buffet.

"Little beast," sighed Erik. "Delinquents or prigs, what are the young coming to, these days? Do go and find Culbertson, Jane, or she won't even be appearing in the *corps de ballet*. I don't know where Susie is—they all seem to have vanished."

But I was already moving towards the house.

Chapter Eight

Once inside, I glanced about me uncertainly. On my left were the Principal's apartments, and a passage leading to a large salon, and adjoining rooms where she received parents or reproved pupils. On my right a swing door gave access to the class and practice rooms. A fine staircase in the hall ahead led up to a gallery, out of which opened rooms where the boarders and mistresses lived. There was a throng of people in the house, mostly parents escorted by small children proudly conducting them on a tour. The perpetual coming and going up and down the stairs and round the gallery made me feel dizzy. I stood there hoping that Culbertson might come by, but she had hidden herself, and I had no idea where to find her in the *mêlée*. Somewhere quiet would be the likeliest solution, and I started hesitantly towards the salon.

It was quieter here, away from noise and crush. I walked down the passage, my feet making no sound on the opulent Wilton. This end of the house was lushly furnished. Dark portraits hung on panelled walls; small highly polished tables stood around; here and there was a fine piece of silver or a freshly washed piece of Chelsea china, and bowls of larkspur, peonies, roses, poppies and cranesbill reflected back their colours from shining surfaces.

I stood in the salon doorway. No sign of Culbertson. I turned, and there stood one of the assistant mistresses.

"Miss Halliford! Were you looking for the Principal? She's giving tea to the directors——" She was wondering if I were important enough for her to suggest an interruption on my behalf.

"No, I'm looking for Culbert—for Caroline. She ran into the house just now, and my brother wants to find her."

"Ah yes, I'm afraid she's a little upset, poor child." Her pale blue glance raked me. "But she danced very well under the circumstances, didn't she? If you'd like to sit down and look at a paper, Miss Halliford, I'll find her for you. They all have their favourite hiding places, and this is a complicated house, you know."

"Please don't bother, I'll go myself, and——"

"It's no bother at all. There are so many people about, which confuses things, but we're quite accustomed to the children's little ways."

As she spoke she drew up a chair and handed me a pile of magazines from a nearby table. There was nothing for it but to obey, with a half-amused remembrance of how quelling such milk-smooth authority had been when one was Culbertson's age.

"Thank you very much."

"It's been a pretty performance so far, hasn't it? Quite a good standard all round, I think, although Dodo Margerison's Adagio was a little shaky." Throwing me this oblique compliment to Culbertson, she left the room.

The magazines were old. I returned them to the table, and sat lazily listening to the tick of the clock, the sound of distant childish voices, and a murmur of conversation which came from the small salon through the further door, like two bees having a summer drone together. It must be a very private conversation, I decided, perhaps some mother or father of a small dancer was carrying on a discreet *amour*. The idea amused me, particularly when associated with some of the parents I knew, and I considered having a tactful fit of choking. They were speaking too low, however, for any such warning to be needed, their voices were soporific as the sea on a fine, lazy, beach day. Soon, they almost lulled me past the threshold of consciousness. In this state, between sleeping and waking, I grew aware that this house vaguely displeased me. Perhaps it was just these quarters. There was a heavy atmosphere about them, something disquieting in the oil-painted stare of the woman with a ribboned cap above the chimney piece. The room had an oriel looking on a yew maze, and was shadowed because the glass armorials were dull blue and green and amber, and filtered out the light.

I found myself shivering slightly. It was curiously as though time had ceased to exist. The house, this end of it, was quieter than it had been. A moment ago a bell had shrilled far away, to signal that the lengthy tea interval was over. Yet still I sat on, wondering where the assistant mistress had got to in her search for Culbertson, and almost hypnotized by my surroundings, and the lowered voices in the next room.

The clock struck a quarter to five. Culbertson, if she was dancing, must be back in the wings. I struggled to rid myself of this lethargy, now that time had reasserted itself.

"Time," said a voice in the next room heatedly, nearer the door, as though corroborating the clock's assertion. "Time, time, time! Zo stupid you take me for, eh? See now, vorse it vill be——"

I sat bolt upright. Without the rest of her speech my ear would have recognized that "Zo" anywhere. The thought of being involved with a Madame Sosostris heatedly rowing one of her customers or dubious foreign friends was too much. With a swiftness and lightness that would have done credit to Culbertson onstage I was out of my chair and the room, and fleeing back down the passage towards the hall where one or two gallery stragglers glanced at me with raised eyebrows. I slowed my pace and, feeling foolish, walked sedately back to rejoin my party in the third row.

They had not yet all returned. Stewart and Nicola were still over by the buffet, but there was no sign of Susie, Cosway, Roger or Gabriella. Erik alone was back in his place, deliberately studying his programme in an effort to stem Mrs. Margerison's flow from behind him. I made my way to his side. "I've completely failed with Culbertson, I'm afraid—even her form mistress couldn't find her for me."

He turned to me with relief. "She came out again when Susie had gone into the house. All blown over, I think. The Principal's plainly sorry for her, came over specially to tell us what that chap with her said about Culbertson's dancing. He's fairly eminent behind the scenes, and apparently his eye is riveted on our young Humboldt's woolly monkey. And not——" he dropped his voice—"on Dodo or Celia."

"Oh good. But I hope Culbertson is not *too* re-inflated."

"Just nicely so-so. Went back to the wings quite happily, but subdued."

I gave a sigh of relief. "I am glad." The second bell sounded its tyrannical call.

"Where have the others gone? They'll be late."

"Putting themselves to rights, I imagine—ah! here they are." Several people rose further up the row to let in some of our party. Susie's face had a glistening flush, unsubdued by powder. She stood on one side to let Roger join me, blocking Cosway as she did so. Gabriella, cool and unruffled, followed Roger in, and Cosway sat down on her other side looking as thunderous as Roger had earlier in the day. I found myself wondering if all other families had these continual undercurrents. Perhaps half the trouble was the peculiar net of relationships that bound us together so inadequately.

Even from where I sat it was obvious that poor Susie's jaw trembled with umbrage, forced as she was to sit between her brother and Madame Sosostris, whose head was shaking too. It was like a couple of china mandarins' heads nodding away side by side. Yes, poor Susie: the garlic would certainly have augmented in this heat. There would be trouble in the Rover going home—thank God I was driving my own car! Stewart and Nicola now rejoined us, causing everyone to rise again, just as the Principal made a second gracious entrance down the gangway.

I enjoyed this half of the performance more than the first. It was gratifying to know that Culbertson had been singled out by the Principal's chief guest. Afterwards, our party split. Roger dashed off to hold a surgery, and I found myself unwillingly pressed into promising a lift to the witch, as Nicola called her. Erik and Susie, with Stewart and Cosway loosely attached, were staying on to collect Culbertson once she had changed and removed her greasepaint.

While I waited for Madame, Gabriella and Nicola to join me I strolled idly to and fro on the gravel drive, now and then exchanging pointless conversation with acquaintances, or listening to one brave lark which had reasserted its claim to an audience. I gazed up into the blue sky. An amethyst haze was definitely there, moving in from the sea. It would be too miserable if that dismal fog crept back unexpectedly on us again. . . .

My three passengers were approaching from the house. I got into the driver's seat while Nicola and Madame Sosostris settled themselves in the back, and Gabriella beside me in front. That bitten-in look was back on her face. She had seemed carefree enough out on the lawn: it was impossible to imagine what had caused the change. She sat looking out of her window and answered monosyllabically when spoken to. I suppressed a brief suspicion that she was resenting Roger's unceremonious departure, his casual farewells.

Nicola had chosen Madame as her back seat companion. I had heard her arranging it: "You must come and sit by me, Madame, because I most terribly, terribly want to pick your brains about the Tarot." Such openness was disarming, as perhaps it was meant to be, but Madame had not been disarmed. She had smiled a little grimly, as though she had seen right through Nicola's childish enthusasim and attempt at exploitation. Now I lent an amused ear to the conversation behind me:

"I bet you have one particular spread you go by, more than any other, don't you, Madame?"

"Ah, as Mademoiselle on the front seat vould say, it is always *comme ci, comme ça.*" She stressed the French words. "Von adapt to the client."

"But how do you go about it? Do tell me, it's fascinating. Do you concentrate, or visualize, or what?"

"My dear child, impossible to pin down the occult. Zometimes is von, zometimes is other."

"But if you were to tell—say, Gabriella's fortune, how would you go about *feeling* it?"

"I vould be very happy to tell Mademoiselle's cards at any time, if she come to see me vill, and tell her all I know." Madame raised her voice a little. She obviously wanted Gabriella to hear, but the latter made no response. I was a bit indignant at such touting in my car.

"It's that there are so *many* cards," wailed Nicola at last.

"You might just tell me how you blend it all together."

"Aha, now ve ask the chef how ve blend the sauce! And I say, is art, is long experience, is feeling, is gift, is much, much knowledge that not acquired can be in little vile."

"Nicola," I said, "that's more than enough questioning. Why should Madame tell us? You don't ask your lawyer to teach you how he does his work." We were now gliding downhill into the town, and could see the great spread of Channel before us. "Look—that wretched fog *is* coming back again." Here and there above the surface of the water floated small banks of mist, as soft and pliant as the breasts of doves; pearl grey, pale mauve, white and grey mingled together like smoke.

"I fear our Jane is right. Ve not much luck have, this summer."

"I'm so sick of it," I said as we began to descend steep Mariota Street. "Will it ever go again?"

Gabriella was silent. She appeared tired, and when we reached our own street I deliberately drew up first outside Madame Sosostris' house.

"A very nice little car," she said condescendingly, as she struggled out of the back. "I vill not say good-bye, Jane, because ve meet so often in the street. Anyvay—come in, all von you, to eat supper vith me, no? Zome pasta; zome dried pears and apricots that soak already three days."

"Thank you very much," I improvised hastily, "but we're going on to my brother for supper."

"Zo." Madame gave me a cynical stare, patted my hand in a spirit of irony, and paying us no further attention opened the door of her house, stamped her feet on the threshold as though to shake off layers of thick mud, and banged the door between us. I drove on to Number 16.

"Old hag," said Nicola. "She didn't even thank you."

"She guessed I wasn't going out to supper. And later she'll look out when you two leave and confirm it wasn't true."

"As a matter of fact Gabby and I are having supper with you here, darling Jane."

"There isn't any. Only eggs; or tomatoes and bacon."

"Eggs again. Do you never eat anything else? She'll turn into a hen one day, won't she, Gabby? And then Roger will put her in his pot and eat her." Nicola began to flap her arms up and down and outwards from her sides, and go, "Cockadoodledoo!" in a way I found extremely irritating.

"Do be quiet, Nicola. You'll have a better supper tonight at home. No, I'm serious. Susie will be annoyed. Gabriella may stay if she likes, but I didn't invite you."

"How very odd, I distinctly remember hearing myself tell Susie that you had."

"And you really shouldn't use quite so many lies."

"Oh Aunt Jane, my love, my darling, in future I'll base everything on your great, great social honesty with Madame S. Don't be a beast. You saw Susie's face. She's in a mood, already. Supper in the old homestead tonight is going to be a rank affair." Nicola pressed her warm cheek against mine pleadingly, leaning over from the back seat. "Please."

"Oh, all right. But your father might have liked supper."

"Now, don't let's go moral. Just cook us a lovely big omelet *aux fines herbes* or whatever, and while you're doing it I'll instruct Gabriella in ze cards vot zay mean."

"I want nothing to do with those cards." Gabriella's cheeks flushed carnation colour. "She's a horrible, vile old woman. I cannot think how you all bear to know her. I have a migraine, so I won't have supper, thank you, Jane. I'll walk on to The Lime Tree House, and go to bed. Thank you for taking me to see Culbertson." She escaped hurriedly from the car, and walked away without looking back.

"Did I upset her too, Nicola?" I said, as we went into the house. "I didn't *not* want her to supper, but there's really so little, and I can hardly face an egg myself."

"Not to worry, she was upset already. By old snakes-and-ladders Sosostris herself. That was the only reason", added Nicola virtuously, "I took the old witch in the back, and put her through a questionnaire. And not because I was inquisitive, my dear Janey."

"I'm sorry." I sat down on the sofa and stared at her. Nicola curled herself up on the floor and began to eat an orange from a wooden bowl. She seemed to need food all the time. Perhaps it was her age.

"How could Madame have upset her? And when? They weren't together."

"Oh yes, they were. When you were waiting for us on the drive. I was in the loo quite a time, it wouldn't pull. When I came out I could see something was up. Madame was all wriggly smiles, and Gabriella looked as though she might die of hauteur." Nicola began to laugh. The orange squirted on my carpet. "Gabby said: 'What do you mean, you didn't know my name before?' and the witch said: 'Vot I say, I mean. And now I tell your surname it is von very vell-known name—to me, anyvay. It mean much, much.'" Her mimicry was perfect. I laughed, unwillingly.

"Go on, Nicola."

"Well, not much more. Gabby said haughtily: 'It is not a common name in France,' and Madame smiled again, like this——" Nicola bared her teeth in a crocodile grin, "and said, 'I do not talk of vot is common, but of vot is vell known to you, my dear.' She put her hand on Gabby's arm, and sort of caressed it. Gabby looked as though a spider fell on her. She jerked her arm away, and said, 'Don't touch me. Don't speak to me again!'"

"Goodness—perhaps she had a touch of the sun. She looked flushed enough, just now."

Nicola shook her head. "It was odd, Jane. She looked icy: frozen. And you know how hot it was. Then Madame saw me, and smiled, and said, 'Ah, little Nicola. You vill persuade your cousin to have her cards told, no? Tell her to be sure and kom— it alvays vise to know the future is.' I said: 'She's not my cousin,' and then we came and joined you; and since they weren't being exactly buddies, at least Gabriella wasn't ostensibly buddying," finished Nicola thoughtfully, "I bundled snakes-and-ladders into the back, and that's the lot. Don't you think I'm socially *adept*, Jane? And can I have your other orange?"

Chapter Nine

That fog did return. On waking next day I could feel the difference in the atmosphere—there was a smothering blanket of damp. The curtains hung limp before open windows, and outside was corroboration of what I'd already sensed: whorls of white smoky fog.

I looked in the glass, with resentment for what peered back at me. A restless night had given me a slipshod gipsy appearance. Some dream had worried me. Although the details were blurred I knew they bordered on nightmare, and my eyes, heavily shadowed, looked back at me enlarged with fright. Given a carnation somewhere or other I could have played Carmen when she sees death in the cards. Then I thought of the Tarot, gave a shudder not entirely caused by damp, closed the windows and began to dress.

I had just huddled into sweater and jeans when the door bell rang. As I ran downstairs I was still unwashed and barefoot. I threw open the door. There stood Madame Sosostris. Her nose wiggled as she took in my appearance. Surely it wanted to get past me, and look behind the door to see if anything was going on. It was that sort of nose, and that sort of wiggle.

"Vell, good morning, dear child. I vonder if you sveet dear child vill be, and give me von—no, two, egg. I vould not ask, but dairyman he not yet been is, and I vithout breakfast go."

How like her, I thought, as I went to fetch them, to say "give" and not "lend". First a pint of milk, now eggs. If I were once too sweet about it we should probably progress through butter to cheese and chicken, until I was providing for Madame and myself and having double shopping expeditions too.

"I'd like them back," I said firmly, "because I'm cooking quite a lot now the children are on holiday."

Madame gave me a penetrating look, and snuffled into her scarf. "If dairyman have eggs, I bring them over."

"Don't bother, please. He always has them. I'll be passing your door at about twelve, and I'll look in for them."

A very charming smile spread suddenly over her stiff features, and I saw that her respect had been won. "Very vell, dear. Vy, Jane, I have not seen you look zo beautiful—almost like Juliette Greco."

It was too chilly to stand out there unfed, discussing my appearance. I shivered ostentatiously. "Nothing on my feet. Isn't this fog foul? One can hardly see across the street." I peered into it. "Why, wasn't that my sister-in-law going past on the opposite side of the road? This mist makes it impossible to see——" Madame turned to look; beads of what I hoped were fog had formed upon the tip of her nose. "But Susie—Mrs. Halliford never shops so early. Perhaps she's run out of food too."

"Zo?" Madame made a cackling sound over the eggs as though she had laid them, and pounced out into the fog towards her house. I saw a hand wave at me triumphantly, and then she was almost invisible, just a grey shadow fading hurriedly away to disappear into thickening mist. I shut the door and went gladly to make my own breakfast.

Afterwards I was undecided what to do. It was not a beach day, so later on I sorted clothes and books for my Cornish trip, now very near, and then returned to the kitchen to make a vast cake which, with luck, might keep Nicola's stomach satisfied for a couple of days. From bitter experience I kept it fairly plain, or a swarm of hungry Cullys and Stewarts would inevitably have descended on me within half an hour of its icing, drawn as mysteriously as bees by flowering clover, and with more devastating effect.

When the door bell rang again I was convinced it would be a second Sosostris visitation, but I was wrong. It was Cosway.

"Hello, Jane. Aren't your feet cold? It's a stinking awful day." He shivered sickly on my doorstep.

"Come along in. I'm cooking."

"How very domestic. Practising to be the perfect housewife, darling?"

"Trying to find some way of assuaging Nicola's appetite. Meat and fruit are so expensive, and she's had all the oranges already. My mouth must look revolting. I've been eating *glacé* cherries. It's probably like glue."

I said this because Cosway was looming closer, and my mood was not receptive as I stood on cold wood with cold feet. Unfortunately it wasn't a deterrent enough remark.

After a minute or so he said thoughtfully, "Well, it wasn't too bad, really. And it's remarkably clean now."

"Let's go into the kitchen then, shall we? My feet are frozen. Both they and my cake need the oven."

"You're a hard woman, Jane. Hard, and imperturbable."

"What did you want me to do? Go to pieces? Melt like chocolate in your arms?"

"Take me seriously, for a change."

"Darling Cosway, I'm very bad at taking people seriously."

"Except Roger."

"Oh, you've got a fixation about Roger." I was exasperated. "Like Susie."

"It's you who have a fixation about him. Do you really think it would be a good idea to marry a man who's had one wife die on him already?"

"Cosway, what an appalling remark! He could hardly help that. Anyone would think he killed her."

"We don't know that he didn't." He wiped a finger round the mixing bowl's succulent mixture. "Old Roger's a doctor, after all."

"You're monstrous this morning. Doctors save life, remember? You shouldn't make remarks like that. The fog's got into your brains."

"All's fair in love and war," said Cosway cornily, making another advance.

"That phrase was coined by an arms manufacturer with a harem in the Middle East." I moved adroitly sideways. "Stop it, Cosway. No, I mean it. Sit down, and have some coffee."

Cosway sat, dejectedly. "Oh Jane, you're being so brisk. You'll end by commanding women paratroopers if you don't watch out."

"I shan't look like them, anyway. Madame Sosostris has just told me I look zo beautiful."

"I call that sinister—I should lock the door at night, if she's going to come here talking like that." Cosway scowled, distorting his usually calm features. "That woman's pure poison ivy. Her tendrils are creeping all over this town." He moved restlessly.

"You seem to take a dim view of everyone today. I can't bear her myself, but I do think you're exaggerating."

Cosway, slumped in gloom, was staring at the table. I felt remorse, for I hadn't meant to be too brutal. I touched him on the shoulder. "See, here's your coffee. I'd just made some, although I seem to have been eating since dawn, like Nicola."

"I can't think how you stay so slim. What was that woman doing over here?"

"She wanted some eggs."

Cosway drummed with his fingers on the table. "Oh." And then, fretfully: "I should avoid her, Jane. She's an infiltrator."

"Easier said than done. You look downhearted this morning. Has Susie been at you about something?"

"Not more than usual. She says I don't pay my share of the electricity, but I do. Jane," Cosway stared at the table-top, "I'm thinking of emigrating. Life in this country's too expensive, and my firm has plenty of contacts in New Zealand and Canada. I'd be off tomorrow, if you'll come with me."

"That's very sweet of you, Cosway, but you know what the answer is."

"That you're in love with Roger."

"That I'm going to America."

"If you want to marry him, Jane, I'll give you some advice even if it's cutting off my own nose, etc. Do it soon."

"I thought we agreed one shouldn't marry a man who murdered his first wife."

"Jane, really. That was a joke. Anyway, all men need to murder a woman now and then."

"It's for me to say 'really', this time. I suppose", I added, "that you're trying to warn me about Gabriella. You think Roger's fallen for her."

"I didn't say so."

"Tactful Cosway. Well, I agree. I think he has. He did. It wouldn't be much use marrying a man who's fallen for someone else, would it?"

"Didn't you make up your mind about America before that?"

"You've got a good memory. Yes."

"Well—in that case, think it over about New Zealand." Cosway drained his coffee cup and stood up.

"Thank you very much, dear Cosway. But you shouldn't base an important question like emigration on whether I'll go with you or not."

"What else would I base it on?"

"What other reasons do people have? A spirit of adventure, a longing for a good climate; if they're on the run from the police, if their debtors are after them, if they just want to get the hell out of here, from depression."

"That last," said Cosway dolefully. "That's the one."

My concern was instant, "Poor Cosway. You look wretched this morning. Are you getting a virus, do you think?"

He gave me a wry smile. "I don't think so. Perhaps I'm just allergic to fog. And Roger, of course. I'm going back to London later today, Janey. Can't stay away too long. If you could really consider a paying guest for a week or two in Cornwall, let me know. I'll eat out, or find my own meals. Cornwall may be famous for its fogs, but it can't be worse than here, and I could do with a holiday in congenial company."

"May I let you know?"

"Of course." He kissed me, and went away into the fog. I looked after him with increased affection. Perhaps we always love our friends best when they are a little unfortunate; not too happy, not too well, not too rich.

At five to twelve I took down an old fishbasket and a mackintosh and braved the fog in my turn. It was now whiter and lighter as, high up and invisible to the inhabitants of Seaminster, the sun attained its midday strength. When I reached her door I knocked loudly with Madame Sosostris' brass doorknocker, and then stood back to stare at the turrets. Like a miniature insubstantial enchantress' castle, white on white, they disappeared upwards into mist.

The door opened. I lowered my gaze to find myself face to face with Roger. There, in that murky street, and with Madame herself lurking beyond him in her hall-sitting-room, I felt an unexpected violent urge to fling myself lovingly into his arms. It was a bleak realization of past stupidity.

"Hello, Janey." He just stood there unhelpfully.

"Hello." I thought of Nicola. She would have given him an eager psychological exposé of the situation, Madame Sosostris notwithstanding. Who would have believed that so late in our relationship I could ever become speechless with him? Vexation unexpectedly brought back my ease. "Roger, what a surprise. I'd no idea you were here with Madame S."

An unfortunate remark on the whole, implying that I might not have come if I had known.

Roger's eyebrows lifted, and then lowered.

"And I didn't know I should find you outside this door. We're not particularly telepathic, I'm afraid."

This was not what we had felt before.

"Not this morning, at least," I said as lightly as possible. "Perhaps fog's no good for ESP." I raised my voice: "I didn't realize Madame was ill."

"Ah Jane, dear child." The enchantress came forward with an ingratiating smile. "Come in, come in. Your eggs is ready. Dairyman, he let me have two, and break box specially, vich most unusual is. Vell—good-bye, Doctor, your opinion thinking over I vill be. And do not you be unvise—in this fog, eh?" She gave the snuffle of amusement which always reminded me of a hedgehog, and peered up at him with an ironic eye.

"I meant what I said: I should advise the utmost caution," said Roger in a didactic manner.

"Ve vill see. Perhaps also I vould advise—Jane vould say I advice give, vould you not, Jane?" She snuffled again.

"If you call in a doctor, you should pay attention to what he says. Shouldn't she, Jane?"

"Ah, she is last person to agree, your Jane. For does she do vot you say?" After this crack below the belt Madame Sosostris beckoned me imperiously inside, while at the same time she edged the door to on Roger. We exchanged fleeting smiles before he was shut out. Madame shuffled in her dilapidated pair of slippers towards her kitchen, where I could distinguish smells of garlic, kipper, pig-bucket, onion and steaming laundry.

"Nice little kitchen of your friends Hamiltons, but you vill find I improved matters have."

There was no difference, except that the Hamiltons had been clean, and Madame Sosostris was not; and that curious plants with swollen leaves, and spots or purple blotches, occupied the window sill, along with a pair of ancient field glasses.

Her eyes followed my glance. "Aha, at my age I only good am to sit and vatch shipping and vide horizon!" But I couldn't help suspecting that she was more likely to use her glasses to watch lover with lover on the beach. That nose, I thought.

"Now, here two eggs for you, Jane. And how is your life? Vell? But from all signs I fear you did not take my advice vith your sveet, dear friend. Zo. You answer vill not." I could feel her staring at me and, against my will, raised my head and looked back into her eyes. The pupils seemed shrunk, very small, far off, and dead as stones. Still I felt they were drawing me at the same time—like a plaster. It was a morbid thought, and even as it crossed my mind I heard myself say, "Cosway may be going to emigrate." And then wondered why I said it. It was as though the words had been dredged up out of my mind without my conscious volition.

She gave a little indrawn hiss; like a snake. "He vill emigrate? Susie's charming brother?" (How Susie would have liked the use of her Christian name!)

"I can't imagine why I said that." She saw my unease, laughed, and patted my arm.

"Zo. Zo. Doctor Roger may vell look out. Cosvay is in your mind. Remember vot I tell you about two men, Jane?"

"It's probably nothing to do with those two, at all."

"Zo, you think not?" Her nose wiggled, her little eyes sparkled. "I vill give you von other piece of advice, Jane, but this von not for you. For Susie's charming brother is: he vould be most unvise to go."

I looked at her detestingly. Everything everybody might do, was to her "unvise". First Roger, then Cosway. And she was so free with her opinion too, without its being asked for.

"You vill tell him?"

"I don't know. I never interfere with what people do." I almost added: "If they're fool enough to let you tell their cards, what you advise or don't is up to them," but a strictly polite upbringing held me back. Again I thought of Nicola. She might have said it.

"You vould say, if they such fools to kom to me are, then I advise them vill myself?"

Talk of telepathy. It was impossible to stay in this house a moment longer. The smell. The stuffiness. Those derisive, hypnotic eyes. "Is your clock right? I've shopping to do...." My hand that held the eggs shook. There was a small chuckle at my side.

"Jane, Jane, vy zo nervous? Herbs you should buy for your health, dear child. Is not vise that at your age health must go."

"There's nothing wrong with my health." I stowed the eggs deep in the fishbasket, and moved rapidly towards the door. "It wasn't me seeing a doctor. I didn't know you were ill."

"At my years, it nothing is. Zome arthritis, zome heart—is vay all flesh go," she replied evasively. I remember thinking it odd that Roger should have called on a patient for anything so slight. Usually he made them go to him, unless they were flat on their backs or had a temperature. He said it kept them active, and gave him time to deal with really ill people, which I suppose was right.

"And what did Roger—the Doctor, tell you to do about it?"

"Oh—he advise against too great busyness." She gave a secretive laugh.

"I suppose your appointment book's very full." I had reached the door, thankfully, and slackened my pace for a polite farewell.

"Is fuller each veek," she replied in some professional pride. "Vait—I show you." She handed me a thick leather-bound book from a bamboo table near the front door. I was incommoded by the fishbasket, and not exactly interested, but I made pretence of glancing through the pages, and they were certainly crammed with names.

"It's very impressive. Now I really must hurry, Madame." I heard her curious little snicker of laughter as the door shut behind me.

I walked down the street aware that fog and damp were a welcome change to the atmosphere, mental and physical, inside that house; and wondering uneasily if Madame really had mesmeric powers; and remembering what Nicola had told me about Gabriella's spat with her.

And also wondering why Gabriella had, in that case, booked an appointment with her for two o'clock.

Chapter Ten

The influence of that eternal fog made everyone bad-tempered. On my doorstep I met Susie, come to complain of Gabriella and the way Erik looked at her.

"Everyone looks at her. From young children to old women. It means nothing."

"Doesn't it?" Susie narrowed her eyes at me, catlike. "What about Roger?"

"Oh, Roger." It was as thoughtful and balanced a voice as I could manage. "Yes, he might well be quite hard smitten."

"And you don't mind?" She sounded incredulous.

"Cosway seems to be all right, still." It was an evasion, and I admit it was also a return of service. To my surprise she appeared to welcome it.

"Oh Jane, dear—if you and Roger are through, do marry Cosway." I gaped at her, and she went on: "Yes—that would be a good solution, I think. He does need looking after, and it's so involving—and tiring. He wants to go to New Zealand, you know. At least, he's talked of it; and it would be bad for him to go alone."

I was now more than surprised. Could this be the Susie who watched every sign of affection between her brother and anyone else so jealously? It was strange. Perhaps she thought anything better than to have me free and at a loose end almost on her doorstep, among Erik and the children. If Cosway really aimed at getting lost in New Zealand, I might as well get lost too.

"Do you know, Susie, I don't really want to go there? And nor does Cosway, so far as I see it. He was just suffering from depression. Anyway, Madame Sosostris says he mustn't go."

"Jane! That old witch has a nerve. When did she say so?"

"Now. This morning. She owed me eggs and I went to fetch them."

"And Cosway had told her he was going to New Zealand? Everyone's taken to confiding in the woman."

"No. I told her."

She flushed angrily to her hairline. Damn, I thought—more suspiciousness. "Wasn't that unwise, Jane?"

"Unwise?"

"Perhaps I'm just a snob, or—— She's such an old busybody. Everything you say goes all over the town. You know how awful I think people are who talk behind each other's backs. I'm afraid it's rather a family failing." She looked at me accusingly. I was sure her obsession with herself made her long to ask me if I had denigrated her to Madame Sosostris. "It seems pretty silly to get involved with her—the whole family appears to have taken to her in a big way."

"It was Roger, not one of us, who brought her to Culbertson's do. And he was there with her this morning." Even as I said it I realized again how odd it was.

Susie echoed my thoughts. "I'm amazed at Roger. One lift seemed enough for him yesterday. Fairly hurried off, didn't he? And I'm not surprised, the malicious way she needled him about his wife."

"I didn't hear that," I said; and thought: "The second person to talk of Roger's wife this morning."

Susie picked up her shopping bag from the floor. "I must go." Her voice was long-suffering. "I do wish Nicola would hurry up and learn more about cooking. Chore, chore, chore, who would be a woman these days?"

"I don't suppose it's all that different to when they cleared out corners of caves and sewed up the bearskins."

"More complicated. Anyway, Jane, what do you know about it? You're still free."

It would have been true to say that I did a good deal for the children without the compensation of a husband to earn for me and sleep with me. But I didn't want Susie's lifelong enmity.

"Anyway," she said in her best martyred voice, "at least

you're taking Gabriella off my shoulders for a bit. You won't back out, will you, Jane?"

"It sounds as though I might get the whole gang as well. You'll be able to have a lovely long rest, Susie."

"Me? I never get a rest. On the rare occasions when we're free of children Erik always wants all sorts of things done for him that he never thinks of at other times."

"I hope they're exciting ones." I was slipping; and she went away giving me a glance of dark suspicion, while I mentally upbraided myself for lack of self-control.

Later on that day, towards two o'clock, Gabriella walked by on the other side of the street, evidently wanting to keep her witch's appointment secret. And soon after quarter to three my front door flew open as though attacked by a Channel gale, and she hurtled into my sitting room, looking so beautiful in a fury that I was glad of Roger's absence.

"Sweet Madame Sosostris," I said obligingly; and stopped, aware of having blundered.

"Jane? How did you know?" Gabriella's hands went up to her hot cheeks. Her eyes were wide, astonished. Perhaps for a moment she also suspected me of witch's powers. Then she asked accusingly: "You've been watching?"

"I was there this morning. She showed me her appointment book, and your name was in it."

There was an awkward silence between us, while I longed to ask what had angered her. She, I think, was half longing to tell me, but in the end her new habit of reserve held her back.

"I—I just wanted her to tell me something, you see."

Yesterday she had shown no signs of wanting even to speak with Madame. To my mind it was more likely to have been the other way about: that Madame Sosostris had wanted to ask Gabriella something; but in that case, why had she gone?

She was nervously pulling at her fingers. "The other people—how very odd they looked."

"What other people?"

"Oh—the man who was leaving as I went in. The woman who came as I went out."

"I suppose most of her customers might look a little odd. Did she give you a pleasant reading? Better than mine?"

"Me? A reading?" She looked quickly down at the floor. What I could see of her face was inscrutable. There was a second awkward pause between us. Then Gabriella said in a controlled voice: "How could a visit to such a woman ever be pleasant? Jane—if you're free, let us go down to the beach, no?"

"In this drippy fog?"

"The sea is still there, in this fog. And no one else will be. It will be quite, quite alone. Just us two. And I want to walk—oh, for miles. Just so that I can work off my energy."

"And your anger," I murmured to myself. If only Madame Sosostris would take a walk and not come back! She was altogether too entangled in our family's hair. I wondered how many other people in this town found her nesting in theirs.

As we went down Mariota Street side by side I asked Gabriella: "How's Culbertson today, after her disappointment?"

"She is a little subdued. Thoughtful. Poor Culbertson."

"Yes—poor Culbertson." Although I must admit it was usually a danger signal when she became thoughtful, and I was more apt to pity other people.

After walking by that lazy, oily and unhealthy-looking sea, we parted company, and I returned to my packing up for Cornwall. Whatever the children were doing, they kept away, and without either Roger or Cosway looking in, and with that pervasive fog encroaching through the windows like an open enemy, I began to look forward to the journey west. There were no definite plans to take the others with me, and I decided that all the effort, if they meant to come, must be on their side. I was going to Cornwall in order to work, and they must understand that from the start.

Parkinson's Law operates efficiently when one is alone, and I filled up the time easily till eleven o'clock. Then, just as I was going upstairs to bed, the telephone rang.

"Jane," Susie's voice came fretfully down the line, "have you got Culbertson there?"

"Culbertson? No, of course not. Why, have you lost her?"

And in that case how bloody silly of Susie not to ring before.

"She said she was going to bed." Her voice rose a tone. "All right, Erik, I am asking her—— She seemed positively eager to go, and I wouldn't have believed it, except that she did seem tired after all that dancing. And she can't have gone out of the front door, because it was locked and Erik has the key in his pocket."

"A downstairs window," I said automatically.

"Yes—that's what we thought. But her own window's open, and Nicola has just told us the wretched br— child has taken to shinning down the drainpipe."

I was thinking hard. What mischief could Culbertson be up to that would take her out at night? The weather was hardly the sort to make children long for midnight beaches.

"Jane, are you there?"

"Yes, I'm thinking. She's not with Cosway?"

"He's gone back to London."

"Of course— I forgot."

"And his flat is locked, and not even Culbertson could climb so high."

"Are you sure Nicola and Stewart don't know where she is? They might all be up to something together."

"Quite sure. It was Nicola came to me about it. Erik's worried, now she's not with you. He's going to get the car out. What's that, darling? Oh, Erik says if a quick look round her favourite haunts isn't enough, he'll phone the police."

"He's right, of course. Susie, don't worry. Tell him I'll go and look too—say I'll go down Mariota Street and along the front. Both ways. And I'll ring up when I get back, see? 'Bye...."

I snatched a coat from the hook behind the front door, and was already going out into the street, when I thought that someone should telephone Roger. It wasn't pleasant to formulate this to myself, but he was usually in touch with the hospital. I went back into the house, picked up the receiver and began to dial. The telephone rang and rang the other end, but there was no reply. Of course he might be out on a late call.... Could have been summoned to an unknown child knocked down by a car....

I suppressed the ugly picture. Surely we were all getting worked up by a simple piece of Culbertson' devilry. Whenever she was too quiet, something happened. It was true she had never gone missing so late at night before, but if she had taken to using drainpipes her absences might not have been discovered. That was all, I told myself firmly, heading into the dark and misty night, one hand on my torch, while I called softly at intervals: "Culbertson, where are you? *Culbertson.*"

The streets were deserted. A small, fierce rain had started, fine rain that drenched in a matter of minutes. I went down Mariota Street flashing my torch from side to side. In spite of myself I grew increasingly worried. Culbertson was catlike in her hatred of rain. There was no one, no family, that is, who would have kept her out so late. Anyway, I supposed Susie would naturally check on all her and Erik's friends. I made a thorough search along the front and beach to the right, and then retraced my steps and searched to the left. The sea was sucking at the pebbles with a small lisping sound, faint but determined at its agelong task of wearing away stone. There was no foam showing white through the rolling mist, just a grey shining where the water began, and a gentle dark heaving up and down revealed the rise and fall of waves. To be alone with a fogbound sea at night is melancholy.

The moon was a blurred disk between clouds, and in her fog-extinguished state was not much more help than a forty watt bulb would have been. I climbed down on to the beach, in a flurry of pebbles. Otherwise, and except for the sea's uneasy movement, it was very still. It was hereabouts the unfortunate stranger had been drowned. I shuddered, and flicked my torch's beam over the stones. Wet and colourless in the dark, by the torchlight they showed gleaming brown, white or purple, and the green seaweed as spinach. I called: "Culbertson. Cully. Culbertson?" and my voice echoed away over the water as though it bounced from one lazy incoming wave to the next. I expected no reply, and none came.

After forty minutes by my watch of quartering front and beaches I was sure Culbertson wasn't in this direction. My torch battery had grown weak. Most of the time I walked with no light, unless I wished to flash it towards some dark corner. The street lamps, anyway, although fog-dimmed as the moon, could show me empty streets, and empty gardens.

I came back to my own ground, and hesitated opposite Madame Sosostris' house. She had two lights showing: one downstairs, one up. Was it possible Culbertson could be there? I stepped off the pavement, and then back again. No. If it were necessary I could go over and inquire, but first I must telephone Susie. Probably they had Culbertson tucked up again in bed, scolded and Ovaltined, and had been trying to telephone. The moment I re-entered my house I dialled their number, and Susie answered at once. She must have been sitting by the telephone, which killed any foolish optimism stone dead.

"Susie? She's not been found? No—nothing. I searched along the beach and front both ways. Is Erik back?"

He was, though Stewart and Nicola were still out with Gabriella, searching the streets behind their house. Now I had reported failure, Erik wanted to ring up the police.

"I'll get off the line, then. Listen—has anyone telephoned Madame Sosostris? There are lights on in her house. No? Well, I'll make sure she hasn't seen Culbertson. I'll ring you back in five minutes to hear what the police say." The heavy weight of dread in my chest felt like acute indigestion. I went out of the house again, and across the road.

Although the lights in Madame Sosostris' house burned steadily upstairs and down, there was no reply to urgent ringing. Cursing the deafness or mulishness of old age I leaned on the bell as though my weight could force her out of bed and downstairs to answer it. There was still no response. A mental image of the old woman lying snug in bed upstairs, refusing to hear, must have raised my blood pressure to danger point. I wondered recklessly if the house could be entered from the back. As I made my way down the side path towards the iron staircase which rose so conveniently to the top floor I regretted not having brought my waning torch; for it was very dark just here, away from all street lighting, and I had to tread with caution and feel my way along the side of the house with my hand.

A few yards from the road my left foot, cautiously advanced, met an obstacle. At first I thought it was a sack left carelessly lying across the path, and I bent down to shove it aside, then did an instantaneous and instinctive recoil, while my heart seemed to leap in my body. Was this why, when I rang the bell. . . ? I stood there in the dark, drawing difficult breaths, and remembered what Madame Sosostris had said only that morning about her heart. Another minute passed before I felt able to kneel down by the crumpled form, search for an arm, and then a pulse. While I was doing this a worse horror swept over me—it was no adult whose heartbeat I was now desperately feeling for, but a child. There was no need even to run my other hand up the neck to the short-cropped hair to guess that it was Culbertson.

There are some dreams, known to most people, in which every action slows down, and each movement takes place as though the dreamer's feet were stuck fast in treacle. My attempts to find Culbertson's pulse felt just like that. In reality it can only have been seconds before my fingers found a faint slow pulsebeat on an icecold wrist. There was no other movement from her. She was certainly unconscious. She might also be badly hurt. How long had she lain there like this? I wondered frantically. For the first time I inwardly blessed Madame Sosostris, for if she had answered my frantic ringing and denied knowing Culbertson's whereabouts there would have been no reason for me to stumble down this path, and find her.

Now it was as though someone else took over in me, someone who knew exactly what to do. I stripped off my coat, and the sweater I wore over my shirt, and wrapped them about Culbertson. I daren't move her, since I couldn't see what was wrong. For all I knew she might have internal injuries. It was possible to guess what had happened: she must have fallen from that staircase. I tore back across the road to my own house, still with that fearful sensation of feet stuck fast in treacle. I snatched at the telephone and dialled Erik's number. This time, mercifully, it was he who replied.

"I've found her—on that side path by Madame Sosostris' house. She's unconscious." I went on talking straight through his horrified answer, breathlessly: "Get Roger if you can, or the police doctor. I couldn't see if she was hurt. I've covered her up, and I'm going straight back——" I heard Erik say something about Madame Sosostris, and responded briefly: "She's no help—she wouldn't answer," and put down the receiver. The automaton that had taken over sent me hurrying upstairs to fetch blankets from the bedroom. With these over my arm and the waning torch in my hand I ran back across the road. What really terrified me was the possibility that in my absence Culbertson's frail pulsebeat had dwindled to nothing.

It was, if anything, slightly stronger. The covering of coat and sweater may have helped. I piled blankets on top of them, and then examined her face and head with the torch, rolling back her eyelids one by one, and shining the beam straight into her eyes. The pupils' response was sluggish. I could see no bruise on her face or forehead, but when I ran my hand over the back of her head I could feel a bump, and my fingers came away sticky with blood. I found myself praying fervently that this was all the damage; heaven knew it could be serious enough. I never want to spend such a bad few minutes again as I spent that night, kneeling there shivering by Culbertson in the dark and misty rain, and waiting for the sound of Erik's car.

Chapter Eleven

"—People are very kind, aren't they?" said Culbertson. "You never know how many friends you have till you're sick, do you, Jane?"

" 'I always say.' "

"Would you like that pineapple? Mrs. Planger brought it, because she says I'm such a dear little girl, but I don't like pineapple."

"When I'm sick I'll want something better than your cast-off pineapples. Then I'll know if I'm your friend or not."

"Dear, dearest Jane, you found me, and you can have anything you like." She waved a lordly hand towards the foot of her bed, which was littered with toys and games and fruit and sweets and comics, like several Christmases rolled into one.

"Have the rabbit with nylon whiskers that the greengrocer sent. It's eaten too much pineapple."

"It's certainly very yellow, and I'd sooner have the plastic snake on a spring. Shall I read to you? You're supposed to keep quiet, you know."

Culbertson wriggled mutinously down in bed. Her eyes strayed towards the window. I closed it.

"Drainpipes are out, Cully darling. I'm a very stern gaoler. As for all these rabbits and things, it should really be bread and water and a cell."

"Oh Janey, you're pretending. I wish this horrid hot bandage could come off."

"Stop pulling it about. The back of your head is bloodied, and Roger says it's to be there, and there it stays." I moved in firmly towards the bed. "Have the last chapter of Moomintroll." Culbertson gave a deliberate sigh, and two large eyes looked out at me over the bedclothes, but I relentlessly picked up the book and began to read.

Roger had been next on the scene after Erik and, as soon as Culbertson had been examined by the light of a much stronger torch than mine, had decreed twenty-four hours at least in hospital. No hospital, however, had had to do with a Culbertson before. The half-dead-looking unconscious child which had been admitted at twelve o'clock that night had turned by five o'clock next day to a small flushed determined creature sitting up in bed with a bandage round its head, and demanding every five minutes at the top of its voice to be taken home. Even sedation didn't help. Culbertson triumphed easily over sedation.

"It's mind over matter," she told the Sister. "I want to go home."

"Better give her a jab," advised the young house physician.

Culbertson gave him a cold look. "You try giving me a jab. Even Roger got a bloody nose giving me a jab for whooping cough."

"There's nothing to stop your Daddy taking you away tonight," said the Sister in a thankful voice, "so long as someone will sit up with you."

"Jane will." Culbertson gave them her sweetest smile, now she had won. "She can shine a torch in my eyes every hour to see if I'm going bonkers. She'll enjoy that."

"A very odd child," said the young doctor confidentially to me, when I accompanied Erik to collect her. "I suppose one must put it down to television."

"Culbertson would be even odder if she watched television," I said, and left him to think that over.

"Had enough of that old Moomintroll," said Culbertson's voice, sleepy at last, from the bed. "I'm supposed to be quiet, you know, Jane."

"You said it, not me."

I shut the book. It was time to settle her down. We were still ignorant of what had made her fall, and Roger said it would be best to wait till tomorrow for questioning; all the same it was odd that she had told me so little of what had happened.

Now she spoke in a slightly scared voice: "Jane. It's a bit horrid not to remember things, isn't it?"

"*Culbertson*. You told that young doctor in hospital you remembered everything, but didn't want to talk about it! He told me."

"Yes. Don't be angry, Jane. If I said I didn't, he would have kept me there in hospital, wouldn't he? And I didn't like it."

"I don't suppose he would have, for a moment." I sat down on the bed. "It's the natural result of concussion." I hesitated. Roger had decreed no questions; but he hadn't foreseen Culbertson in a lather. I asked casually: "How much don't you remember? Do you remember going up there?"

"Up the stairs? Yes." She reflected for a moment. "And I remember the cards she put out. Perfectly."

"She being Madame Sosostris, I suppose. She put them out for you?"

Culbertson went down a bit further in bed, but above large eyes her forehead had flushed a revealing pink.

"Culbertson?"

"I was just looking. Through that little window. It's such a nice, clear little window," said Culbertson defensively.

"Dear, dear Cully, I'm afraid you're not a nice, clear little girl. Having some unclean fun again, weren't you? And now you see", said the model Victorian aunt, "what comes of it."

It was never much good being moral with Culbertson. "That man Philby, that Daddy talks of, didn't ever fall downstairs, so far as we know," she pointed out logically. "But it was a pretty dull evening really, Janey. Pathetic. She'd moved her table, so I couldn't even see who the cards were for. She's got a lovely mirror, you know" (I remembered it—all gilt ribbons and sighing ladies with enormous breasts, and a bad glass), "and I remember trying to look so I could see in it, sort of, and then nothing more. So I don't know how long I don't remember, do I?" There was a note of panic in her voice.

"It couldn't be very long, surely. What time did you go out?"

"I don't know."

"Susie says you went off to bed at half-past eight, and Nicola says you were still there at half-past nine. So how long after Nicola looked in do you think you went down that drainpipe?"

Culbertson stirred restlessly, and winced.

"Look—don't bother about it any more tonight. It will all come back bit by bit."

"All? Promise?"

I couldn't promise. "Most of it, I'm sure. Perhaps not the very last bit, but who wants to remember falling downstairs, anyway? You were unconscious for five hours at least, and according to Roger amnesia, if it happens, goes at the rate of a minute an hour."

"What's amnesia?" She looked frightened.

"Sorry—loss of memory. But I'm going to get into trouble making you talk too much. Here's your pill. Do you want to say good night to Susie, or anyone?"

"Daddy, please."

"Lie still, then, and I'll fetch him for you."

I went away to find Erik, and tell him about Culbertson's loss of memory.

By morning I was tired, to say the least. I had sat up all night with Culbertson, now and then dozing off, and at intervals getting up to shine a torch in her eyes, although the need for this was now really over. None of us had slept the night before, when she lay unconscious in hospital, and by now I was reeling drunk with need for sleep, and correspondingly cross. I was short with my patient when she slopped her face-washing water about, and outspoken with Susie, whose idea of a good breakfast after my vigil had been two meagre slices of toast. Culbertson had wanted me with her, and I had been glad to stay; but I felt that I deserved better at Susie's hands.

"You're horrid cross, Jane," said Culbertson, bursting into tears, which was most unlike her.

"Oh lovey, I am sorry. I'm not really cross with you, truly, I'm just very tired."

Culbertson threw her arms round my neck and hugged me. "I know. I love you. I wish you could marry Daddy. They did in Egypt. Are you going back to bed, now?"

"Yes, I think so. Susie will clean your room," I said with determination, "and Nicola will come and keep you amused."

"Could I have my plastic snake, please? Jane, before you go, I've remembered something else."

"Why, that's marvellous. I told you you would."

"Yes. I was trying to see in that lovely glass because they were quarrelling."

"Madame Sosostris was?" I was far too sleepy to care, almost too sleepy to register what Culbertson was saying.

"Yes, with whoever it was. Couldn't hear what they were saying of course, except bits of her voice, it's such an owly sort of screech."

"Oh well, it will all come back, I expect, if you're starting to remember already. I'll look in and see you when I've had a sleep. And Roger'll be along later, so don't try and hide anything from him, will you?"

Rocking slightly on my feet I walked back to Number 16. Dairyman, as Madame Sosostris called him, was just depositing two bottles of milk and half a pound of butter on my doorstep.

"How's the prizefighter doing?" he greeted me.

"She's a lot better, thank you."

"That was a nasty fall she had," he went on conversationally, as I opened my front door.

"Heard about it, did you?" I found myself dimly hoping that no one knew of Culbertson's spying habits.

"You know this town." He grinned at me. "But do you know if old Madame across the way wants any milk today?"

"Doesn't she have a standing order?"

"No. I ring. Yesterday there was no reply, and I left a pint on spec. It's still there, on her doorstep."

"Oh well—perhaps she's gone away." That would have explained why I could get no answer.

"Left her lights on, in that case."

"People sometimes do, because of burglars."

"Not more than one, Madam, generally. And that old Madame, she's close."

I looked across the road, towards the turreted house. In my

dulled mind something urged me to undesired, unsought action. I longed for bed, but an inner voice accused me of selfishness. If it hadn't been for Dairyman I would have forgotten Madame Sosostris. He himself had taken no action other than gossip. Numbers of people must have come to consult her, rung her bell, and then shrugged casually or angrily away. Even in this misty daylight it was possible to see the two lights burning in her house. The same two lights which had burned there as I knelt outside by the unconscious Culbertson. Again I recalled her words, which I had put down to a sense of drama, about her heart.

"I noticed those lights burning the night before you say you left that pint."

"Did you, now?" He was suitably impressed.

"But I'm so tired from being up all night, and anyway there's nothing I can do." I bent to pick up my milk and butter. "Just to put our minds at rest, I'll ring my brother and ask him to check up about it."

"Well, Madam, kindly get him to ask her if there's more milk needed?"

"Yes, I will." I went into the house.

My bed was calling almost audibly; but my conscience called louder, although telephoning seemed an intolerable burden. I would have rung the police, but doubted my ability to explain things clearly.

"Erik? Oh good, I thought you might have gone to the office already. Nothing's wrong, it's only that Madame Sosostris' lights are still on, exactly as they were the other night, and the milkman hasn't been able to get a reply since then, he's just told me. Well no, I know you can't, but if she's ill or something no one can break into her house, can they, without calling the police? You do it, will you, because I'm too tired to think clear any more, I'm going straight to bed. Yes, all right, tell them I asked you to, but don't let them disturb me about it—I couldn't bear it." I staggered upstairs, keeping my eyelids open with an effort, and fell into bed in all my clothes.

Chapter Twelve

That was Culbertson's bell ringing. I never knew they had bells in the children's bedrooms but, since they had, it was typical of Culbertson, I thought, to put her finger on it and keep it ringing when I was tired, so tired.

"Do be quiet, Culbertson," I said, struggling to wake up. It was like having taken too deep a dive into green and siren-singing depths, but at last I twisted up in bed. The clock on my dressing table said three o'clock; yet it was light for 3 a.m. And Culbertson, damn her, was still ringing her bell—there must be something really wrong. It was not till I had pushed my feet into slippers that I woke sufficiently to understand it was now three o'clock in the afternoon. I had been sleeping heavily for six hours, and it was my own doorbell being relentlessly rung. Nothing serious could have gone wrong with Culbertson so late as this, surely? I rushed downstairs, and flung open the front door.

A young policeman regarded me in astonishment. "I've been ringing a long time, Madam," he said reprovingly.

"I was asleep. I've been up all night nursing my niece."

"I'm very sorry to disturb you, then. Could you spare me a moment?"

I was still half asleep, and my first thought was that the flash young man had sold me a stolen car.

"Please come in." The constable followed me into the sitting room. I sat down on the sofa and looked at him.

"Won't you sit down?"

"Thank you, Madam." He sat, rather as though in an electric chair, then took out a notebook, and portentously made a note. "It was you who asked Mr. Halliford to ring us up, Madam."

"Oh. Oh, yes. About Madame Sos—the old lady across the road."

"The milkman had spoken to you, I understand."

"Yes. He didn't quite know what to do. Those lights had been on a long while. Did you—I hope there was nothing really wrong with her? She told me her heart wasn't good, but old people say things like that, and I hadn't paid much attention."

"When did she tell you that?" He made another note.

"Two days ago. She owed me some eggs and I went over, and I met her doctor coming out."

He nodded, without asking who her doctor was. Perhaps he knew.

"Is she ill? I am sorry."

He cleared his throat. He looked suddenly very young and uncertain of himself, and his words came out pompous and faintly absurd. "I much regret to say, Madam, she is dead."

"Oh—how dreadful!" I gazed at him in some distress. "How dreadful to die all alone like that. I feel awful about it. I might have thought about it more, and rung up earlier, if it hadn't been for my niece's accident. It drove everything else out of all our minds." I had a horrible vision of Madame Sosostris gasping away for breath, unable to summon help or reach the telephone.

Again he cleared his throat. "What time did you ring her bell that night, Madam?"

"It must have been almost midnight."

His pencil was very busy. "That would be just before you found the little girl unconscious at the side of the house?"

So Erik had gone into details, when he told them we found Culbertson. I did hope her spying habits were not already common knowledge, and wondered how he had accounted for her presence there.

"Yes. Just before. I thought Madame had gone to bed and didn't want to be disturbed. Then she went out of my mind till the milkman drew my attention to her. I hope—I hope she didn't have a very bad time." It sounded plain silly. "I mean— I hope she just became unconscious, and that was that."

"I'm afraid not," he said, in a constricted voice. "You see, somebody killed her. She was knifed in the back."

Again I felt as though I were skin diving—this time into a deep black hole which excluded air. I put my hands up to my temples, felt the pulse that beat strongly there, and had one of those terrifying moments when one knows the pulse can stop.

"What did you—she was *knifed*?"

His face looked completely stolid. It was impossible to guess what went on beneath its surface. Here in Seaminster Regis knifings were unusual; his experience of them must be limited.

"Yes, Madam." A pause. "Do you know of anyone who would want to do a thing like that?"

"Good heavens, no."

"You saw her the morning of her death. Did you see anyone else there?"

"No. That is—I already told you: her doctor was coming out."

"She spoke of no one else she was expecting?"

"No."

He frowned. "It seems odd she didn't keep an appointment book."

"But she did."

He leaned forward eagerly. "You're sure of that?"

"Positive. It was on that little bamboo table, by the door. Quite a large book. You can't possibly miss it."

He looked at me curiously. "It's not there now. What a pity you didn't look inside it that morning, Madam. You might have saved us a lot of trouble. You didn't, I suppose, by any chance?"

"Yes, she showed it to me; but I didn't notice any names." Her two o'clock appointment could hardly make trouble for Gabriella, yet instinct told me not to involve my family too closely with Madame Sosostris, now she had come to this appalling end. I could already guess what the next question might be, and hastened to forestall it. "You think it could be one of her customers—clients, killed her? It seems suggestive, if the book's really missing, doesn't it?"

He was noncommittal: "We have to cover everything. You saw nothing that struck you as odd, the night you rang her bell?"

"Nothing. I was too worried, anyway, to notice much."

"I quite understand. Madam——"

"Yes?"

"About the little girl."

Here it was. If only I knew what Erik had said; what they had already asked him.

"You want to know what happened?"

He avoided this. "I want to know what you think happened."

"It's difficult, isn't it?" I replied evasively. "You see, she's got some loss of memory."

"Very usual, with concussion. Have you any idea what she was doing there?"

This still gave me no lead on what Erik might or might not have said. I plunged: "Well—we're a bit ashamed, as it happens, of a dreadful habit she's developed. She's as inquisitive as a monkey, and nothing stops her."

He gave a sudden grin which made him look even younger.

"My sister was just the same. Our Dad walloped her for it, but nothing made no difference. If it's any comfort to you, Madam, she grew out of it."

I relaxed. "I must say, it is. Well, Culbert—Caroline, was fascinated by Madame and her cards. They had real drawing power for her. We knew she'd taken to prowling round there to see what she could see, but we never dreamed of her doing it at night. No scoldings or punishments had any effect. Roger—Madame's doctor, I mean—only spoke to me about it the other day. He thought Cul—Caroline was, well, pushing her luck."

His face had gone grim. "He was right, wasn't he? The old lady may have been killed some time while the little girl was lying out there unconscious."

"Yes—must have been."

He caught me up sharply. "Must?"

"Caroline told me this morning, just before I left to come home, that the last thing she remembered was hearing Madame quarrelling with someone."

His gaze was intent. "Someone? She was up that staircase, I suppose? Did she see who it was—a man, or a woman?"

I blushed for Culbertson. "No," I faltered. "She couldn't. She was trying to see, and that's the last thing she remembers."

He was looking down at his notes. "I see," he said slowly.

"That puts her in an awkward position, doesn't it?"

For a second or two I failed to understand. When I did, it was a nasty shock. "You mean—you mean she may be the only person who has seen the killer?"

"Yes, Madam, that is exactly what I mean."

"Then we must keep it completely dark where she was found." I stared at him in acute distress. "Only the family and the police know, so far as I know."

"That might not help us, might it?"

"Why not? Surely so long as nobody knows she was there, she's not in any danger?"

"Can we be certain nobody knows?" It was his turn to stare at my appalled face. "Did the murderer see her through the window, as she saw him, or her? Did she fall down the staircase, or was she pushed? How will we know when the murderer becomes aware that she is still alive?"

I could only stare at him in dumb horror.

"It's important for her to recover her memory," he said, with horrifying gentleness.

I walked back to The Lime Tree House half an hour later. After one glance I had carefully looked away from Madame Sosostris' house, for outside it a police ambulance had just drawn up, and the house's turret eyes, as blind as usual now that the lights were out, looked down on a horrid bustle beside the front door. Once that house had been a gay family house, and now it had progressed to the sinister ill-fame of a house that should be haunted. So houses, like people, could develop the wrong way.

The young policeman had asked me if I knew who any of Madame Sosostris' clients were. I had replied that it was difficult to say, because nearly everyone in the street had taken to consulting her now and then, even in a shamefaced way; which skated delicately over the subject of Gabriella.

"You rang her bell that night because you were searching for Caroline. And when you got no reply, the little girl's er hobby——" he smiled faintly—"was what suggested to you a search round the side and back?"

"Yes, I'm afraid so." There was no need to say that I had been intent on forcing an entrance, and had stumbled on Culbertson by accident.

Then he had left, murmuring of another look for the appointment book. As I walked up to Erik's house I wondered how much my sister-in-law and brother had been told already. The young policeman was skilful at keeping his information in separate boxes. Soon enough I knew the answer. Susie came to the door in her most agitated mood: tears and anger fought for priority. "Oh Jane, it's too much! I said she was an unsavoury woman, but you would all go dashing round there. As for Culbertson, if there was a whip handy, I'd use it. What are we supposed to do now, would you tell me? Keep two armed bodyguards with police dogs in her bedroom? And many murderers aren't caught, I've read the statistics somewhere, so we're in for a life sentence unless she recovers her memory——"

"Hush. I wouldn't shout it down the street, if I were you. The idea is to keep it quiet as possible about Culbertson. Only the family and police know where she was found."

"And the murderer."

"Probably not, if she slipped on that staircase by accident. I see Roger's here." His car stood outside, against the kerb.

Susie shut the door with a bang behind us. "And a lot of help Roger's been. He says she can get up. I should have thought peace and quiet in bed for at least two more days."

"You think Culbertson in bed is a recipe for peace and quiet?" But she side-stepped my question, and reverted to her grievance about Madame Sosostris. "She was just the sort of creature to get herself murdered. She was maddening, simply; well, remember the uncivilized way she came to Culbertson's do? Must have absolutely rolled in garlic, like a dog."

"You don't get murdered because you eat garlic, Susie," I protested mildly, although I was used to Susie's heartlessness, and saw no real point in protesting. It struck me suddenly that Susie also was what might be called the born murderee.

"I can't think what Roger's doing up there. He promised to come straight down again, because I've made him tea. Now you'll want some too." She looked at me accusingly. "You go up and fetch him, will you, Jane? Culbertson does hang on to people so. She can come down if he says so, instead of lying about."

As I went upstairs I leant over into the hall and asked, "Where's Erik?" What I really wanted was a private talk with my brother.

"He thought it best to come back from the office. He's working through some papers in the dining room, and doesn't want to be disturbed." Whether that was Susie's invention, or what he had really asked, it could hardly be gainsaid. I went on up to Culbertson's room. The door was closed. I pushed it open. A heavy draught came to meet me. Culbertson, in full chatter, a nightdress and her bandage, was sitting on the window sill. Roger stood just beside her, with his hand on her shoulder. The window was wide open.

"You see, I could reach it if I leant down, entirely by myself, without any help," she was saying. "It's a nice bit of jasmine, isn't it? Just what my sick room needs."

Roger looked round, and smiled at me. "You couldn't reach it," he said, "but I can, if you'll just get out of the way."

"Do you want to bet? Look, if I——"

"*Culbertson,*" I precipitated myself forward, "you are not to open that window at the bottom, or go down drainpipes, or do any silly idiotic things after concussion, do you hear? You might get dizzy and—and fall again. You shouldn't encourage her, Roger. Trust a doctor to show total lack of common sense."

"Oh Janey, you're getting just like Susie." Culbertson turned the discontented face of convalescence towards me. "Did you have a nice long sleep?"

"All right. It was interrupted by——" I stopped and glanced sideways at Roger. He was looking at me intently.

"By the police!" yelled Culbertson excitedly. "Oh Janey, I've had a super time with them too. Dixon of Dock Green. Nicola and Stewart are wild with jealousy."

"I don't suppose they've experienced anything like it before," I said faintly.

"Do you know, they told Erik they hadn't?" Roger began to laugh, and Culbertson froze into great dignity.

"They said they were grateful to me, Roger. You know they did."

I glanced at him again.

"They only asked her how she fell, and if she saw anything unusual," he said reassuringly.

Culbertson intercepted our glances.

"Ohh—something's happened. I know all that secret stuff, making faces. Has Madame Sosostris been burgled? What a thrill. Maybe I didn't fall down those stairs—maybe I was pushed. Perhaps she was rowing with a burglar——" she put both her hands up to her face, pushed at her temples as though she would force herself to think. "I wish I could remember."

"You heard a quarrel, did you?" Roger picked up his doctor's bag off the bed. I leant between him and Culbertson, and shut the window, and locked it.

"Only half a quarrel—just her side: screeching. I only made out a few words: 'Zo you expecting are——' and 'vot you take me for, eh?'" Culbertson's mimicry was not so good as Nicola's. "Oh Janey—I haven't got my jasmine!"

"Nicola will get you some. There's plenty in the garden. Do hurry up and get dressed, since Roger says you can come down. Susie's getting tea."

Culbertson sprang lightly on to her toes, pirouetted, and clutched at her head. "Ow. Jane, you'll never guess some of the things I told the police. It would turn Susie's hair purple."

"And mine. And the Chief Constable's too."

"I said you could explain anything they wanted to know by telling the Tarot. That made them sit up. But of course they can ask old Madame S., can't they? She's the only person down here who hasn't sent me——"

"Come on," Roger shepherded me towards the door, "she'll never get dressed till the audience is gone."

Culbertson stuck out her tongue at him. "Do you know, Roger," she said severely, clutching at the back of her head, "even that hurt?"

"Don't do it, then." Outside the door, he stood still and looked me in the face. "It seems years since I saw you, Janey. You're pale."

"Since we were all at that hospital does seem like centuries," I agreed.

"I've missed you, Janey."

"I've missed you too."

He put his arm round me, and we walked downstairs together. I thought his mind was fully on me, but he said abruptly: "What's the point of keeping this from that child? She's bound to hear of it sooner or later."

"Some of Susie's doing, I should think."

"Culbertson must learn not to chatter about where she was."

"I'll have a word with Erik. Oh Roger, how are we going to keep her safe, without putting the fear of death into her?"

"It may not be for very long. Anyway," he smiled faintly, "Culbertson's full of nerve. We're much more likely to fear death than she is."

Chapter Thirteen

Susie was waiting for us in the kitchen, where Stewart and Nicola occupied one end of the table with all the paraphernalia which surrounded any of their more advanced ploys. I caught sight of a long dead bat, and shuddered.

"How's your patient, Roger?" Susie poured boiling water on the tea-leaves.

"Better and stronger than most of us, as usual. It would take an atomic explosion to damage Culbertson seriously."

"Is she coming down?"

"Yes, she's on her way," I said; and added boldly: "I've still eaten nothing today but those bits of toast, Susie." My terse remarks that morning must have had effect, for she graciously offered me a variety of food, from sardines to semolina.

"She doesn't want that sort of thing at all," said Nicola scornfully, rummaging in the fridge herself. "Here, Jane, have some of these sausages. They're good and meaty—I'll cook them for you."

"You didn't wash your hands after that bat," said Susie with some asperity. "Meaty will be the word, and——" But I interrupted her to say, "Susie. I've been thinking. There's something I really should tell the police: Culbertson's do. You remember, everyone split up for a bit——"

"Here, Nicola, I'll do those sausages." Susie got up from the head of the table. "You'll burn them all on one side. Come and pour out for me instead." She bent her head over the pan. "Yes? Culbertson's do?"

"Madame Sosostris was having a row with someone."

"With whom?"

"I don't know."

"You mean it was someone you didn't recognize?" Susie

turned her face towards me again, then glanced at Roger.

"I didn't get a chance to recognize him—or her." I described my flight into the house after an emotional Culbertson, the unintentional eavesdropping which had followed.

"If you couldn't even tell if it was a he or she, then I should drop the idea, Jane. I think the less this family gets involved with a thoroughly unsavoury case the better."

"Are we sure she should drop it?" asked Roger judicially.

"It sounds like blackmail." Stewart's interruption made me jump. He had seemed entirely involved with his dreadful bat.

"What does?"

"What Madame S. said to this person, whoever it was. If our Janey tells the police they might find someone who did see them together."

"Blackmail," said Nicola thoughtfully. "I wonder."

I did, too. I always had wondered just how Madame Sosostris could afford the Hamiltons' house.

"Leave the whole thing alone, Jane," said Susie stonily. "The less Culbertson's involved, the better, I should think."

"It's vitally important for Culbertson that this killer's found."

"Wouldn't it be better not to stir him up? Wretched Culbertson, she would involve us all with something like this. Here are your sausages, Jane."

"They'll have a gorgeous overtaste of bat." Nicola put out a very dirty hand and broke one of my sausages in half. (Susie gave a loud, desperate sigh.) "Susie thinks marriage is a horrid business—the growing up children side of it, I mean. You can't really taste the bat."

"I'm not exactly disappointed. And Susie's entitled to her opinion. All children haven't such filthy habits as you have, either."

"Cosway doesn't mind us half so much. He never seems to *notice* things."

"Cosway appears not to notice them, but has very sensibly remained a bachelor," put in Roger.

Nicola gave him a scornful glance. "That's all you know. Cosway had a very attractive wife. At least, Susie says she was, didn't you, Susie? And he divorced her. He was only twenty-three when he married, and he got taken in. That's what Susie says."

"Did you know that, Jane?" Roger sounded surprised.

"I thought everyone knew it."

"That's why he blinks so much, poor old chap," said Stewart. "Doesn't like what he sees. Or so Dr. Fosborough would say."

"We all get taken in." Roger skilfully helped himself to one of my sausages. I looked rather sadly at my plate. "Janey is in the habit of taking us both in at the moment. Watch out for me starting to blink at any time."

"You couldn't blink, Roger. You've got the natural bold stare of the deceiver, when you're not looking deceptively modest." I gulped down two sausages quickly. "Remind me to tell you my theories of marriage—in all the reasonably successful ones I know the woman has the man by the scruff. A quiet, firm grip, kind and controlling and barely noticeable, like the way you hold back a bull terrier who wants to fight——"

"Thanks very much for the warning," said Roger. "Before I start thinking of marriage again, I'll——"

"What has become of Culbertson?" interrupted Susie.

With one large reflex action, we all leapt to our feet. It was the awful measure of the difference in life now and yesterday. Stewart was first through the doorway, Roger and I behind him, while Susie and Nicola were disputing the passage round a chair. How could we, even momentarily, have forgotten? Culbertson had been left alone, and——

She was descending the stairs in a stately manner. There was a serene smile on her face. The bandage had developed a sideways slant. She stopped when she saw us, and the smile faded, to be replaced by a look I knew all too well. That hesitant, deprecating look on Culbertson's face was a sign she had been flagrantly disobedient in some way.

"What are you all stampeding for?" she asked sweetly.

"We've been waiting for you."

"When you're sick it does take a long, long time to dress." Culbertson's firm bare feet resumed their downward tread. "Is there any tea left?" She passed through us as though we were invisible and headed for the remains of Stewart's sugar bun.

Then she stood on her toes and experimentally moved one strong leg to and fro. "It's already made my muscles slack. I must do a work-out after tea."

"Leave it one more day," advised Roger.

"I was working on a test piece. If I did about twenty minutes it wouldn't help much, but it would be better than nothing." She had a small practice room high upstairs, with a *barre* rigged up by Stewart where she did her exercises with ferocious concentration to music supplied by Erik's old record-player.

"I shouldn't go up to those attics all alone," said Susie.

"If you do I'll come and watch," and, "You'd much better pay attention to what your doctor says," I and Roger interposed simultaneously. Then we exchanged looks of despair. We were overdoing it; how was discreet chaperonage of Culbertson to be achieved without turning her and us into nervous wrecks?

"I'm not likely to faint, am I? If I'm dizzy, I'll yell."

"Your muscles won't go completely to pieces in one day," said Roger very firmly. "So you can bloody well oblige us all for once by a little obedience."

"Oh Roger, what a nasty word."

I saw the muscles in his jaw tighten. "It's not nearly so nasty a word as he might have used," I put in hastily. "And he's dead right, anyway. Culbertson, behave."

All our nerves were frayed. It looked as though we were in for a general scene, but luckily Susie acted for once with a modicum of common sense. She gave Culbertson a push which sent her sliding on to a chair, and dumped a cup of milk beside her and another sugar bun upon her plate.

"Here, feed up, you silly child. You look a most horrible colour, it puts me off my food to look at you. I'll ask Daddy to have that record-player disconnected for a week, if there's any more trouble tonight. You really have caused quite enough."

There was a general silence, full of surprise. Susie's usual complaining tone had no effect on the children, and to hear her speak with authority took them all aback. Culbertson scowled at the bun, but began to eat. And a fortunate diversion was created by Gabriella appearing suddenly in the doorway, and saying, "Tea—how good. I'm so very thirsty. I've been such a long, long time with the police."

There was another silence. Culbertson's soft seal's eyes grew round and large, and two gimlets appeared in the middle of them. Roger was staring darkly at Gabriella, with his brows twitched noticeably together. He was always staring at her, these days. She went to sit beside Culbertson. "They were quite friendly and nice. They are always taught to be pleasant in this country, not so? Except for ban-the-bomb, and long hair."

"You've got long hair, Gabby," said Nicola.

"Yes, but I do not look as though I study to smoke cannabis. They have found the appointment book, Jane. It is just as well I went, not so? They told me when I left. It was stuck in a litter basket, up a back street."

"So all our troubles are now ended," said Nicola joyfully.

"You're a clot, my sweet sister." Stewart handed Gabriella a bun. "No, it wouldn't be stuck in a litter bin if it had anything compromising in it. And nor would the police have told Gabriella."

"You said there would be two," I reminded Roger.

"Two what?" asked Susie. Her voice had taken on a shaky fretful note that, like Culbertson's hesitant face, we knew from experience.

"Two appointment books. One for the tax people, and one under her woolly drawers or her mattress. You'd better tell them."

"I was probably wrong." Roger's face wore a stony look. "She may have kept it all in her head."

"If there was a second book, the killer needs it. Or has it already, of course," said Stewart.

Culbertson was looking very intently at her plate. Nicola, with equal concentration, at Culbertson.

"Madame Sosostris was killed, Cully. Someone stuck a knife in her back. She was probably killed some time when you were there."

Culbertson raised her head and stared at Nicola. Her eyes were dark and unfathomable. Very, very slowly she nodded her head up and down, as though something she had wondered about were now quite clear.

"Nicola," said Susie explosively, "you little brute!"

"Don't be too Fauntleroy, Susie. You can't have lived with Culbertson so long and not realized that she'd know all about it by tomorrow, at latest. How were you going to explain that Stewart's sleeping in her room tonight?"

"Nicola is quite right, you know, Susie."

She gave Roger a furious glance. "Erik should have decided."

I said hastily: "It's all right, Culbertson. It's just a tiresome precaution. They'll catch the person who did it soon."

"They'll have to get it quick, before it gets me," said Culbertson with appalling logic.

"There's no question of 'getting you', if they didn't know you were there. So it's got to be kept dark, you see? We can't remember telling people at the hospital where you were found, and we're not going to talk about it to anyone outside this room."

"They'll know if they pushed me. If they saw me looking in and came up, and thought they killed me."

"We think you fell."

"I've got to get back my memory, haven't I, Roger?" She was gazing at him with a soft, dark glance. "Bloody damn quick."

"Don't say bloody damn," said Susie automatically. Under the circumstances her cleaning up of Culbertson's conversation struck me as funny.

"Worrying won't bring it back."

"Four minutes." Culbertson looked pensive. "Four little, little minutes." (" 'A little grave,' " I thought, " 'a little, little grave.' ")

"They'll put a police guard on her, won't they?" asked Gabriella.

"Not if they don't want to draw attention to her. It will be subtler than that."

I stood up and pushed back my chair. I said in a light, false voice: "You probably saw nothing at all. You probably weren't up there at the time."

"You forget she heard them quarrel," pointed out Roger.

"Anyway, it's most likely someone she'd never get a chance to recognize, and who knows it."

"Could be one of us," Nicola reflected ghoulishly. "Roger was Madame's doctor—he may have done illegal something-or-other, and she knew it. Gabriella hated her, for no reason anyone could see. Cosway had a positively morbid obsession about her beastliness—he could easily have nipped down from London on a train, and back again. Or just lain low somewhere."

Culbertson was now decidedly white, and I really could have murdered Nicola. She must have seen my expression, for she subsided in an uncharacteristic way.

"Don't let Nicola's idiocy upset you. The police don't seem to be worrying us too much, do they? They'd want a very, very strong motive for that sort of crime. Gabriella, you've not told us why you went to them." It would be best to turn Culbertson's detective mind a more academic way.

"Ohhh, why? Welll—you know I went to have my fortune told, that afternoon." She looked round at us with her usual friendly expression, and gave Roger a confiding smile which annoyed me. "As I was part of Culbertson's family, I thought they had better know, not? Also I wanted to tell them what way she had struck me as a woman, which was not nice. They thanked me—oh, much. They said it was this sort of impression that might help. And they gave a—a hint, it was suggested she knew many, many—I am not sure of the word, but it meant not pleasant, people."

"Sordid, perhaps?"

"Oh Jane, you are clever." Again she looked round at us with that friendly smile. "You all think I was right?"

"Very sensible, anyway," said Roger. "Pretty, pretty Gabriella. Who would ever believe such prettiness went with such common sense?"

"I would. I think Gabby's very shrewd, really. A shrewd pretty dolly," said Stewart. "Aren't you, love?"

"If anything happened to me in this house," Culbertson spoke as though working out a problem in arithmetic, "that would make the police sit up and think twice, wouldn't it?"

"It would indeed. So don't you go after any more jasmine when we're not looking, Cully, or it might make things awkward for us all. Not that we wouldn't mind for other reasons, too."

"Of course, people can get in from outside," argued Nicola in her helpful way. "Look at all these burglaries there are."

"Then the best, best thing would be for us to go away." Culbertson raised troubled eyes to me. "Let's come with you to Cornwall, Janey? And not tell anyone outside the family. He wouldn't follow us to Cornwall, Janey? Would he?"

"Of course not," I said quickly. "That's a very good idea." Or, I supposed it was, if that house on Bodmin weren't too isolated. There was a dog, anyway. That generally kept intruders off. And the police would have to know. . . .

"Nicola and Stewart, and me and you; and Gabriella and Roger and Cosway." Culbertson looked politely at Susie. "Would Daddy and Susie come too, Jane?"

"My dear, there may not be room for all these people. I'll have to telephone the agent first." In spite of poor Culbertson's situation my heart was sinking. Susie and Erik! How would any work get done?

"I don't think Erik can possibly get away just yet," said Susie, relieving my mind. "Also, I might be against your going down there, Culbertson. Jane will have to be out, and it could be a difficult place to keep an eye on you."

"I'll ask Daddy. Daddy thinks a lot of Jane."

Culbertson's lower lip stuck out mutinously. Susie's lips tightened. Roger's, unfortunately, twitched. Here we go again, I thought, in real despair. "I'll have to find out from the agent," I repeated. "And if Erik can't come I certainly wouldn't take you down there unless Roger or Cosway or both of them can get away too." I could just visualize Nicola taking Culbertson and me along a dangerous path, with a killer waiting at the end.

"My dearest aunt, how you hurt my feelings," said Stewart. "I've always greatly fancied myself as a cross between Sherlock and James B."

"But Roger's so strong, and Cosway's so clever."

"Thanks very much for that second warning against matrimony," said Roger loweringly.

"Oh darling Roger, I didn't mean it quite like it sounded." I sighed, feeling particularly inept just lately; and I could hardly be surprised when he said, "I'll certainly come—if Gabriella will. I can't wait to see what Isolde would have looked like in her adopted land."

I couldn't avoid bitterness: "Gabriella had definitely better come—as far away from the Seaminster police as possible. Nicola says she was having quite a spat with Madame Sosostris at Culbertson's do. Didn't you say so, Nicola? Oh yes—I'm sure you did. Madame Sosostris made some very dark remarks about people they both knew."

Roger only smiled sympathetically in Gabriella's direction. "I should think nearly everyone who knew her had a spat with poor old Madame some time. As now seems obvious. Well, I must be getting along, Susie—got a short list of patients for tonight's surgery. But if Culbertson needs another sedative, just let me know. I'll even risk giving her a jab—so long as Janey volunteers to hold the arms."

Culbertson twisted her placid biscuit-coloured face into a rude grimace beneath her crown of white bandage. She no longer looked nervous, but slightly self-important, as though already aware that every adult round her was likely to be indefinitely at her beck and call. Roger gave her a searching look as he departed after kissing me in an absentminded way. Not that I blamed him for being absentminded. It was not a situation that gave prominence to love.

"I'll share Cosway's tent on holiday, and we'll have that dog," decided Culbertson. "Although I'm not very pleased with Cosway. He hasn't sent me even a 'get well' card."

"He doesn't know you were cloppered."

"Of course he knows, Nicola." Susie began to clear away the tea things. "I rang him up and told him yesterday. I forgot to tell you that he sent his love."

"What's love to Culbertson, or she to love?" put in Stewart rhetorically. "She wants her hurt head assuaged with a present. She's a demanding little beast, aren't you, Cully? There'll be cold looks for people who turn up with small bouquets at the Garden."

"It proves they mind about you," said Culbertson sadly.

"He's coming down soon, my dear. He'll probably bring something for you then."

"Oh Susie," I said anxiously, "you didn't tell him where she was, did you? Because he might tell other people, since he can't have heard yet about Madame Sosostris."

Susie considered. "Yes—no, I don't think so. I just said she played truant after dark, and got concussed by falling. In any case, Janey, Cosway's not a chatterer. Now, that girl, Roger's secretary—Pamela whatshername, she's a talker. So I hope Roger was discreet."

"Roger could hardly be described as a chatterer, either."

"Oh, my dear, I hope not. Don't sound so hot about it, Janey. I wasn't insulting him. Look—it's after six. Would you like to go and ring up Cosway, and ask him about Cornwall?"

"I'd sooner ring the agent tomorrow, first."

"As you like, but——"

"Didn't you hear the telephone?" Erik stood in the doorway, rumpling his hair with an inky hand. "It's Cosway. He wants to speak with Susie or Jane."

"You go, Jane," said Susie generously. She never missed a chance of pushing me at Cosway now. It was as obvious as her previous attitude, though so different.

I went out into the hall, and through to the drawing room. The telephone was by the window, on a small green table.

"Hello, Cosway?"

"Oh Janey, what an awful lot of things seem to be happening round about you." Cosway's voice, divorced from his face, managed to sound almost as fretful as Susie's. Perhaps it was the line. "Poor old duck, who could have done that to her?"

"Who? What?" I asked stupidly, before I recollected myself.

"Madame S., of course. It's in the evening papers. She was an unpleasant enough old girl, I'll grant you, but people don't get knifed for being unpleasant, or there'd be hardly anyone left. Do please take care of yourself, Janey, your little house is near, and you're alone."

"You think I'm so unpleasant that I'm bound to be the next?"

"You know I don't. But it's most unwholesome, so near home. Lightning-Struck Tower, and all."

I had completely forgotten that prognostication.

"Janey? You still there?"

"Yes, I'm here."

"It really is horribly near home." It was this aspect that appeared to be worrying him unduly. "I suppose you've thought no more of going down to Cornwall with the family? It sounds much healthier."

"As a matter of fact, I had. We were just saying it might be a good plan. I was going to ring the agent tomorrow, and find out how many rooms there actually are."

"Good—good. Don't forget I've got a tent. Could I come?" There was a hesitant note of self-deprecation in his voice.

"Oh Cosway, I'd like that very much. So would the children. Roger and Gabriella are probably coming too."

"I see. Well, that makes it quite essential for my presence, doesn't it? I shall look forward to the fuchsia hedges. Dear Susie isn't joining us?" He sounded anxious.

"I hardly think so."

"Not that I mean to be unkind, or unbrotherly, but——"

"Dear Cosway, I understand you perfectly."

"Well, here's this awful pipping noise——" Cosway's voice rose in the hopeless shout that penetrates no pip for long—"good-bye, my sweet Janey; let me know just as soon as you can about Cornwall, and I'll make——" pipppipppippp went the telephone, and we were cut.

I went back to the others. "Cosway's coming. If we all go, that is."

"Why did he ring?" In spite of Susie's new attitude to us, there was a jealous note in her voice.

"It's in the evening papers. Madame S., I mean."

"I'm glad dear Cosway's coming. Roger's changed a lot just lately." Culbertson moved a sharp glance from me to Gabriella like someone playing chess with a seal's eye. I gave her my best poker stare. This game was not played to suit Culbertson.

"If I take you with us, Culbertson—that is, if Erik agrees——" avoiding Susie's eyes—"you must promise to co-operate. Not start dodging us, or anything. It would be too worrying."

"I wouldn't." Culbertson looked like a maligned seraph.

"I'll do all you tell me, Janey."

"And all Roger and Cosway and Gabriella tell you, too?"

There was a faint flicker deep in the seal's eye.

"Culbertson?"

"I'll try," she said at last reluctantly. Then she brightened. "It's a bit of a star part really, isn't it? Mine, I mean. So much for Dodo Margerison."

"You see, Susie?" said Nicola. "I told you you were being too Fauntleroy. Culbertson's tough."

She was tough, all right. I quailed when I thought of supervising that tough spirit on Bodmin, a killer real or imaginary lurking in the background. Before leaving that night I went to take a look at Culbertson's room. The window was wide open again, and a nice bit of jasmine flaunted itself upon her dressing-table.

Chapter Fourteen

On thinking it over we were really not too scared for Culbertson. It seemed much likelier that she had fallen than been pushed or knocked on the head. As long as we all kept quiet about where she was found, and the police were being very discreet, it appeared that any danger to her was probably less than a chance of being run over. Resolutely I thrust from mind a memory of Madame Sosostris' voice saying: "Zome fog. Zome danger. Much bravery needed." Telling too of accidents, of a journey, of someone underhand; and particularly of a "stubborn young person", too close a Culbertson description. But if death had been seen for someone in the cards that day, I reflected, most probably, poor woman, it had been her own. As for fog—it was not only in our minds and hearts, but outward, visible, as well. When I locked up my house I could only hope that the west would be more welcoming than the so-called sunny southeast.

In spite of Susie we were really off to Cornwall after all. The three children were crammed into the back of my Fiat, and almost hidden beneath picnic baskets and luggage. Cosway's tent was strapped on the roof rack; while its owner, wearing a cableknit sweater filled with natural sheep oil, sat beside me in front, a large map extended on his knees and a netted pack of fruit beneath them. Roger was joining us the next day with his own car. Gabriella had gone up to London, and would join us later, like Roger, but by train.

The police had been helpfulness itself. Pushed on by the family (Susie excepted) I had finally told them my story of the row I had so nearly overheard in the Principal's drawing room at Culbertson's school. They had questioned us all, and promised to make further inquiries. Of Culbertson's Cornish holiday, so long as suitable precautions were taken, they approved. We were to keep in touch with local police, who would be told of our coming, and let our own Inspector know at once if her memory disgorged anything new and helpful. Nicola had kindly reiterated that the killer might be one of us, and had offered to keep a special eye on me—but I think the Inspector hadn't greatly taken this to heart.

"Culbertson's got a message for you, Jane," said Stewart's voice from the back seat.

"I'm often, often sick, when I'm in the back," said her martyred voice. She was squashed almost out of sight and shape between her elders.

"I'm very sick in the back," said Cosway firmly. "Always. And because I'm bigger I'm sicker, and my sick is more horrid."

"Anyone who doesn't like my car can walk. Or can travel wrapped up in Cosway's tent on top. Let's get it quite clear to start with that three hundred miles of grumbles is out. Have you got the glucose barley sugar, Cosway?"

"It's in your side of the dashboard, Jane, my darling."

"Damn." I drew up at the side of the road, to search amongst oily dusters. While I was busily engaged Roger's car drew up alongside, and his face peered in at my window.

"Hello, Janey. Lost the ignition key?"

He was given to provocation these days. I moistened my lips, and forced a smile: "Roger—please would you bring down that very heavy suitcase you'll find in my hall? It's full of books and things. And there's my typewriter too. And five large bunches of overripe grapes."

Roger raised his eyes heavenwards. "What were you going to do, if we hadn't met?"

"Ring you up tonight, of course."

"I see. Clever Janey. And were you going to dematerialize your doorkey and send it to me over the line?"

I felt myself turn pink as I handed it to him out of my bag. Cosway made an amiable choking sound beside me. It would be nice if they were both going to behave like this all the time in Cornwall.

"I've got an envelope," said Cosway kindly. "Janey could have put it in the envelope."

"Yes, but has Janey got a stamp? If you knew Janey as well as I do you'd know that Janey never has a stamp. Nor a pen either. Anyway, Janey, you're not really going to work, are you? You're going to look after Cosway and me, one or other of us, for the rest of your life."

"Here's the barley sugar." I handed it over to the back seat.

"Jane is being very lofty. She's not revealing anything." Cosway stroked my bare left arm in the way which had annoyed Roger so much before.

"I mustn't hold you up—or keep you from anything." Roger gave him a look of ice which could have penetrated even the oily sheep's wool. "See you, Janey. If you have to put me in with you or Gabriella I shan't mind at all, but I very much draw the line at sharing Cosway's tent."

"Janey's practical. We'll have the whole place ready by the time you come."

"I hope so indeed. Well, then, Janey, mind that whatsoever thy hand findeth to do, do it with thy might; for there is no work, nor device, nor knowledge, nor wisdom, in the grave, whither thou goest——"

Roger gave me an amiable nod, which barely concealed a ferocious glare, and drove away brandishing my key. I restarted the car with an unnecessary roar. He may not have meant to dash my spirits with the darkness of his words, but it was a bit much having Roger be so Biblical in the middle of the street.

"Now keep your mind on your driving, won't you, Janey," besought Cosway, "always remembering that the race is not to the swift nor the battle to the strong, nor yet favour to men of skill; but time and chance happeneth to them all."

"Let's put paid to anything out of the mouths of babes and sucklings," said Stewart, stuffing Culbertson with barley sugar.

"Janey's like the virtuous woman in Proverbs who brought food from afar," added Nicola. "Hasn't Roger got sarcastic and bossy lately? It's since Gabriella came. I must ask him why."

"I wouldn't, if I were you."

"Janey's got bossy, too." Culbertson was plaintive. I had

expressed myself strongly to Erik about the jasmine, and her window was now permanently secured, except for one small top pane.

"That jasmine was the turning point. You've toughened me, Culbertson."

"Roger was all right about my jasmine. He was encouraging me to get it, till Janey came in having kittens."

"You've made that up."

"I didn't make it up, Nicola! He said he'd hold my feet."

"I told you all doctors were mad." I gave way at the roundabout, and headed out of town. I was conscious of Cosway's stare, and glanced briefly sideways to see that a frown had settled on his face. Conversation about Roger never seemed to please him much. "What's the matter? Am I going the wrong way?"

"No, you're quite right. You stay on this B road till you reach the next A. You know all the next bit."

"And then we'll go through Midhurst, Petersfield, Winchester——"

"If you like. You can by-pass Winchester."

"Oh Cosway, no! I did that once with Roger's car, and ended up going round and round Southampton."

"Right. Through Winchester then, and on to Romsey." Cosway's tone was curt. Perhaps it did seem that Roger's name had been unnecessarily dragged into the conversation. The trouble was that I still thought naturally in terms of him and me.

"The thing is," said Nicola's voice behind my ear, "they didn't find the weapon."

"Of course they did, you never listen to anything," scoffed Stewart. "It was her paperknife, wiped clean. No use to them at all."

"Killers often act so domestic," sighed Cosway. "Always a duster handy."

"Can't we discuss something else? Look—we've left all that behind us now—I'm sick of it. Did you know, Cully, people sometimes see seals in Cornwall? With luck we might get a photograph, if Stewart's brought his camera."

"What they see is a projection of Cully."

"Nicola wants an orange, Janey."

"Already? They're under Cosway's feet. Anyone who wants real food had better give plenty of warning, because I'm stepping up the speed now."

"Dear Janey, do please remember what I said about 'time and chance happeneth to them all'."

We had the usual sort of run anyone has with three children in the back. Not that Stewart or Nicola really came under that heading now, but Culbertson in a car was a substitute for any number of five-year-olds. She felt it incumbent on her to establish supremacy. By the time we reached Romsey I was flagging, with a distinct sensation that several dozen Cullys had been restlessly chewing things, asking questions, or muttering dire prophecies of car-sickness behind my ear for hours.

"Like me to drive, Janey?"

I shook my head. Although the Fiat was a bit bogged down by all the weight she was a pleasure to drive, and I was reluctant to give up the wheel.

"I was thinking we might soon stop and eat somewhere."

"There was a place several miles back," offered Culbertson.

"Lovely shady bit of forest ahead."

"Do let's find somewhere in the sun, Janey," begged Nicola, while Cosway declared himself never happy unless he could lunch sitting down decent at a pub.

"Or I'll have frightful indigestion, and be most unpleasant. You aren't really suggesting I should torture myself with hard-boiled eggs and cheese sandwiches, are you?"

"Not at all. There are some prawn and salad things in pots."

Cosway groaned. "Baked to full bacterial strength under Culbertson's boiling-hot knees, I have no doubt. Any beer?"

"Cider, or tea."

Cosway unwrapped his legs from the fruit. "What did I come on this trip for, I wonder? Sensible old Roger not to get away until later. I should drive into this hideous lay-by, Janey, if I were you, before the children start fighting in the back."

"You wanted to sleep in a tent near the wine dark sea. You

murmured something about roughing it. And I'm going to pull up in that sunny patch of forest just ahead. Culbertson, what's that odd squishing noise I can hear?"

"It's my feet. They've sort of got in amongst some sandwiches." Culbertson bent down to make an examination. "Tomato and egg," she said, coming up again, "and I think sardine. Can you smell it? It's on my sandals and some towels, and the back of your seat."

"With prawns! Jane, what has come over you? Still, I must say, this does seem a nice little clearing you've chosen, very nice indeed." Cosway got stiffly out of the car, and stumped about sniffing. The smell of his sweater in the hot sunshine was considerable, and when Nicola joined us with the prawns the natural scents of high summer in the country were obliterated. However, the day was dazzling, we had left the fog behind us, and not even thoughts of all those miles to come while Cosway's sweater fought for supremacy with Culbertson's feet could lower my spirits, now rising like new bread. Something else did, though.

"What have you got there, Cully—a bread tin?" asked Cosway.

She plumped down beside me on her knees, clutching a rectangular object wrapped in a striped beach towel. "Jane's Tarot. She was actually leaving it behind. You didn't mean to, did you, Janey? I just slipped it in. If only it's kept clear of sardine——" She unwrapped the box as carefully as though it were a baby, and laid bare the cards. Like a visitation Lightning-Struck Tower and Black Magician gazed blandly up at us as though Madame Sosostris' ghost had specially arranged them there.

Cosway and I stared at them in horror. "I can't think how you can bear to look at them," I said, trying to hide annoyance.

Culbertson smiled at me, and re-wrapped her treasure. "I'm going to do some interesting research while we're away."

"Have you remembered anything more, Cully?" asked Nicola curiously.

"She won't." Stewart rolled over on his back to stare up between interlaced fingers at the sky. "At least, Roger says the chances are she won't get it back for weeks—months, even. He says it's unlikely she'll remember quicker than that."

"And when did Roger say he was coming down—in two days?" asked Cosway; as though thinking something over.

"No—tomorrow."

"And you mean you really can't remember things before you got concussed?"

"Four minutes," crooned Culbertson self-importantly. "Four whole, whole minutes. At least, I should think as much as that."

Cosway shook his head. Already he had silently munched his way through three prawn pots. I removed a fourth out of reach.

"Is that mine? Thanks," Nicola scooped it up. "I say, Janey, have you fixed your arrangements for America?"

It was my turn to shake my head. And I refused to ask myself why I was still holding back.

"Ow," said Culbertson, rising suddenly and kicking over the unstoppered cider in her movement, "I was sitting on a wasp."

We drove into Plymouth around eight, and I drew up outside the hotel chosen to receive our unsavoury carload.

"Well, I'm glad a lot of people coming here probably look and smell just like us." It was Erik's idea that we should stop the night in Plymouth. Now, tired and aching, I was thankful we had reluctantly agreed. It was one thing to arrive alone with two cases, swallow cold food and cider, and fall into the nearest un-aired bed; another to turn up with a party of querulous unfed children ripe for rowing with each other, who would probably get bitten by the dog. Tomorrow we could collect the house key from the agent, report to the police—like undesirable immigrants—and settle in, in peace. I don't know why the word "peace" should ever have occurred to me but, curiously enough, it did.

Next morning I woke early to a day of brilliant sunshine, and chivvied the sleepy children and a sleepier Cosway out of bed. I stuffed them with a gigantic breakfast, vainly hoping they would need less feeding later, and organized an early start.

"I say, are there any oranges?" asked Nicola, as we left the Tamar behind. "Jane, the sky ahead's rather grey. I do hope——"

I did, too. All too often while its next-door neighbour Devon basks in blue skies and bluer seas the Cornish peninsula, so narrow and so sea-surrounded, retreats into its sea mists and sea weather as nebulous and unreliable as its own legends of saints and kings. Cosway looked depressed. He might not have minded a westerly gale, but the creeping drizzle we were meeting was another matter. As we drove into Bodmin our spirits sank further with a discovery that the drizzle was rapidly converting itself to thick white wreaths and puffs of fog, which curled across the road in front of us without warning, and made an ordinary drive into a mortal danger.

"Culbertson's brought it on us with her Tarot."

"I haven't."

"You have."

"Look—that's the agent's. I'm going to stop, although there's a no parking sign. If anyone's rude you can say I'm delivering something."

"Deliver Culbertson. We're all tired of her."

"I hate you, Stewart. Ow, that's my ankle."

Our holiday had begun on the wrong note. Inside the agent's a depressed-looking man, stout and bald with thick glasses, looked me up and down in a discouraging way, and sniffed. He either had a cold or was rude by nature.

"I'm Miss Halliford, and I've come for the keys of——"

"Ah, yes. Mr. Cromarty's out. He was going with you, to see that everything's all right, but he's been called in the opposite direction."

It seemed an odd way of putting it. Perhaps the seals were calling him, or the voices of drowned sailors; or an eccentric Cornish saint.

"Could you come instead?" I ventured.

He sat down fatly and definitely, as though adhering to his chair. "Unfortunately I must remain, to hold the fort."

Conscious that the enemy was probably myself, who had interrupted his depression and cup of coffee, I asked, "How am

I going to find my way round those unmarked lanes in this fog without a guide?"

"Haven't you a map?"

"Are all the lanes on a map?"

"On the Ordnance Survey ones, yes."

"I haven't one of those. Could you possibly lend——"

"Unfortunately, no."

There was a slight silence, while I also adhered to a chair, more from damp than desire. "Look, I've got a carload of children parked outside here, and——"

"Of *children*? Mrs. Walter Wart understood expressly there was only one child."

I refrained from saying that nothing could be more express than Culbertson. "The other two are almost grown up."

"I see. Young adults." It sounded threateningly sexual. Foreboding shone in the poor man's eyes. Long hair, pot, guitars, C.N.D., I could hear his thoughts. In one moment he would be finding a loophole to wriggle out of this let; and although just then I would have preferred two up, two down, almost anywhere else, the thought of catching and redirecting Roger and Gabriella, now speeding to join us from different directions, was too much.

"I expect Mr. Cromarty has left some fairly definite instructions, at least?"

He sighed, stood up again, and began to rootle in a side drawer. "He did say—where did he put, ah, yes——" He held out two large rusty keys, loosely joined together with a piece of wire, and a sheet of paper showing a wild sketch of Cornish lanes, or a condemned electrical system.

"You take this road here, you see, and then that, and then this, and then that. If you should get lost——" surely he almost put in the words "don't come back here"—"there's quite a useful landmark in the shape of a disused tin mine. A chimney, you can't miss it. There was a very terrible disaster there, once. Twenty men, entombed." He stared at me through his spectacles. He might have been mourning, or thinking of something totally different.

"You have paid your deposit, I think, Miss Halliford? Good.

Then if you would just sign here——" He pushed a paper across to me. I signed without thought and then remembered that they say women always do that, and wondered in a moment's panic if I had left him all I possessed and Culbertson.

"Good," he said again, and took off his spectacles and polished them, revealing pleasant brown eyes, mild and sad like an Alderney's. "If there's any other way I can help you——" He looked hopelessly at his chilling coffee.

I explained that Gabriella and Roger would be joining us, and asked him to give them the same directions he had given me, if either of them turned up lost.

"You are expecting a doctor?" He put on his spectacles again, and looked at me anxiously. However, we got this one sorted out and then, just as I was leaving the office, I found four large tins lovingly thrust into my arms. They bore the legend: "Bowser—Meaty, Treaty, Trendy: keeps *your* dog on the ball."

"Mrs. Walter Wart was wondering——" he drew in a breath, as though conscious of over-alliteration, "if you would kindly feed the dog a Bowser every day? Any expense you may be put to, she will naturally take off the rent. She will be greatly obliged to you, Miss Halliford. The dog is in the kennel."

"Is there a tin opener? I don't believe we've got one."

"I'm sure Mrs. Walter Wart will take it off the rent," he repeated, and now his sad brown eyes looked so desperate and his forehead so sweaty that I went without demur. The children were keeping warm by fighting in the back of the car, and Cosway was huddled in front looking more miserable than ever.

"Here—take this map." I thrust it at him, and threw Bowser into the back seat, which effectively stopped the fight. "These are the keys, all rusted-up, and we've got to stop at an ironmonger's to buy a tin opener for Mrs. Walter Wart's dog."

"Oh don't let's start the holidays being so bestial," said Stewart sadly from the back seat. "I can't have my best aunt vivisecting on Bodmin, what will the *Seaminster Gazette* say?"

Chapter Fifteen

We found our way moorwards as best we could. It took some time. The roads were alarming in the fog, and the car made odd grunting noises like a young pig. As far as possible I followed the directions on Mr. Cromarty's map, sketched in with a wanton disregard for truth or distance. "Look out for the landmark," I was soon begging the others, although there were lots of disused tin mines on Bodmin, and not even the largest, dirtiest stone chimney was likely to be visible through the cottonwool fog. Nicola added to our gloom by asking if Mr. Ross (as we had inevitably named Mr. Cromarty's sad partner) had revealed whether the twenty unfortunate miners were still at the bottom of the mine, and if so could she and Stewart get a rope and go down and see? Depressed by the curious morbid buoyancy of adolescents, I replied with a firm "no".

In the event it was neither Mr. Cromarty's inadequate map, nor Mr. Ross's invisible chimney, which led us to our goal, but the distant hungry barking of Mrs. Walter Wart's dog, who through some psychic canine sense had discerned the wavering approach of his Bowser. A smell in the back of the car more full, glutinous and salty even than yesterday's sardine, showed that Culbertson had put the new tin opener to good use, and was gravely sampling a lump of something like furry brown whale. "It's not bad at all," she said, pushing down the lid again and cutting her thumb as she did so, "you could live on it if you had to."

"You could die on it, too," said Stewart, energetically removing himself from the vicinity, as far as he could.

"Be quiet, all of you. We'll miss the dog barking."

The car grunted on across the moor. Now a pleasant smell came in at the windows, the spongy damp aromatic smell of summer moorland heavily drenched by rain. The dog, which had been silent for a minute or two, struck up again nearer at hand. A stone wall appeared out of the mist—so much for Cosway's romantic fuchsia hedges—and a small unpainted wooden gate. The barking came from the direction of some decrepit buildings further to the right. The house loomed over us, looking larger than it actually was, because of fog. It had a pointed porch which housed, charmingly enough, some unexpected lilies. This was the only visible spot of charm. Bleak, undressed stone can look so very grey in mist. The roof was slate, ornamented with orange lichen: a sure sign of damp. The building was long, rectangular, all grey: even the window paint was grey, and the hessian curtains which shaded every window.

>   *"Frisch weht der Wind,*
>   *Der Heimat zu,*
>   *Mein Irisch Kind*
>   *Wo weilest du?"*

murmured Cosway. "Let us hope that Roger, or Gabriella of course, will bring something cheerful like a love potion with them."

"Two love potions," stressed Nicola.

"And one for Culbertson and the dog," added Stewart, "because by the growling I can hear...."

"Please may I give him his Bowser?" Culbertson spoke with unusual politeness, and was out of the car before anyone could stop her. We were all silent with horror, and the growl itself subsided into a suspicious kind of whuffling whine. As Culbertson approached the kennel a huge black furry shape darted out of it and began strangling on the end of a chain. Spleenish choking noises interposed with a clash of jaws and teeth replaced the whine.

"Cosway," I said faintly, "get out. Do something."

"My dear Jane, my legs have turned to water, I do assure you." To our shame nobody got out. Stewart voiced a hope that Roger was bringing anti-tetanus with him, and we were near a hospital.

"I know there's an asylum."

"We may well need it. Look at Culbertson."

"Do get out, Cosway."

"Not me."

Culbertson stood just out of range, holding the tin firm between her hands. "You're a very silly dog," she said, when the choking had choked itself to silence. "I've brought you a tin of Bowser. Lovely, lovely Bowser." She raised the tin to his nose, slid her arm round his neck, and began to ruffle up his ears. He squinted up at her with a most evil expression. His eyes were bright green and wolfish. Now he had stopped throwing himself about we could see he was an ill-fed German sheepdog.

"Culbertson," I moaned in a low voice.

"If you interrupt now he'll undoubtedly bite her," said Stewart.

The dog appeared to be considering. It was plain he had never come across a Culbertson before. He half closed his eyes, and lowered his head. Culbertson began to rub the back of his neck. "There," she crooned, "there. Nice, nice, nice little dog, aren't you? You never guessed you were a nice, nice little dog, did you?" The dog, which certainly hadn't, made a coarse moaning sound like, as Cosway afterwards elegantly put it out of child earshot, a sailor making love, and began alternately to lick Culbertson's other hand and the tin of Bowser with indiscriminate affection.

I got shakily out of the car.

"Action broken off," said Stewart following me. "Troops, the next objective is that front door. Do the keys fit, is it wired, has Mrs. Walter Wart laid a minefield by those lilies?"

With the exception of Culbertson we were soon standing in the hall. The house was not quite so formidable inside as out. It was painted white downstairs, and blue up, and had tiled floors and rush mats. There was not an excess of comfort, but at least there were some efficient-looking electric radiators, which relieved me so much that at first I failed to notice the dreadfulness of the kitchen, or even to respond badly to Nicola's cheerful call from upstairs that she had found some darling little nests of mice.

"To business," said Cosway, who had been looking rather

ashamed of himself about the dog. "Nicola and Stewart, you can unload the car. I'm going to warm up this house, first. Janey, darling, what about brewing us all up some coffee, to raise our spirits?"

"It's a good idea. I bought some milk, from the hotel." I went out into the rain, with the children. "Stewart, do you think Cully's really safe with that dog?"

"It may well be the other way round. Poor dog." Stewart went to look, and came back to report, "It's all right, a love-in has been declared, by the shape of things. They're both sitting in the kennel, sharing Bowser."

"That's all right, then, but I hope she won't want to sleep out there."

"Not Cully. She likes the warmth. I say, Jane, do you realize this dog will be a godsend? No intruders are going to like it much. If it and Cully are thick as thieves we can somewhat relax."

"I'm not quite happy, all the same. I was always taught that German sheepdogs are unreliable. Poor thing, anyway, one tin of dogmeat's not enough for an animal that size. I'm sure you're not meant to chain dogs up like that, these days, and leave them alone. It must have been here all night." I felt indignant with our landlady. "I'm going to buy beef for him every day, and take it off the rent."

We spent a busy and productive morning, for once unhampered by Culbertson. Nicola gave herself up to a zealous airing of beds. Cosway and Stewart volunteered to unpack for everyone, and I retreated to the kitchen with such stores as we had, and brought it into as much order as I could. A simple unappetizing meal was already in preparation when Cosway entered in an agitated way. He looked over his shoulder as though expecting to be followed, shut the door, and advanced on me holding out a paper. His face was almost green.

"Jane! Look at this—quietly. Where's Culbertson?"

"With Dog. What is it?"

I took the paper from him, saw that his hand shook, and glanced at the date. It was today's. "Where did you get this?"

"In Plymouth. I've just finished unpacking, and I started to have a browse through, and look what's in it——"

I was soon disturbed enough myself. Some bright young reporter, seeking a good story, had stumbled on the Seaminster murder. Even as my worry grew I appreciated the thoroughness and nose for news of his reporting. From whom had he discovered Madame Sosostris' nickname, extracted her connection with our family—and, worst of all, from where could he possibly have discovered Culbertson's involvement with the case: her amnesia, the precise place she was found?

"Cosway, do you think he knows we've come to Cornwall?"

Cosway looked dazed. He sat down at the table and stared at me. "Who—that reporter?"

"Him, too. I meant, the killer. Cosway! Do you think so?"

"It's not in the paper, about Cornwall," he said at last.

I read it again, slowly, then sat down opposite him. "It may be in the next article," I said grimly. "Besides, quite a lot of people knew I was off to Cornwall. Culbertson simply must get her memory back. Until then we'll never know if she saw anyone, although we know she heard them quarrel. Of course she might not recognize the person—still, she is the only one who can identify him or her, so far as we know, isn't she?"

"So far as we know, she is," said Cosway judicially.

"What about getting this reporter to say that she's found her memory, and saw no one?"

"That wouldn't help—if the killer knew she did."

"Did she fall—or was she pushed? And how much did she see?" I drummed on the table with my fists in frustration. "*Where* did this man get his information from?" I cast my mind back to that night, and the next day. The hospital, Dairyman—— Had I, had Susie, Erik, or anyone else, caught up in that nightmare, talked without realizing it? Had—as seemed all too likely —Nicola, or Culbertson herself? Until that young policeman had come knocking at my door there had been no need to blanket anything. We all assured each other there had been no leakage, but did we really remember quite as clearly as we might? Susie, for instance, over tea in the kitchen, had said: "That secretary of Roger's, Pamela whatshername, she's a talker." Had Roger absentmindedly talked in front of her?

"It's no good us sitting here, fussing. Come on—better call the others in for lunch. Then we'll go and report to the police. With that paper."

Cosway flapped his hands in a distraught way which reminded me of Susie. "Do we let the children see it?"

"Nicola and Stewart, yes. But Culbertson——" I thought for a moment. "I simply don't know. We don't want her getting overbold, but—— Look, Cosway, let's leave Cully out of it, till Roger comes."

"Why till Roger comes?" A sulky note had entered his voice.

There was no reasonable reply. It had been an instinctive reaction on my part.

"What can Roger do about it, that I can't?" Cosway stood up, came over and put his arms round me. He was bending his head to mine when the door into the passage flew open, and there stood Culbertson. She looked us up and down with interest.

"You do it quite differently from Roger," she informed Cosway. "He's more violent. Jane doesn't stand a chance, do you, Jane?"

"Culbertson, go away. Go back to wherever you've left Dog."

"I haven't left Dog. He's here. He got bored with the kennel, didn't you, Dog? So I've let him off, Janey, and I hope you don't mind, because he's really very sweet, he just hasn't been loved before, and——"

Sure enough, behind Culbertson loomed a shaggy shape. The calves of my legs went rigid, and started to prick. Once I was bitten by a dog, and even now my calves had not forgotten it. Dog, however, seemed prepared to accept me courteously as the provider at second hand of food. His sharp green eyes smiled at me, and he waved a dirty plume of a tail to and fro.

"There," said Culbertson, "you see!"

She was premature. I don't know if Dog was shortsighted or short-nosed, but he had evidently overlooked Cosway's presence. Perhaps the sweater with its rank sheep smell now struck some chord in his German sheepdog's heart, raised some need to bully any sheep on sight. His head went up, his ears stiffened, his tail grew fierce and pointed. The muscles of his throat began to quiver in a sinister fashion. He crouched—"Help!" cried Cosway—and launched himself. There was a thud, a crashing of kitchen chairs, and Cosway lay spreadeagled and winded on the ground, with Dog on top of him.

"Oh Dog!" wept Culbertson, "you aren't nice at all."

I launched myself less adequately on top of him. Cosway, beneath us both, struggled for breath. My hands went round Dog's throat, and squeezed, but his coat was too thick beneath his chin for him to feel me. He showed no inclination to have at Cosway, but simply lay there, his jaws open, his pink tongue lolling out. Then he turned his head to stare me in the eyes. He was not ferocious, only bothered. "What next?" he might have been saying. "What do we do now?" I began to suspect he was a bit touched in the head. Cosway had got his breath at last— his diaphragm must have been extremely strong—and was signalling me to get off.

"I'll really murder you, Culbertson," he managed to utter, and accompanied it with a look that made Dog growl and quiver.

"Stop it." I hit Dog over the forehead with the palm of my hand. "Culbertson—make Stewart open up another tin."

"I say," said Nicola's voice from the doorway, "do you know, you look just like a layer sandwich, or a tram?"

At the sound of a new voice Dog went into a thrashing motion which meant he was trying to stand up. I took an extra pull on his scruff, and we came upright together. He seemed to look on me as his oldest friend, poked his nose into the palm of my hand to lick it, and then turned to Nicola with a courteous grin of all his teeth.

"Where's Stewart, Janey?" she said. "If we can just get him accepted too, we can keep Dog in the house, can't we?"

"Do you call this acceptance?" asked Cosway angrily from the floor.

"But he hasn't bitten you—biting's the acid test."

Cosway forbore to comment, but gingerly sat up, and felt the back of his head.

"Speak to Cosway nicely," directed Culbertson, as she crouched by Dog and took him by the ear. Dog crouched, too, and fixed Cosway with his sharp green glance.

"Now, Culbertson—leave well alone. He thinks you're sicking him on. Let Cosway make friends with him quietly."

"I'm choosy about my friends. Come here, you bad animal."

Dog advanced in a neutral way. Cosway very bravely held out his hand. Dog held out his nose. Hand and nose touched, with mutual suspicion. The nose sniffed, the hand quivered slightly, Dog backed, Cosway rose, and the worst was over.

"Now," said Cosway, dusting himself down, and trying to act as though Dog didn't exist, "where has Culbertson gone, Nicola, and where's that paper?"

"She's gone upstairs, I think. What paper?"

By the time we had all rushed up a narrow wooden staircase, impeded by Dog who would come too, Culbertson had locked herself in the lavatory.

"Culbertson, come out at once. That's Cosway's paper."

"I'm busy," said a dulcet voice. "You'll upset my rhythm."

"You're reading an article that you've no business to read."

"I'll come out when I've finished."

"I'll never take you anywhere on holiday again."

Silence.

"Hello," Stewart's voice rose from the bottom of the stairs, "something's cooking on your stove, Jane. Is that old Dog up there?" He came up after us and gave Dog's tail a familiar tweak. Dog bowed his head lovingly, pressed it against my thigh, and turned a tolerant eye on his tormentor.

"Erik should apprentice them all to a zoo," said Cosway, bitterly. "Jane, I'm really very worried. Let's have lunch quickly, and then go to the police."

"About this awful danger I'm now in?" piped up the dulcet voice behind that locked door.

"About the way I need a guard from you and Dog."

hurry, feeling it would be weak-kneed to give up and return to warmth and comfort. My head was down against the rain, and next time I glanced up a bank of fog had appeared from nowhere to blot out the chimney and my way ahead. Only the sound of Dog barking his head off somewhere beyond that bank of mist encouraged me on. The others could be heard shouting, and I quickened my steps, to walk straight into the bank of mist as though it were seaspray. As I did so someone came running out of it, running unevenly because of the tussocky grass, and gasping hoarsely for breath. It was Gabriella. I gave a warning shout, but she saw me too late and cannoned heavily against me. We clutched at each other to prevent ourselves falling.

"Jane—oh, Janey! It's Culbertson—the chimney. . . ."

The icy air seemed to have got into my throat. For a second I could say nothing at all.

"She fell—oh, that bloody Dog. . . ."

"How far has she fallen——?" The words came out as though between slabs of ice. Before my eyes was a picture of a coal-black shaft leading to the burial spot of twenty men.

Gabriella seized my hand. "I'm sorry, Janey—she's on a ledge, we think. I don't know how long . . . Roger says quick, get a rope. Even get the trunk straps from the car."

Together we stumbled back up the road. A car crawled out of the mist behind us, and passed at gathering speed. "We should have—asked them—for a lift——" panted Gabriella.

"Better not—explanations—might have—held us up."

The car disappeared beyond the house, and after that we ran in silence. In spite of haste it was at least ten minutes before we had collected rope, trunk straps, and a horrified Nicola, and reached the road's nearest point to the chimney, this time by car. Dog came whining to meet us and then galloped back as fast as he had come. We found Roger and Cosway, white-faced, bending over the shaft, the sinister mouth of which gaped amongst the rubble like an entrance to the underworld. Stewart was a foot or so down, feeling with his feet for some edge of crumbled brickwork which might hold. For a moment, looking into the shaft, I could see nothing, hear nothing. Then, as the wind which had been keening round the chimney momentarily

A small "yes" floated up from the shaft. Its depths were terrifying, and I could only admire Stewart's calm. He had taken the rope from a reluctant Roger, and was now tying it professionally round himself. Then he leaned backwards over the shaft, letting the rope take all his weight, and tested it.

"You've got that O.K.," he told Cosway. "Nicola or Gabby or someone, go back to the chimney and yell out if anything goes wrong." Gabriella and Nicola exchanged a look. A yell wouldn't be much use—but they both went. Stewart took the attached trunk rope in his hand, said, "Light the candle, Jane," and let himself over the edge. I flashed the torch against the shaft wall, then deliberately looked away. I could hear Roger's and Cosway's breathing rise loud and louder from nerves. Dog lay behind them, rigid as a statue, and I realized all at once that we should have locked him in the car. . . .

After what felt like two hundred years Stewart's voice could be heard shouting up at us, "Hold it—I've reached her."

"I can't manage——"

"Yes, you can. Don't twist. *Under* your arms. . . ."

At one moment there was an awful slithering sound, which made me nearly sick: I learnt afterwards that it was only Stewart's boots scrabbling against the wall.

Then, after an age of anxious watching and listening, there was a tug on the double rope. Stewart's voice rose from the depths: "Haul away—gently. Gently."

And a moment later Nicola's voice behind me said on a note of anguish, "It's slipping——"

Roger and Cosway were both hauling on the rope. Gabriella and I grabbed it behind them. We flung ourselves down in the grass and rubble. The rope, I thought, was slipping through my fingers—and then I saw Stewart's head appear above the shaft. He was holding to the edge with one hand as Cosway and Roger finally hauled Culbertson up and over it. I rolled on to my face in the long grass, and lay there thanking God. Beside my ear Gabriella was being sick. And Dog—Dog had to be withheld by Cosway from welcoming Stewart and Culbertson so thoroughly that they might all three have ended down the shaft; and in the chaos that followed, the general relief and all the comforting of

Culbertson, he suddenly made a great roaring noise in his throat like a Caribbean hurricane and for a change flung himself on Roger and knocked him down and sat on him.

"How nice I'm not the only permanent victim after all," said Cosway.

"Horrid old Dog." The resurrected Culbertson seized hold of his muzzle and shook it to and fro. "You nearly killed me."

"What made him do it, Cully? Were you teasing him?"

"No, I wasn't. He was behind me, and I just felt a push, and I went over."

"Were none of the others near enough to stop him?"

"I don't know, I wasn't looking." Culbertson, who had held up bravely till then, although pale and shocked-looking, began to sob quietly as she had down the shaft. "Let's go home, Janey. I want to go home, now."

Later, while Gabriella and Nicola were cleaning Culbertson's green knees and feet in the bath, Stewart came quietly into my bedroom where I was doing up my face.

"Janey, are you quite satisfied that that was Dog?"

I looked at him in the glass.

"I've no reason to think otherwise. Why—aren't you?"

He frowned through his spectacles. "I simply don't know. It was misty. We were all looking for those bloody flowers. Dog was jumping around."

"Gabriella seemed quite sure it was all right."

He gave me a narrow look. "Oh, she was, was she? Well, if you ask me, no one was noticing anyone else very much."

Stewart's thoughts and now mine were almost too monstrous to be aired. "Look," I said, "we can't start believing this, without any reason at all. We'll go round the bend."

"Or perhaps down a shaft," said Stewart grimly. "You know what I think, Jane? I think Father ought to come."

I considered. "Do you seriously believe that Cosway, Gabriella or Roger, pushed Culbertson over the edge?"

Stewart looked at me miserably. "No. I can't. And yet Culbertson has had another accident, hasn't she? And no one really saw what happened. And—and look at this." He held something out to me. It was the blue sweater Culbertson had been wearing.

"What about it?"

"Look at the back."

I could see nothing unusual, except that there were green streaks where Culbertson had lurched against the wall on her way up.

"Did you see Dog's paws? They were full of filthy black mud from wallowing in the boggy bits we walked through. There are no paw marks on the back of this sweater, see?"

"It might not have come off on her, if it was a brief push."

"No? Did you see old Roger's back after Dog bounced him? Covered."

"He hit Roger fairly hard. He could have brushed against Culbertson with his shoulder."

"I've just asked her, casually, if he did, but she thinks she felt two paws."

"Or two hands, you mean. She might have been mistaken."

Stewart gave a hopeless shrug. I stared at my nails. Cosway. Gabriella . . . Roger.

"You think I ought to tell this to that Sergeant?"

His lips curved into a wry expression. "He'll ask us all in turn if we saw anything suspicious. And all in turn we shall answer 'no'. Including me. If anything odd happened, the only people who are in the clear are you and Nicola."

"Stewart——" I suddenly believed my own words, and the relief was tremendous. "You know it's all such a lot of nonsense?"

"Is it? I think it is. But I don't know. Do you think you can afford to take the slightest risk, Jane?"

I was silent. I knew what would have happened to Culbertson if there had been no ledge.

Stewart sat down on my bed and gazed at me. He looked suddenly very grown up. "Which of them is it, Janey, that you can't bear to think of it in connection with?"

In spite of his grammar it was all too clear what he meant.

The blood ran into my face.

"Cosway or Roger?"

"Stewart, that's entirely my business. . . . But even if I didn't care for either of them, it would be an appalling thing to imagine, or hint, about them—about Gabriella, too. And what possible motive could any of them have? Do you think I should ask them?" I heard my voice rise a note.

"No. I'm sure you should get Father."

"Which amounts to telling them."

"It would be reasonable enough for you not to like the responsibility of Culbertson, after this."

"Erik's too lazy to come, unless I really jolt him. And the telephone's in the hall." I was discussing it with Stewart as though he were older than I; practically leaning on him, I noticed with such amusement as I could raise.

"We're out of beer," he said reflectively. "You could nip out in the car and fetch some from Bodmin, and telephone from there. No one need know you sent for him. They could wire tomorrow to say they were coming——"

"They?"

"Susie will certainly come too. They'll have to put up somewhere, of course, and perhaps Culbertson could be with them. With any luck, nothing more will happen." He stood up. "Well? Don't you think I'm right, Janey?"

"Perhaps. Underneath, I think we've maybe got a bit hysterical."

"If anyone here is a murderer, underneath they've maybe got a bit hysterical, too."

"And if it's all glossed over?" I asked. "Do you realize what the future's going to be like? Intolerable."

"If we bring it out into the open, that's going to be intolerable. And frighten Culbertson stiff. Besides, I'm more optimistic than you, Janey. The Seaminster police struck me as pretty good; and Culbertson may recover her memory."

"I'm sure it was an outsider," I said, suddenly feeling more lighthearted. "I'm sure we've just lost our nerve."

"As you like, Janey. But ask Father to come—yes?"

"I'll go and get that beer," I said.

Chapter Seventeen

Stewart had been right, and I was thankful Erik and even Susie were coming. My brother hardly took what he thought my unlikely suspicions seriously, but he was so horrified by Culbertson's second fall that he was jerked clean out of his indolence and into a sense of responsibility. As I drove back from Bodmin with the beer I reflected that when Nicola had seen me as that overburdened woman in Proverbs she had almost shown second sight.

We all longed to ask Culbertson if her second fall had jogged her memory, but Roger said she was suffering slightly from shock, and to question her might be unwise. I contented myself with a certain amount of cosseting and insistence on her going early to bed. Nicola, at a look from Stewart, announced airily that she was dead tired herself from shock, and making waffles, and she and Culbertson went off together, while I marvelled at Stewart's effortless control. Dog also accompanied them, for he had obstinately taken to sleeping in their bedroom, against all Nicola's protests about the horrible smell of what she described as pure ripe Dog. Sometimes I suspected that he slept on Culbertson's bed, or even in it. At least, with him there, she must be additionally secure.

Stewart and I had decided that since Erik was coming there was no need to tell the police of the whole dreadful incident—not yet, at least; unless in a most casual manner, hinting that we would think it wiser if the shaft were somehow blocked because of danger to roving tourists or children. This also relieved me, for the thought of that charming though not very intellectual Sergeant questioning Gabriella, Cosway and Roger at my instigation made me blench.

So, with Erik's arrival timed for twenty-four hours ahead, or at the worst forty-eight, I had set myself to make a plan which would keep Culbertson safe and happy, as well as unsuspecting of nebulous dangers. The weather was supposed to be finer with, at the worst, sun and showers. Cosway and Gabriella spoke of taking a bus somewhere further afield like St. Ives. Stewart, I noticed, pressed Roger to go with them, but he declined, saying he would lend them his car, and stick around with me and the children in mine; he thought it would be good for Culbertson not to overdo it. Until Erik arrived I would sooner have stuck around with the children by myself, but I knew that determined look when it settled on Roger's face; for one reason or another he was set on our company, and no efforts would dissuade him. I must admit I was glad to see him part lightly with Gabriella; and after all, Stewart and Nicola would be around as well. . . .

Then I thought, with an access of horror, that this couldn't be me, thinking such cold and hideous thoughts of those I knew so well, and particularly of Roger. What ugly chance had brought someone like Madame Sosostris into our lives, with her train of squalor and violence? I remembered her inharmonious voice with its grating foreign consonants, speaking her mad words of Queens and Suns and Emperors, and Kings of Cups and Swords. . . . Danger, she had said, danger, "You must be very brave, Jane," and had spoken of another woman, and taking care. And "for you there is varning—if it is good or bad, if you have not open eyes, you not see". There had been too that spark of good, like gold shining in a mine. In a mine . . . I shuddered at my own involuntary thoughts.

It was now hard to prevent myself saying things like: "When Erik comes——" We had agreed on the telephone that he should send a telegram saying that he and Susie were taking an unexpected holiday. Yet although my brother's discretion could be relied on I winced in spirit whenever I looked at Roger and realized that the moment must inevitably come when Susie would drop some resounding and probably deliberate brick.

It's a curious fact that whenever people are expecting future good the jealous gods promptly dispatch evil on their heads—as was the case with ourselves and Madame Sosostris; whereas when nothing is expected they sometimes reverse the process, and send an undeserved bonus down instead.

It was a minor bonus, that day out with Roger and the children; but we weren't prepared to cavil at the size of bonuses. When we set out I was determined to forget all unpleasant thoughts—in the sunlight they seemed ridiculous anyway, and with Stewart present to look after Culbertson the most accidental harm could scarcely come to her. Roger himself seemed to have thrown off the withdrawn moodiness that had haunted him just lately, and we might have been back three months ago when we were happier in each other's company.

We went first to Restormel. "Positively no climbing, do you hear?" I heard Stewart murmur to an unusually subdued Culbertson, as we walked up the slope to the great round Norman keep that broods over a wooded valley of the river Fowey. People speak of castles crowning a hill, and no better description exists of Restormel, which is just like a neat, round, arrogant crown deposited on a hill top. The day was sunny, with a sky endlessly blue and streaked with tracings of mares' tails cloud that spelt turbulence in the higher atmosphere. The moat had just been mown, and there was the sweet juicy smell of fresh-cut grass.

"I wouldn't mind living up here," said Roger, lifting his arms above his head and taking in deep breaths. "A toy train in the distance, a toy river, and a minute untroubling sort of town tucked away down the valley. And all the width and trees and space to play with by oneself."

"A bit cold in winter," said the more practical Nicola. "Nothing to stop the winds sweeping up at you from all quarters of the valley, and circling round you like a witches' coven in full flight."

I stirred uneasily, disturbed by the subterranean drag at my mind that the word "witches" caused.

"What's the matter, Jane?"

"Nothing." I sat down on the grass, and Roger sat beside me and put his arm round my shoulders. I dug my fingers into the turf, the cut blades of grass and clover and birdsfoot trefoil; I lifted them to my lips and smelt the cool green tang of summer. I smiled at Roger and he smiled back: there might never have been disagreement between us. I could have wished the children miles away—and my wish was almost granted for they went running across the moat into the keep, and disappeared together, with shouts and laughter. Except for birds, and the children, and the keeper in his hut down the slope, the castle was deserted.

"Janey, we don't seem to be annoying each other today," said Roger. "What do you think about us?"

"That you've been exceptionally cross lately," I said thoughtfully. "And there's Gabriella."

Roger's arm stiffened slightly. "What about Gabriella?"

"I call that a shifty question, Roger darling."

"She's unhappy, I think, poor child. Had a lot to contend with—she's confided in me. She says it helps her."

"She could have confided in me."

"She's obviously someone who finds it easier to confide in a man. I've only been trying to cheer her up."

"Is that so? You've only been looking at her as if she were Isolde."

"I think she probably is Isolde," said Roger simply. "So what's that got to do with it?"

"As Tristan said."

"You couldn't be paying me the compliment of feeling jealous, could you, my dear love?" He lay down on his back and pulled me down beside him. "Here we are in a wide green double bed. In forty years' time here we might be in a narrow green double grave. How long before you make up your mind to jump one way or the other, Janey? How long before you know if you love me?"

"I know."

"And what about the jump?"

I thought reluctantly of Gabriella. "By the end of the summer I should know that too, shouldn't I?"

"I would have thought it might be better if——" Roger sat up, and stared down at me, and thoughtfully stroked the side of my face; and Nicola's voice behind us said, "Hello, are you sunbathing, or are we terribly in the way? Culbertson would start climbing, so Stewart brought us out again."

"You're terribly in the way," said Roger patiently.

"Sorry, but one can't help being alive." Nicola shook back her plaits and squatted down beside us. "If you want any advice, I expect we can give it. This has been going on such a long time between you both, hasn't it?"

"It's a wonder it's been going at all, with you around," said Roger.

"We can have a walk round the outside, if you want to go on stroking Jane's face in that indecisive way," offered Stewart handsomely, "but I should think we may have broken the spell a bit."

"You'd think that, would you?"

"Don't be cross, Jane." Culbertson plumped down in front of me on her knees. "Have a bullseye, unless you want to kiss Roger. He doesn't like peppermint." The round dark seal's eyes studied my face impassively.

"All this dither is just a question of your generation," said Nicola helpfully. "Now, your generation——"

"Look, Nicola, we'd sooner you didn't give us a lecture on how *your* generation is sexually aware. Let me tell you that there's never been anyone in this world from six weeks old to ninety-three who hasn't been sexually aware, see? The surface is different sometimes, that's all—but sex hasn't just been discovered, however surprised you may be to hear it."

"Why, Jane," Nicola was enchanted, "if we could just get on now and discuss your marriage, we——"

"And neither Roger nor I are going to have what you'd call this super sort of day turned into a session of group psychotherapy."

"I can't say I blame you, my dearest aunt." Stewart bent down and gave me his hand and pulled me up on to my feet. "We'll try not to conduct yours and Roger's ripe *amours* for you, snail-like though they may be. And it is a super sort of day, isn't it? There aren't words to describe it."

" 'Rarely, rarely, comest thou, spirit of delight.' "

"Is that for Jane, or the day, Roger?"

"For both, of course."

" 'And after many a summer, dies the swan,' " murmured

Nicola, gazing down into the empty moat with an adolescent's full enjoyment of melancholy. I rather wished she hadn't.

"Come along," Roger walked off ahead of us towards the castle, "I'm going to show you all the chapel which is in this guide of Jane's. A chapel will do Culbertson no end of good."

After the chapel Roger's informative zeal gained on him, and we doubled back on to Bodmin to show Nicola the stained glass at St. Neots, and then on to Minions because Stewart insisted on making everyone walk to the sinister Cheesewring, where the width of sky and view caused him to say that it made the surroundings of Restormel seem suburban; and eventually Nicola said for heaven's sake, it was too much, she could feel her agoraphobia coming on, and hunger too, and was there anything to eat?

"I'm tired." Culbertson dragged her feet. "I want to go and lie on a beach and sleep, and perhaps find somewhere with a seal, Janey?"

It was rare for Culbertson to feel tired, and I looked at her anxiously. "I don't know if you see seals at this time of year."

"We mustn't show Culbertson to a seal, it will get no end of a shock wondering where she had those legs from."

"We'd better buy some pasties, or sandwiches or something."

"Roger? You hear...."

"Very well, Janey. But I'll drive. I know this part of the world better than you, and I know just the right place for Culbertson. Not too many people, because you have to walk some way downhill to it—and uphill on the way back."

Roger's perfect place was anything between ten and fifteen miles off.

We walked down to it loaded with carrier bags and bottles acquired in Liskeard. The sun burned on our uncovered heads. The air was bleached with middle of the day light. The gulls were white harsh-voiced ghosts sailing in from the glitter beyond, to trail limp yellow legs arrogantly above us. The ground was harder here than on the inland moor, the grasses tougher and blonder. The scent of the sea was strong and salt, and transferred itself to our skins so that, pressing the back of my hand against my mouth, I could smell and taste the roasted salt. The sea itself, when we eventually climbed down to it, had small gentle waves colourless and translucent as jellyfish, which curled and hissed very quietly round rocks and pools and stones. Further out it was the colour of pure jade.

Culbertson gave a great sigh of pleasure.

"Dog would have liked this. Poor Dog." She sat down on a boulder, and methodically began to take off every stitch.

"Culbertson, be decent," said Stewart severely. "Put your pants back on. There's an obvious retired colonel over there."

Culbertson cast the colonel a scornful glance, and curled up like a nude blonde shrimp on her rock.

"I don't think he likes little girls," said Nicola, peering, "he's got a gorgeous little boy with him."

"It's probably his son," I said desperately, as a pale woman in a bright pink bather cast a glance our way. "And if you children must prove your awareness all the time, do prove it in lower voices. There was something to be said for Albert and Victoria. Culbertson, please——"

"O.K.—after I've bathed." Culbertson genially rolled off her rock into the sea, where her round biscuit-coloured face grinned back at us amongst the little waves.

Roger pulled his sweater off over his head. "Let's all change and bathe. Will you, Janey?"

"I don't know." I hesitated. "I'm hungry."

"I will, anyway." Stewart hurriedly sprang up. "Where can we change? Coming, Nicola?"

"Not me. I'm hungry, too."

"You'll have cramp if you wait till after lunch."

"I'll bathe later." Nicola pulled a carrier bag towards her, and began investigating its contents. Culbertson swam to and fro just offshore, making a weird buzzing sound to herself which drifted across the water. "Culbertson thrives on the valley of the shadow, doesn't she? What's in this paper bag?"

"If you've changed your mind, I'll go later too, Roger," said Stewart, sitting down again.

Tired in all our limbs with the blissful tiredness of too much sun and sea, we climbed uphill again. Only Culbertson seemed in her usual form, as she marched ahead of us up the steep sweet-smelling slope, with its exhausting ruts and sudden rises. As she climbed she plucked at the purple-blue scabious or threw back her blonde head to watch a hawk stooped on wings still as death against the sun. We reached the road, and were delighted to find an ice-cream van pulled up beside it. Thankfully we assuaged our sea-thirst, and then climbed into the car. At the last moment Culbertson provisioned herself with a second ration—a prodigious coloured rocket of an ice, almond green, purple and yellow.

"It will poison her." Roger took the wheel.

"Nothing could poison Culbertson. She's a reincarnation of Rasputin, didn't you know? I'll have a piece when you get to the yellow, Cully," said Nicola.

We drove home very pleased with ourselves. I leant against Roger's shoulder as he drove along the bumpy lanes, and watched the walls and hedges rush up ahead of us towards a milky six o'clock sky which contained a westering pale gold sun. The fields were fresh as limes, where their colour was undissolved by too much light. There was a gilded look about everything, and the sun had even gilded us as well.

We reached the cottage shortly before seven, not having hurried ourselves. A car stood outside it.

"I know that number," said Roger. "It's Erik's."

I was silent, stiff with self-consciousness.

"Daddy—how marvellous," said Nicola, and added differently: "Susie too, no doubt."

"I'll have to sleep with dear Cosway." Culbertson appeared to look on this as the summit of pleasure. "Nicola can muck in with Jane."

"They're staying in an hotel, I mean, they'll have to——" I realized anew how chancy this was going to be.

Stewart said nothing. He had an uncanny knack of not doing the wrong thing. All my peace and heavy sun-steeped relaxation drained away from me, leaving me tense and watchful. Roger was looking at me, although he said nothing.

"Well, hadn't we better get out? Your car's back too, Roger, so Cosway and Gabriella must be here."

"Janey——" began Roger thoughtfully; and then obviously changed whatever he was going to say into: "It's to be hoped that Dog hasn't practised his pet parlour trick anywhere near Susie. A fairly long way to come, just to drop in, isn't it?"

I went hastily into the house. Admirable Stewart said behind me: "How like Daddy—you think he's petrified for good, and then he suddenly surprises everyone."

Unfortunately I also heard Roger's mild reply: "I don't feel that he really surprises Jane very much."

Noise came from the kitchen. I opened the door, and was immediately greeted by Dog. When the dust raised by a whirling feather fan of tail had subsided I was able to take in Cosway and Erik seated at the table surrounded by cans of beer, Gabriella stirring a large pot over the stove, and Susie, immaculate, tired, and plainly very cross.

"Darling Erik!" Hypocrisy was written large across my face. "What a lovely surprise. What are you doing here?"

Susie shrugged and pulled a grimace, obviously in no acting mood. She opened her mouth, but luckily Erik forestalled her. "My dear Janey," he rose and came to kiss me more effusively than usual, "how are the children?"

"As well as can be expected." Roger spoke drily behind me. "I've not known you worry over their health before, Erik."

"But this summer has been definitely odd," murmured my brother. "Don't look so worried, Janey, we're not descending on you here. We've settled into an admirable local hotel; at least, I'm sure the beds and breakfasts will be admirable. We did send a wire to say we were taking a small holiday, and Cosway and Gabriella have opened it."

"As a matter of fact," Susie got in a word at last, "we needn't have come, because——"

"Well, we could have gone somewhere with more settled weather than Cornwall," added Erik hurriedly.

"I wonder you didn't." Roger lounged over to the table, picked up a can of beer, and started to open it. All the time he kept looking at me in an unnerving way.

"Oh Daddy," Culbertson flung her arms round him, "it is

lovely to see you, and I frightened a colonel on the beach. Hello Susie."

Susie gave her a bright cross smile. "Head quite recovered?"

"Yes, thank you. Do you like Dog?"

"Not very much."

"Oh Susie, he's a lovely Dog, we were thinking of bringing him back with us—at least, I was."

"Jane, there's such good news," Gabriella turned round from her cooking pot. "You tell them, Cosway, I must concentrate on herbs."

"Did you have a nice time?" put in Nicola.

"Lovely. We went to St. Ives. Cosway, tell Janey——"

"Erik had a pleasant surprise this morning, just as he was starting," Cosway addressed me.

"Oh? What was that?" I could feel Stewart behind me breathe warmly down the back of my neck.

"The Seaminster police rang him up." Cosway sipped his beer.

"Nothing like a call from the police to start the day well," said Roger affably. "Go on."

"In the classic phrase, a man is at the station helping them with their inquiries into Madame Sosostris' death."

"Oh." I closed my eyes. Thank God.

"Is that all you can say, Janey? Oh?" Roger was still watching me narrowly.

I put a hand on Culbertson's shoulder, and pressed it.

"What else is there to say?" I asked faintly. "Except that now Culbertson needn't worry if she doesn't get her memory back." I looked at Gabriella, at Cosway, at Roger, and it was as though a black shadow shifted away before my eyes. Except that Roger, very still, had taken in my threefold glance.

"Now we can all relax," Gabriella smiled across at me.

"And we might have gone somewhere hotter than Cornwall." Susie stood up. She was in a real rage. "Is there nowhere more comfortable that we can sit than in this small dark kitchen smelling of that awful Dog?"

"There's a sitting room, with potted palms. We usually stay in here."

"Take me there, will you, Jane? I'm stiff as a board from car seats and that endless drive. Erik never seems to feel a thing." She gave me a glance of malice, no one else was speaking in the room, and her voice rang like a bell of doom. "Poor Janey, you needn't worry any more, need you? I really do believe Janey thought one of you——" her glance strayed from Gabriella to Cosway, and then lingered heavily on Roger, "was trying to push Culbertson down that shaft!" She made a good exit, without looking back.

"It wasn't Janey," said Stewart bravely, "it was me."

I don't think anyone believed him. Gabriella looked absolutely appalled. Cosway gave his beer a faint, reflective smile, and murmured: "Hmm. I don't think I care much for that idea of yours, Janey. And I'm quite sure that Roger, when he thinks it over, will agree with me."

Chapter Eighteen

So we all relaxed, like puppets whose strings the puppet master has let fall; at least, the others did. As the party's pariah I found it less easy to lose tension. However loudly Stewart claimed responsibility for the suspicions that had been levelled at a worthy, reproachful trio I, the adult who had summoned Erik, was held solely to blame and to possess an unjust and monstrous cast of mind. Roger soon made it plain that Cosway's forecast of his reactions was correct; and if he any longer felt an urge to quote Shelley for my benefit it could only have been those stanzas that begin: "Away! the moor is dark beneath the moon," and lead on to "profoundest midnight". He seemed continually preoccupied with Gabriella. Perhaps they shared their indignation against me. Even Cosway, formerly so unwavering if a little clown-like in his love, implied it would be long before he was likely to forgive completely. While what finally embittered me was that Culbertson, after listening gravely to all sides of the question, gave it as her plain opinion that I was mad as Susie— a statement which didn't endear her to her stepmother—and that Roger should take me to Dr. Fosborough as soon as we got home again.

"——because I said it was bound to be Dog who pushed me, and Roger wouldn't do a thing like that, even if you think he might, Janey?"

"Bless you, Culbertson," I said as Roger and Gabriella moved ostentatiously out of earshot, "for making everything worse."

Since my love, rather than Culbertson, was buried in that deep shaft on Bodmin, there seemed little to be done with the rest of my holiday but work. Gabriella was unlikely now to keep her promise to be my secretary. So Stewart, who was obviously unhappy about the way things had turned out for me, volunteered instead. He came with me next day when I decided to do some research on local history, and wrote up my notes for me afterwards as we sat on a sunny headland, eating sandwiches, and hearing the gulls' hoarse crying overhead which inescapably reminded me of yesterday before this plunge into disfavour had taken place.

I would have liked to skin Susie alive, if not actually, then with my tongue, but she kept well out of my way, and was for once acting the part of a fond stepmother. At their hotel she had got into conversation with a woman head of some charitable organization for the blind, who was getting up a local show. Fired with a longing for reflected glory and gratitude, Susie offered up Culbertson's dancing. The offer was accepted with as much pleasure as even Susie could desire, only failing to win Culbertson's approval or co-operation.

"You're a selfish little beast," said Susie hotly over tea, to which Stewart and I had returned heated and dusty with our well-filled notebooks. "Don't you care at all about the blind?"

"You don't," said Culbertson accurately. "You want to preen yourself over Mrs. Haileybury rhapsodizing about your darling stepchild in a costume of dirty white swansdown that someone's daughter wore last year as Miss Muffet. Be lucky if we don't catch a pint of fleas. If you think I'm going to lower myself for a load of mucky amateurs who don't know ballet from tap, you're wrong. And I do care about the blind, but they'd do better at that mucky show with a performing bear. It's off."

"Erik!" wailed Susie. "Are you going to let her speak and act like this?"

My brother was usually unhelpful when appealed to between his children and his wife, but for once showed himself surprisingly firm on Susie's side. Mrs. Haileybury, I reflected, must have surpassing charm.

"Pack it in, Culbertson. We've promised for you, and that's the end of it. The show's tomorrow, and you've only to dance two pom-pompity little solos, which you can do on your head. Susie will take you in to try on the costume tomorrow."

Culbertson opened her mouth as though to argue. She looked

at Erik, and decided it was useless. The round seal's eyes turned on Susie with a laser beam stare.

"Thank you, Erik." Susie spoke with some dignity. "I'm glad you've decided to show a firm hand at last, even late in the day. Be ready at half-past ten, Culbertson, do you hear?"

"I hear," said Culbertson with such sweetness that I shot her a considering glance. In direct conflict with Susie she had never yet been beaten, and I was as interested to see what would happen as any *aficionado* could be in the fortune of his favourite matador. Susie saw my glance.

"And I'll thank you not to back that child up against us, Jane. We have quite enough trouble without you abetting her—and don't frown at me like that, Erik, you've got a blind spot about Jane, *and* the children too."

Culbertson went off meek as a mouse the next morning. Susie's smile was bland with victory as she drove away in my Fiat with her stepchild beside her. Two subdued eyes looked back at us under a rounded fringe of fawn hair, and a small hand waved graciously as the Queen Mother's.

"I know that look of Culbertson's," said Stewart as we went back into the house, "and if I were Susie and Mrs. Haileybury I'd get the fire hoses ready, and the tear gas out."

It was my own feeling exactly.

The morning was now grey, and overcast with heavy cloud. The others of our party had scattered to do local shopping, while Stewart and I set to work on our notes, all solid background material. At twelve o'clock a triumphant Susie returned with her captive. "It wasn't so bad, was it, Culbertson?"

"It depends what you call bad."

Susie gave a tolerant laugh. "Mrs. Haileybury was enraptured. The costume's really charming. She said Culbertson looked just like a dear little swan."

It was odd how Susie seemed bent on her own undoing.

"There's nothing wrong with the costume, Jane," said Culbertson, "except that it's too tight, and the other child who wore it had a dirty neck. We're rehearsing this afternoon, aren't we, Susie?"

"You know, she's really quite reasonable when someone puts their foot down," Susie told Erik just within earshot. Culbertson raised her meek head, and gave me a long, very sweet smile, which curdled my blood. "It's a pity dear kind Mrs. Haileybury doesn't want me to be Red Riding Hood, isn't it? I could have taken Dog along to wolf her up."

We all ate lunch together, Roger still much concerned with Gabriella, Cosway a little kinder to the pariah, and then Susie said: "Culbertson. Are you coming to watch, Erik?" And drove them away in my Fiat without asking if she might.

At half-past two, just as we were thinking of an expedition to Tintagel in Roger's car, the telephone rang.

"Hello?"

"Oh Janey," Erik's voice was worried, "is Roger around, or has he gone out?"

"He's here. Want to speak with him?"

"Please."

I hesitated. "Nothing wrong, is there?"

"Culbertson."

A cold hand seemed to slither down my spine. "Oh Erik—no!"

"Just a bug, I should think. Heaven knows where she got it, probably accounts for her unusual co-operation," said Erik with a father's natural gloom. "I don't think she's putting this on——"

"What happened?"

"She went green at rehearsal, turned dizzy, fell—— Then she was sick as a dog."

"Susie must be sick too. Hold on, I'll fetch Roger."

"There's a good girl. I suppose I may have let her dance too soon after her concussion, what do you think?"

"I should ask Roger."

They had a brief talk while I reflected that Culbertson had seemed in stalwart health. Then Roger came into the kitchen and spoke directly to me for the first time that day. "Susie was for taking her to the hotel, but it's almost as quick for them to bring her here. Since her appendix is out, I don't think we need worry too much. Probably some virus, as Erik says. We'll have to put off Tintagel this afternoon."

"Of course. I'll get her a hot bottle ready. Can I put her in your room for the present, Cosway? It's much closer to the kitchen and us all, if she's got to be in bed today."

Cosway sighed, in a pernickety way. "Oh very well, Janey." He seemed to have forgotten his hostility. "Just give her a basin, won't you, there's a sweet. And a towel over my pillow."

"And borrow Gabriella's atomizer with Fleurs de Rocaille in it." Roger grinned at his obvious dismay.

"And don't let her have that Dog on my bed," shouted Cosway after me up the stairs.

From the bedroom window I witnessed the drama of Culbertson's return. There was a pause after Erik drew up outside, and then Susie helped her from the back. For a moment Culbertson considered something. Then she nodded doubtfully, and they advanced, till her hand rose suddenly towards her mouth; she leant hard against Susie, gave a wail, and was sick in a widespread manner over her stepmother. I ran hurriedly downstairs. Roger had gone out on to the path and picked up Culbertson to bring her in. Susie, finding it harder to sustain the role of stepmother than she had that morning, followed them, her dress held as far away from her body as it would go.

"Poor Culbertson," I commiserated, "are you feeling horrible?"

Roger whisked her expertly upstairs. "She'll feel worse soon, by the look of her. Better make it two basins, Jane, if you can find them. Has anyone got a thermometer?"

No one had, till Cosway admitted to one in a drawer. "Travelling's so dangerous, even in England." He went upstairs to join the patient and her doctor, while I went to the kitchen in search of an extra bowl. I put fruit juice in the fridge, in case Culbertson got thirsty later, checked on the possibilities of invalid food, and then rejoined the others round the sickbed. Roger had just finished his examination.

"She hasn't a temperature yet, but she'll probably have one later. She's got some normal colic—normal for this sort of attack, I mean. Could be a virus. Could be she's eaten something. Did you eat anything suspect before your lunch this morning, Culbertson?"

"*Please*, Roger——" she whimpered, and was sick again.

"All out, except Jane." Roger shooed the others away before him, and followed them.

I laid Culbertson back on Cosway's pillows, remembered my promise about the towel, fetched it, and placed it under her head. I fetched a stick cologne from my bedroom, and rubbed her forehead with it. I pushed the hot-water bottle up against her feet, and sat down on the bed and held her hand. She was sick again during the afternoon, and her colour faded alarmingly. On the principle of giving her something to be sick with I fed her glucose in water at intervals. Later she revived slightly and said she felt sleepy. I left her drowsily laid out flat on her back, and went down to join the others for tea. Dog was creeping up the stairs, and when I went back later he had justified Cosway's worst anticipations.

"Dear Dog," said Culbertson weakly, "he's so companionable on a bed."

"Well—that was a very extreme way of not dancing for Mrs. Haileybury, wasn't it? I don't know who can be feeling worse—you, or Susie who has a dress and new shoes ruined."

"Roger thinks I had a virus, Janey, didn't you hear?"

"Roger hasn't had a good look in the fridge, and I have. Culbertson, did you eat half a pound of butter, half a pound of lard, six eggs, and some olive oil?"

Culbertson gave me a very weak, wry grin. "You can't think how the lard stuck, Janey. I'd awful trouble getting it down."

"None getting it up. You're an expensive child, aren't you?"

"I'll pay you back, out of my pocket money."

"No need." And then, very subversively, considering all theories of solidarity amongst grown-ups, I said: "Susie's face coming up the path was quite enough. Send the pocket money to Mrs. Haileybury for her charity."

"Are you going to give me away?"

"I ought; but this time, no."

"Susie was pretty beastly giving you away, wasn't she?"

"She was tired," I said hurriedly, sidestepping this adult acuteness. "Is there anything else you want? Something to read?"

Culbertson considered. "No thanks. I'm sleepy. Dog and I will sleep it off together."

"You look a bit too married in Cosway's bed. He's going to be cross."

She closed her eyes, and gently caressed Dog's ears. "He wouldn't be cross to a poor sick child."

As I went softly from the room I heard her voice again. "Janey? Could I have your Tarot, just to look at?"

I hesitated. "Why do you want those horrible cards?"

"They were a costly present," she said with dignity, like someone in *The Young Visiters*. "Don't want to read, but they're something to look at."

"All right. I'll bring them up to you later."

As I left the room Dog's tail was disappearing into Cosway's bed. When I reached the kitchen Cosway himself looked up at me from the rocking chair with an agonized expression.

"That Dog has disappeared. Where is he?"

"How should I know?" I evaded basely. "Where are Nicola and Stewart?"

"In the sitting room, forcing Erik and Roger and Susie to play a hard game of Scrabble. Susie is unusually subdued. Roger thinks of lighting a fire, in spite of these heaters and the fact that it's August. Not at all like yesterday, is it? Cornwall doesn't seem constant."

"Dear Cosway, what did you suppose?"

"One always hopes for miracles. Come and join me in my loneliness. I've had enough of my sister for the present."

"You've got a more forgiving nature than Roger or Gabriella," I remarked, as I fetched my notes and settled myself at the kitchen table.

"Gabriella is a wilful girl. Cela se voit."

"Roger might try to realize I was in a difficult position."

"Roger has been irritable just lately, hasn't he? He's always a person of fairly dark moods. Cela se voit, aussi." He shut his eyes and rocked to and fro in his chair. Presently he said: "How's Culbertson?"

"Virus wearing off."

"Virus, my sunburnt foot. I suppose she ate all the food that's missing from the fridge. Don't worry, I shan't tell Susie. Imagine actually eating half a pound of lard—it shows will power that I find positively unnerving."

"I know—once Culbertson decides on something, she never lets up. She's still fixated on that dreadful Tarot, in spite of what happened to poor Madame Sosostris; I've promised to take it up to her later."

"I will not have witchcraft practised in my bed. Not that kind, at least."

"You've not much choice." I bent over my work again, but I was glad of Cosway's company. This house was cheerful only when one was surrounded by people; or it may not have been the house, it may have been the moor, so large and old and desolate, that lay around it on every side, with its bogs, its tors, and—I glanced out of the window, to see why the light had grown so grey—its encroaching mists. Out there in the gathering gloom anything unhallowed might be crouching, things from the Stone Age, the Bronze Age, dark emanations, gods or demons from the dawn of time. When the telephone rang in the hall the sound was startlingly modern and out of place. I opened the kitchen door just as Erik picked up the receiver.

"Yes, it is," I heard him say. "Yes. Oh yes, Inspector——"

I leaned up against the doorpost and listened shamelessly.

"I see—I must say, I'm sorry about that—— No, she hasn't. She's in bed. Been sick. What? Oh, we think a virus."

Someone the other end spoke at length.

"It is disquieting, Inspector. Very. Sounds as though she had a lot of ugly customers—— Yes. Yes. I'll look in and see them, then. Thank you for letting me know. We'll keep in touch. Good-bye."

"What was that, Erik?"

For once my imperturbable brother seemed upset. "Seaminster police." He gave Cosway a bothered look. "We've been basking in false security, it seems they've let that fellow go."

Cosway sucked in his lip. "Not enough evidence?"

"He's convinced them he didn't do it. Still, he was a tough type, and just as certainly knew a lot about Madame S. My son Stewart is acute: she was most thoroughly engaged in blackmail, the town was full of Mr. and Mrs. Xs—they perhaps proliferated elsewhere, too." He sighed. "Jane, it's been awkward for you, I know, but I'm glad you called me. I'm sorry you've had the rough edge from Roger, though."

"And Cosway and Gabriella too," said Cosway indignantly. "Don't overlook us. Jane got the rough edge all round, and she deserved it—I'm surprised she hasn't been fingerprinting us: she and Culbertson are a pair."

"Don't be so brutal to poor Jane."

"Cosway, I wouldn't marry you or Roger for a million—*Culbertson*! Go back to bed at once, do you hear?"

We all three looked upwards at the banisters. A small figure in a long nightdress was draped across the rail, peering down at us. In the background hovered Dog's patient form.

"Was just coming down to tell you I feel sick again," said Culbertson with dignity. "And the telephone happened to go."

"I left a bell beside your bed. Mrs. Walter Wart's bell with a pisky on it."

"Was that what it was?" She raised two despairing hands. "You haven't brought the Tarot, Janey. Please, dear Cosway, fetch it for me? It's in the sitting room."

"Very well, I'll bring it," said Cosway reluctantly, and lumbered away. At a stern look from Erik, Culbertson hurried back to bed, and my brother followed me into the kitchen.

"There's another thing, Janey, which might help the police. They're looking for a small blue book—this chap they held tipped them off about it, so he was useful in a way. It's her private appointment book, and he swears blind it exists."

"Like Roger thought."

"Oh, did he? But I'm afraid——" Erik sighed—"if the killer found it, it's gone for good. Still, don't look so worried, Janey—come and play Scrabble, it will cheer you up."

He put his arm round me, and we went out into the hall where we found ourselves face to face with Gabriella. She looked a little awkward, as though we might suspect her of hovering.

"Are you not coming back to play Scrabble, Erik?" she asked quickly. "I thought I would just see how Culbertson is——"

"Cosway's there."

"Oh, then—we will all Scrabble, no?" She took Erik by the arm, and led us to the sitting room; but as soon as Cosway reappeared I crept out and went upstairs to Culbertson.

She was lying flat with her arms round Dog, as though she had successfully defended him from Cosway's wrath. "If I keep very still, Janey, that nasty feeling goes away."

"You needn't try to pull the wool over my eyes. When will you learn that other people's telephone calls are none of your business?"

"You were listening too, Jane." Her eyes were reproachful. "It does concern me if I'm going to be cloppered. And I do feel dizzy. I knocked my head again when I fell. It's not too bad, but don't tell Daddy, will you, he'll fuss?"

"I'll tell Roger. I should stay in bed, if I were you, and not go cantering round the house."

I walked over to the window, and leaned my forehead against the cold window pane. I stared out across misty Bodmin, and wished I had been born in the Bronze Age, and were dead.

"Poor Janey. You're upset. Is it Roger or Cosway?"

"Roger's been unspeakable all day." I was still angry, and forgot I was talking to a child. "But when Cosway does it too, then I really feel stabbed in the back."

"I'm sorry, Janey."

I turned round, and she was sitting up in bed looking altogether too earnest and adult. "Forget it. It doesn't matter."

"But it does. It's all because of me, isn't it? And you've always been so nice to me, Janey." The round eyes stared at me solemnly. "If there's anything I can do, just let me know."

I was moved by her comic intensity. "There won't be, I promise you that; but thanks all the same."

I stayed with her a little, and when I went back downstairs found that Erik had disengaged himself from Scrabble again—which by this time had reached a height of noisiness guaranteed to cover all absences—and drifted once more into the kitchen.

"Something else, Erik?"

"I said that I was glad you called me, Jane, but I just want to tell you that I was speaking generally. The old woman certainly had an unpleasant clientele, and I'm happier near Culbertson at present. But I've had a talk with Stewart since I came down, and he admits he panicked—well, it was a beastly situation, Cully and that chimney. Enough to put the wind up a boy of his age. I think he did very well."

"So do I."

"Yes. But I made him go back over the whole thing, as a lawyer would have done—really shook up his memory. And he doesn't think any of them could have been near enough to—to, well——"

"Push Culbertson over."

"Exactly. It must have been that damned animal of Mrs. Wart's."

"There were no paw marks on her sweater."

"If he prodded her with his nose, and leant against her——"

"It could have felt like it," I agreed.

"So I hope I've relieved your mind a little, Janey? All we have to do is guard Culbertson from strangers."

I felt laughter rise in me; bitter laughter, and choked it down. "It's certainly a relief. We won't have to worry any more, will we, about anyone here."

Erik shot me a quick look. "Things do blow over."

"What a comfort that always is, isn't it? So long as they blow in the right direction, when they do. 'Frisch weht der Wind, der Heimat zu——' "

"What's that?" He sounded startled.

"Oh nothing; a quotation from *Tristan and Isolde*, that's all."

Chapter Nineteen

No wind blew next morning, anyway. The returned fog had crept in close, wrapping the house in spirals and coils of sliding, moving, tremulous mist. Erik and Susie were cut off from us except by telephone. With Culbertson under our eyes there was no need to trouble about intruders, although we made the gesture of locking doors and latching windows. Cosway seemed to have thawed again, for which I was thankful, since Roger was taciturn, and sat reading most of the time by a fine fire in the sitting room; and Gabriella was too often with him.

Nicola and Stewart were strong and gay, which made them intolerable when housebound, and by lunch time my head had begun to ache. After the meal Culbertson joined us. With her usual resilience she had almost recovered, although she had been sick once more in the night.

"It wasn't my virus," she said, winking at me, "but I bet it was that horrible French *infusion* Gabby rushed in and insisted on giving me, last thing. I threw most of it out of the window—what I didn't throw up. Frogs and snails, and puppy-dogs' tails. *Primitive*, it was."

Gabriella went bright scarlet.

"Culbertson," I said, "that's very rude. And did Cosway say you could bundle yourself up in his dressing-gown?"

"I like it. It smells of Cosway." She threw Gabriella and Roger a disconcertingly adult glance. Evidently I wasn't the only one to suspect what they were not meant to see.

"Cully dear, I do bath," said Cosway plaintively.

"It's not a dirt smell. It's your special smell. Like Dog has a special smell. And Gabriella——" again that adult glance—"smells of Fleurs de Rocaille. Roger likes Gabriella's smell, don't you, Roger?"

"Good French scents are mostly pleasant."

"Oh. I thought you specially liked that one."

"Cully, you're not laying out that Tarot again?"—for I saw she was carefully arranging cards on the hearth—"I can't bear it."

"Just the right day for fortune-telling, with all this mist about," said Nicola ghoulishly. "Don't be so damping, Jane. Go on, Cully, tell me my disastrous future."

"I read them up in bed this morning, but I don't quite know how to make you count them out, Nicola."

"It's the ones I pick that count, isn't it? I'll just shuffle, and choose, and——" Nicola handed down the result to Culbertson, who spread them before her on the floor.

"It's good," she said professionally. "All cups and pentacles."

"That's hearts and diamonds, isn't it?" Stewart bent down to see. "Think of Nicola with a heart."

I escaped kitchenwards to make the coffee, because I still found the associations of those cards profoundly disturbing. By the time I returned Stewart and Nicola had grown bored with Culbertson's stumbling interpretations, and were engrossed in a game of vingt-et-un with matchsticks. Culbertson carefully laid out another spread. Then she left the cards fanshaped where they lay, and joined in her brother's and sister's game.

Roger stood up to take the tray from me, and remained staring down at Culbertson's cards. "What have you put out here?"

"It's something the witch used to do."

"Madame Sosostris?"

"Yes—the witch."

I looked where Roger was looking. "Does it mean anything?"

"I should think so indeed," said Culbertson, gazing up at us, and using the dulcet voice I mistrusted so well.

"There are my old friends the Black Magician and the Emperor," I said. "It's not unlike one of the spreads she did for me. But I didn't have those five cards at the end."

"It looks sinister." Nicola peered at it over her shoulder, and then returned to her own game.

"Just the day for something sinister," remarked Cosway, coming to see what we were staring at. His eyes narrowed when he saw the chosen cards. "So that was the witch's choice? Does it give you an unpleasant feeling up your spine, Jane?"

"They always do. Here's a cup for you."

"A very curious choice," said Cosway, pondering.

"Does your spine crinkle, dear Cosway?" inquired Culbertson as she grabbed up Nicola's matchsticks and added them to her hoard. She looked from him to me to Roger, and I recognized the familiar gimlet in the seal's eyes.

Cosway looked thoughtful. He said, "Not really," and then to Roger: "How about yours?"

Roger looked as though he were in a trance. He said, "What?" absently. And then, "Oh—mine always crinkles till I get my coffee. Your preoccupation with those cards is morbid, Culbertson." And stepped over them to put the tray carefully down on a table by the fire.

"Have a closer look and see what you make of it, Jane," invited Culbertson. "Those five last black cards mean death."

But Cosway was bending down to sweep the fanshaped spread together. "Here you are, Janey, I should put them right away, if I were you. I'm inclined to agree with Roger about Culbertson's state of mind. One shouldn't tempt the fates."

"With this fog outside," I stared at it and shivered, "you don't need a witch's cards or Culbertson to cause dark premonitions of some kind."

"Harm won't come to anyone Jane loves, I don't suppose," pronounced Culbertson oracularly, "because she's always been so nice——" which made Gabriella look at me and give way to what sounded like cynical laughter.

Next day the weather capriciously reverted to heat and sun. There was still a hint of haze, which made Nicola sigh with satisfaction, and say summer looked settled in at last. Erik rang early. Susie thought it would be a good day for Tintagel, and if they brought the drinks would we get a picnic ready? By the time Gabriella and I, still no warmth between us, had prepared sandwiches and food for nine hungry people my yesterday's headache had returned in full force, and the attraction of Tintagel shrunk considerably in my eyes; particularly when I compared what this trip with Roger could be like, with the one we had taken already to Restormel.

"You're not crying off, Jane!" said Culbertson, outraged.

"Yes, I am. I've got a stinking headache, which gets worse whenever I think of all that climbing up and down at Tintagel, and how hot it's going to be. I shall have a lovely day all alone in the cool."

"You'll feel fed up later, when we've gone," said Nicola.

"I can always come and join you, can't I?" Not for the first time I blessed my own car. I heard Culbertson mutter, "It's not her headache, it's Roger of course; horrible Roger——" which worried me slightly. I did not want Culbertson to be too partisan about the way things went.

Everyone tried to dissuade me from my plan—everyone but Roger, that is, who remained coolly aloof from the argument, even when appealed to by Nicola. His indifference hardened my determination not to go. Without regret I watched them all drive off twenty minutes later, Dog's head peering sadly out from the rear window of Roger's car. To my practised eye he looked as likely to be carsick as Culbertson, and I thankfully went back upstairs to bed, with a bottle of aspirin for company.

The house felt very still, and I found it harder to relax than I expected. Now and then I got off my bed and went to the window, to look at the moor rolling away to the tors and misty sky. And the moor looked back at me as though it might come in and get me. One particular tor was like a definite personage, very old and malign. "You think I don't know that you're watching me," I said aloud in a persecuted way, and returned uneasily to bed. Gradually I relaxed, and eventually fell asleep.

It was half-past two when I woke. The day was still very hot, but the sky had clouded slightly, and from the bronze-coloured clouds on the horizon and a sense of electric tension in the atmosphere I guessed thunder was approaching. The heat had removed my appetite but I went downstairs and dutifully ate the sandwiches which had been left behind for me; and then carried a soft drink out into the garden. The air felt almost unbreathable. I was too restless to settle, too restless to work, too hot to go for a walk. I sat on the stone wall, sipped my drink, and stared at the disk of sun haloed by bronze haze. My headache was better. I wished I had gone to Tintagel. Against my will I visualized Roger with Gabriella amongst the ruins. He was right about her being unhappy, I thought, but that was no reason why he should provide a cure.

The drink was finished. I went back into the house, and looked round for something to do—something unconnected with my work. Perhaps I could take a look at the linen, while there was time. Mrs. Walter Wart had specified that she was leaving hers, but she hadn't foreseen quite such an invasion, and although the children and Roger had come reinforced with towels and sleeping bags—Cosway and Gabriella had forgotten —the situation required careful juggling. I went up into Roger's room, where the linen cupboard was, to plan a campaign. It was an airing cupboard too. When it was hot weather he complained, and when it was colder he was the envy of the household.

His room was kept almost ferociously tidy. Dog had never got a foothold here. I stood in the doorway, and looked at it, and wondered if Gabriella had got a foothold, and then reproached myself for sordid mental spying. An examination showed that my fears of linen shortage were justified. I prodded hopefully at a lower shelf, but it proved to contain only stiff white tablecloths and another nest of mice. Mrs. Wart had left her laundry book here, a bit tattered and torn, with a limp leather cover. Or perhaps it was an inventory of linen. . . . I flipped it open, and frowned. It was no list of towels and pillowcases I held but a form of engagement book. Printed-in times, and scribbled-in names.

A horrid breathlessness seized me. I carried the book over to the window and looked at the cover in the light. It was a faded blue. A good many of the centre pages were loose or missing. There was no name and address inside, no absolute reason for me to connect it with Madame Sosostris. Still I knew, with inescapable, telepathic certainty, that this was her private appointment book. In Roger's room.

I turned over the tattered pages, searching for the one that could resolve the question of Madame Sosostris' death. I was eager to find it, yet afraid to see set down in the dead woman's handwriting the confirmation of my worst fears. The page, with several others, was missing. It was hard to think why a murderer should keep the book after tearing those pages out. It was mad to do it. It was mad to kill, of course; it was not logic which was likely to be a killer's strongest point—— And Culbertson, with Erik and Susie all unsuspecting, had gone for a happy day out at Tintagel. Rocks and sea caves—and headlands hundreds of feet above the innocent-seeming summer waves. I looked at Roger's clock. It said half-past three. I might be already, by some hours, too late. . . .

I went out of the room, and down the stairs, and heard my running footsteps on the tiles as though they were someone else's steps. A voice said "Jane" behind me, and amazement swung me round. My arms went out to balance the sudden pirouette. I said: "Who's there?" in a frightened voice, and was relieved when Cosway came out of the kitchen, on his face his bemused and amiable smile, his spectacles slightly askew.

I breathed "Cosway darling——" and flung myself thankfully into his arms. At first he failed to respond—from surprise, I think—and then he tightened them about me. "I must say, Janey, I didn't quite expect—— Not that I'm not glad—— But anyway I made an excuse to come back, and——" I felt his mouth on mine, and said, "Not now," and pushed him away as eagerly as a moment ago I had clung to him. Poor Cosway looked as though he were being brainwashed.

"Where's Culbertson?"

The look deepened. "With the others, of course, but——"

"Come on. We've got to go and find her—fast."

"I don't quite see——" His tone was injured and plaintive.

"Don't argue—I'll explain in the car. What are you doing, Cosway?"

"Getting the drinks. I'm not very popular with anyone because—— Well, I had to have an excuse to see how you were doing——" He was pulling a rush basket with Erik's carefully packed drinks out from behind the kitchen door.

"If you don't come at once I'll start to scream."

"Have you been sitting in the sun, Janey? It's——"

I seized his free hand and dragged him after me. "Oh Cosway, shut up and hustle——" He made vague complaining noises in his throat but I paid no attention. "Which car did you come in?"

"Roger's. Shall I let you in round the other side?" He was being brisker now.

I hesitated. "No. We'll take mine."

"Janey, I'd better drive, you appear to be so——"

"I drive faster than you, and I know my own car."

"It does seem——"

I had climbed into the driving seat. "Do get *in*."

With a resigned and fearful expression Cosway followed me, the basket of drinks rattling on his lap.

"I'd be extremely glad if you'd explain——"

"I will. I just want to get started first."

"It seems to me you are started, you very nearly had that wall—— Oh Jane, do take care, dear, didn't you see that van?"

"I missed it, didn't I?"

"By a centimetre, I should imagine——"

"Right, left? At these crossroads, I mean?"

Cosway seized my arm and screamed. An army lorry on summer exercises drove across in front of our bonnet.

"There were white lines."

"Very stupid of them to pay no attention, then."

"It was we who paid no attention." Cosway wiped the sweat from his face. "Are we going to drive all the way like this?"

"Perhaps I am driving a little fast." I slowed slightly.

"People usually drive at about thirty in these lanes."

"I'm only doing fifty now. Do you always grind your teeth when you pray?"

"Only when I'm frightened." He ground his teeth for what seemed a very long time, while I paid more attention to my driving. Eventually his breathing slowed again. "Now, Janey. Are you quite sure you haven't sunstroke?"

"Quite sure. I've found Madame Sosostris' appointment book."

There was silence, as we swayed round a corner, except for the clashing of bottles on Cosway's knees. Then he said flatly: "You can't have. Don't be stupid, Janey. The police found it long ago, in that litter bin. Don't you remember?"

"I tell you, I have." I swallowed. "And of course I remember. But this was her private one—her second string. The one the police are looking for. You know, they told Erik the other night. On the telephone."

"My love, I haven't got telescopic ears, unlike our little Culbertson."

"But Erik told us, in the kitchen—— No, of course, you'd gone upstairs to her. Anyway, I——" I took a deep breath, and said steadily: "It was in Roger's room." I felt rather than saw Cosway look at me, and I said defensively, "I wasn't taking the chance to search you all, if that's what you think. It was in the linen cupboard. I wanted some sheets."

"Yes?"

"Well, that's all. I found it."

"Is her name in it?"

"What does it matter? Hell—I don't know. I don't think so."

"Is Roger's name in it, then?" asked Cosway rather too patiently.

"No—no. Some pages have gone."

"If her name's not in it, nor Roger's, then I don't see how you know it's her book."

"I just feel it is, that's all—I know it."

He gave a sigh. "Janey. Did you bring it?"

"Yes, but you'd better not handle it. Fingerprints."

"My dear Janey, you are being dramatic, aren't you? Did you handle it?"

"Do you think I'm making this up? Yes, of course I handled it. It's in the pocket of my jeans."

"Then the original fingerprints are no doubt quite obliterated. All the same——" The bottles clanked again as he placed them on the floor of the car. He drew out his silk handkerchief. "This side?" His hand slid into the pocket, and delicately withdrew the small oblong book. He laid it on his knees.

"You see now why I'm in this tearing hurry."

"I'm not yet convinced there's a reason." Again, I could feel his gaze on my profile. "You believe this about Roger, Janey?" I felt a moment's sharp shame; for remembering Roger's foot dribbling that stone over the edge of the mining shaft; Culbertson telling me that Roger had urged her to lean from the window to pick jasmine——

I said: "I don't believe anything. I'm just hurrying." And wished there was no shadow of doubt in my voice. "It could be you. Or Gabriella."

"Throwing the blame deliberately elsewhere?" There was a note of disbelief in his voice, mixed with amusement. "Or Stewart. Or Erik and Susie. Or even you, Jane, if we count that Dog really pushed Culbertson down the shaft."

"Which is why I showed you the book, and I'm now hurrying off to push Cully over a cliff?"

"That's just sunstroke—or hysteria. Now you have to get rid of me en route."

"Cosway, you don't believe any of this, do you? You think it's funny."

"No, I don't. And particularly not if you're going to run down these three approaching children. You attend to your driving, Janey, while I examine your find. I'm sorry", he added softly, "that you think it's Roger. I'm really sorry for you, Janey."

I stared straight ahead of me, speechless. The car's wheel was wet. My hands weren't sweating from heat alone. It was like driving on and on through one of those landscapes with no end and no clear definition in bad dreams. The whole land was blonde and sepia in the light of approaching storm, all other more wholesome colour had been sapped from it. The hedges were shadows, the roads a white glare, the sky the colour of a bronzed and smoky pearl. The heat flowed round us in great dragon breaths. We approached the coast and could see the ocean stretched wide before us. Then we were driving through the village of Tintagel itself, at a speed its tourist-jammed streets scarcely allowed. The Victorian hotel called King Arthur's Castle loomed up before us on the cliff as we followed the winding road that led towards it. Beyond, stretching out into the sea, was the island which carried the ruins of Tintagel, and the crumbling cell foundations built by the cenobitic monks who had settled there.

I ran the car in behind Erik's, and we got out. I saw Cosway slide the book into his pocket, and he answered my look of inquiry by saying: "I wouldn't think it was too definite——"

"Ought you to be handling it?"

He shrugged, and put a hand on my arm, and pointed. "It's that way down—to the right. It's almost a lane, at first."

"I know. I've been here before."

Dust rose about my feet. I was wearing espadrilles bought long ago in Spain. Sometimes, when I think of it, I can still hear my feet pad-padding on that path, as I scurried on, trying only to think of Culbertson, and what might have happened. Cosway's hand took me by the wrist, and pulled me back. "You'll fall, if you keep going at that rate, Jane."

I shook him off. "We must hurry." The heat was fierce, the horizon now ominously shrouded. Behind that heat could be felt the threat of storm. I wiped my hand across my forehead, and screwed up my eyes against the glare. Just then the shrouded distance was irradiated by running cracks of light, in the same crazy pattern as cracks in dried-up mud. Thunder echoed along the rocky coast, so exposed and vulnerable. Effortless, like a sleepwalker's, my feet found the steep grassy slope and padded downwards. Cosway breathed hard behind me. Over my shoulder I said: "Where did you leave them all? Were they —together?"

"Yes. On the beach. Lazing around after lunch. I wasn't too popular because of my—er, failure with the drinks."

"There's an eating place."

"They still felt misused. And Erik and Roger wanted their own particular brands of poison for later in the day. They could have bought some in the village, if we hadn't all carefully left most of our cash at home."

As we went on down we met knots of resentful tourists trailing upwards. Distantly other knots of people could be seen hurriedly descending the alarming steps which wound down the causeway from the island. Now I could see the beach—the tide was out—and the dark tunnelled caves; the small restaurant to the left. Amongst the people defiantly ready to sit out the storm I could see no sign of the others, none of Culbertson. Then a familiar voice shouted at us from somewhere to the right, where a sloping cliff rose above the level of our heads. I raised my eyes. Gabriella and Erik were sitting high up against an outcrop of rock, in a small patch of shade.

Gabriella made a megaphone of her hands, and called, "Too —hot—on—the beach."

"Where are—the—others?" I called back, after the same fashion.

"Susie—with children—in the—tea place."

"Roger?"

Gabriella made an outward gesture of her hands, as of one who does not know, and beckoned. I shook my head.

"Go and join them," I told Cosway. "Tell them. I'll go on down."

"I'll come with you."

"But I'd like Erik to come."

"Don't you think we should hurry?" Cosway gave me a friendly push, and I stumbled on down, after waving to the others.

The sky near the horizon now had a crazy craquelure of lightning like a drying mud pack. Tintagel loomed high above us, with its nightmare steps, its ruins, its tiny people scurrying from the storm. The sky looked as though it might begin to boil above our heads.

"Like a Samuel Palmer," said Cosway appreciatively.

"What makes you think of things like that just now?" I muttered pettishly. We had reached a steep stony path with steps, and one of my ankles gave, painfully. I had to stop for a moment, nursing my foot. As I straightened up again my eyes were focussed on the rout of tourists, and then by chance I shifted my gaze upwards, and cried out.

"What is it?" asked Cosway, staring.

"Dog. I'll swear I saw Dog right right up on top. Just for a minute. And then he went over that rise. The farthest one."

"Oh nonsense, Janey. You're seeing sunspots. I don't suppose awful great animals like Dog are allowed up there."

"I tell you, I did. And where Culbertson goes, Dog goes."

Sweat that had nothing to do with the day pricked out all over me. "To get that monstrous animal up there is just what Culbertson would do. And just what your monstrous sister would be too outrageously lazy to stop. She's probably told Nicola and Stewart they can go off somewhere while she keeps an eye on Culbertson, and then went to preen herself in some bloody loo or other. Come on."

"And where have you plotted Roger in all this?" asked Cosway amiably.

"Have you got money—for the tollgate, or whatever it is?" I limped hurriedly ahead, Cosway following with what I felt was diabolical calm, feeling in his pockets for change. And then I hesitated. "Or do you think we should investigate the tea place first?"

"On the whole," said Cosway, in his most deliberate tones, as though he had just cleared his mind for a decision, "I think not."

Chapter Twenty

No one else was waiting to pay the entrance fee, and the stream of descending tourists had slowed to a trickle. The man who took our money raised his eyebrows, and gave a whistle.

"You going up there now, Madam? Had a good look at the sky?"

"I think my niece is up there." I was chafing with impatience as he slowly counted out the change.

"She'll come down, if she's any sense."

"She hasn't."

As he let us through I could feel his eyes on us in wonderment. Cosway pocketed our tickets, and we began the dizzy climb up those stone steps.

"We should have brought a mackintosh for you, Jane."

"I'm going to keep my breath for the climb."

"Don't twist that ankle again."

"No. It's fine now."

That was all we said, until we were three-quarters of the way up. At a bend where people could pass me easily, I stopped.

"Need a rest?"

"Yes."

We were silent, looking down at the sea, now so far beneath. The reflections of that terrifying sky were almost copper colour. It was sullen water, water that might have been poisoned by the waterlogged monster whose bones made islands in the misty distance. The sense of space and silence was overpowering. Even the gulls floated silently between us and the sea, as though the heat had made their hoarse constant crying dumb. I was panting, and the sweat ran down my spine. Cosway leant against the rocky wall, and said nothing. I looked at him and saw his usual placid countenance.

"Pardon me——" I stood back beside Cosway, and a woman dragging a little boy by the hand pressed past us. She also, as the attendant had, gazed at us in wonderment.

"I expect that's the last," said Cosway.

I had stopped panting. "Come on."

"Don't exhaust yourself, Janey. I don't think there's all that hurry."

"You don't believe Dog and Culbertson are up here, do you?" I couldn't mention Roger. It was essential to keep my thoughts off him as much as possible.

"I should think it's unlikely."

"Oh Cosway, you are so irritatingly placid."

"That's funny. I don't feel placid at all."

"The storm's going to be horrible, anyway. Doesn't this place feel odd in it? The others are going to think we're mad, if they see us up here."

"Perhaps they'd be right. To be struck by forked lightning on Tintagel would be a notable death."

Again we climbed in silence until high, high above the sea, and a long way even above the silent circling gulls, we reached the narrow entrance to the ruins, and could see ahead. Green paths, green enclosures. The crumbling remains of walls. To our left a tussocky climb upwards over the headland, scattered with these low grey stones. Straight ahead of us, and to our right, a tremendous drop to sea and beach. I looked across to the cliff where Gabriella and Erik had been sitting. The two of them had gone, perhaps to join Susie and the children, perhaps back to the car. I glanced up at the sky, and the storm seemed to be walking towards us with a giant's determination to crush and destroy. It was like being inside a cauldron, waiting for the water to boil.

"We're alone up here," said Cosway. "How strange it feels."

"Do we go separate ways, or stick together?"

"Stick together. And shout for Culbertson."

"Culbertson. Cully! Culbert—son. . . ."

We went hurriedly along a green path in single file, and then scrambled up over the rise to our left.

"I should think this is the way to the highest point," said Cosway.

"Culbertson?"

There was no answer. All was silence, except for a sudden rumble of thunder which seemed to shake the sky. The grey stones about us were marked with huge drops of rain, which as suddenly ceased.

I was frightened of finding Culbertson, and of not finding her. I thought of the monks, who had sat placidly praying in their cells through just such storms as this now gathering about us in its wicked strength. "And there was war in heaven: Michael and his angels fought. . . ." I had never been so conscious of how formidably immense would be eternity.

We reached what must have been the highest point, and looked around us. There was nothing to be seen but the ruins, the island, sea and sky.

"Not here," said Cosway. "You imagined things, Jane."

"There are some more ruins." I pointed south-west of where we were standing. "And all sorts of little gullies and things, as well." I made a sweeping movement with my arm. "We can't see it all from here." But I believed him right, and I had made an error. Ought we to hurry back, or go on?

Cosway was looking round him. "Awe-inspiring, isn't it?" I heard him murmur. "No legend does it justice, on a day like this. It's pure Wagner. If you lay down on that stone, Jane, and flames were lit around you, it would come straight out of *Siegfried*."

"Do quell your imagination—keep it for what we do next. Oh!" A spear of lightning had shot out of the sky, down to the surface of the sea. It was as though Wotan had hurled an answer back. "If Cully's up here, we must find her." My words were drowned in thunder. I felt as though someone had taken hold of the top of my head and shaken it. I clutched at Cosway. He put an arm round me and held me to him soothingly: "We'll find her, if she's here." And at that moment Dog's eager head appeared out of a small gully some way in front of us, and he gave a woof of astonishment and came bounding to my feet; where he bowed himself on his stomach like a very small dog indeed, shaking in a cowardly way. Unkindly I heaved him up by shifting my feet, and pushed him back in the direction he had come. "Go on, Dog—take us to Culbertson. Find Cully...."

"Find Culbertson, Dog," echoed Cosway in tones suited to the majesty of Tintagel. With his tail low and dejected poor Dog slunk ahead of us, now and then looking back over his shoulder for encouragement. As we followed him the rain began cascading in hard spearthrusts as though it would drive us flat into the earth. "Can she be still here?" I asked Cosway anxiously, blinking my eyelids in a furious attempt to see. "She can't have had another fall, can she?" Even to myself it was impossible to acknowledge a fear of where or how or why she might have fallen.

I was chafing with impatience. Dog's mind seemed not altogether on his task, he was just wanting comfort like a puppy. His backward glances lingered on us as though he hoped we would relent; but all I said fiercely was: "Good Dog—go on. Find Culbertson." And at last he suddenly turned left and made a sort of dive, and following him I found myself at the entrance to a stony tunnel, open at both ends—for what purpose, or at what age, it was impossible to tell—and here just inside the entrance sat Culbertson, curled up in a small determined shape, and gazing out with a connoisseur's pleasure at the encroaching storm. There were two empty packets of Toblerone beside her and she was just finishing a third.

Like all people who have been thoroughly scared my first reaction was peevish indignation. "You little beast, Cully! What the hell are you doing alone up here? And where's Roger?"

"Isn't it a super storm? I gave Susie the slip and came up here to see it, with Dog. Come in my tunnel," invited Culbertson, standing up and effectually blocking the entrance, while Dog fawned on her feet. "Roger went to explore that very deep cave, I think. Do you want him? I thought you really liked Cosway best."

"Let us in to shelter," begged Cosway, hunching himself against the unkind rain. "There's a lot of room in your burrow."

"Cosway!" I said suddenly, putting out a hand and catching at him. "Have you got that book safe?"

He looked startled. "Why, I hope so——" and automatically

he drew it from his pocket, held it in the shelter of his coat, and showed it to me.

"Why, you've got my little book again," said Culbertson, peering too, "my nice little book that I found in your room when I was sick ... the one I hid in Roger's cupboard."

"*You what?*"

"Don't be cross, Janey. I wasn't really stealing—and I'm sure Cosway took it first. His name's in it, but lots further on than anybody else's, and——"

I flung myself backwards against Cosway, preventing his advance. All the disconnected ideas that had been jostling each other so unproductively in my head twirled suddenly like the pattern in a kaleidoscope to fix themselves in one clear, definable, evil form. Delusion gave place to the ungovernable terror of one who stumbles suddenly on an *oubliette*, before the final and irretrievable fall. Dog bounded up and stared with puzzled eyes. Culbertson was staring too, going pale at my extraordinary reaction. In bleak and gibbering terror I could only mouth at her: "He did it then—he's the killer. Run, Culbertson. What a bloody fool I've been ... *run*. ..."

And mercifully for once she was obedient. I don't know if it was my warning, which must have seemed incredible to her, or some sixth sense operating for her protection, but she let out a terrified squawk, and turned, and ran blindly back up the tunnel, Dog following at her heels as though tied to them. Cosway struggled to free himself from my frantic grasp on his jacket, and had almost succeeded when I grabbed at him again. The impact of my body sent him reeling off balance, and flung us both to the soaking ground. All the time thunder rolled overhead, the rain battered and bewildered us, the slippery grasses betrayed our desperate attempts—his to free himself and stand upright, mine to gain a firmer foothold so that I could act as a dragging anchor on his efforts to get away. As the rain slackened for a moment before it renewed itself in tropical violence I glanced up and saw with almost unbearable relief Culbertson's backside and Dog's streak of tail disappearing over a hillock on their swift way down.

"All right," said Cosway's voice in my ear, calm, amused,

and ordinary. "You can stop fighting like a lioness to protect its cub, Janey. I couldn't catch her now, even if I wanted to. She's faster than a bird in flight."

We were face to face, breathing deeply, kneeling on the soaking grass. Between us lay that damning little book, drenched black already by the rain. I put out a hand for it, but he was quicker.

"Even if you destroy it, there's still Culbertson." I scrambled to my feet, shakily, too limp with shock to try and follow her, too unreal for fear. I wouldn't have feared for myself anyway, since there had been no time to grow accustomed to the idea that Cosway, who said he loved me, could want to harm me. It would have been the fear of someone confronted unexpectedly with the unknown. And I was filled with a sensation of utter disbelief. Roger was obviously by nature a fairly violent person, but I had never suspected it of Cosway—which was surely why I'd been so irrationally blinded.

Now he stood up too, pocketing the book, and then took hold my wrists. "Come on, Jane."

"Yes, we'd better go down," I said dully.

His answer was slow in coming: "Yes. . . . But I'd sooner talk to you alone, first."

"Not up here? In this?" The rain was still torrential. The storm centre drifted over us, towards the south. It was a fitting background for what had just taken place.

"We could shelter, for a few minutes; couldn't we?"

I looked at the sky, and back at Cosway. Everything was grotesque. It was as though I had double vision, and were seeing two of him. The Cosway I knew, and the Cosway I didn't. Yet through it all ran a thread of relief: that it was not, that it never had been, Roger. Unthinkingly I followed Cosway to Culbertson's hiding place, out of reach of the rain.

"It won't go on long. Too violent. You're soaked, Janey." He sounded so much as usual. We sat down side by side and I stared at him. Nothing he could do now could avert what was coming. Whether we climbed downwards to the others, or they climbed up to us, the result would be the same, since Culbertson had got away. It still didn't enter my head to be afraid of him. I felt pity, and horror, but not fear.

"I could never have killed Culbertson," he said, as though making some comment on the weather. "If she recovered her memory it would have been just too bad."

"You were going after her."

"That was instinctive."

"Yes?" I said drily. "Another instinct might have followed. It did once before. The shaft."

"What an appalling idea, Janey. That must have been Dog." He sounded so indignant that I hardly knew whether to believe him or not. All I could remember, with brutal clarity, was his eagerness to take the rope from Roger and go down to the ledge.

"You never really considered me as an alternative to Roger, did you? It was no flattering faith—you were just too terrified for him, to consider anyone else. You were like someone mesmerized. And then, you wouldn't really have thought it of me, would you?" He looked at me sadly, and I was almost moved by his pathos. Almost. "I'm not violent by nature, I'm not a violent man, you must believe me, Jane. I'm weak. It just happened. Things just—happened."

"Madame Sosostris—happened?"

"Other things happened. First. Things I couldn't help."

"What things?" I whispered. "What other things, Cosway?"

He was staring out into the rain. Here, at the heart of the storm, there was temporarily a strange brooding silence.

"It feels curiously timeless, doesn't it? Timeless," he murmured. "Time is, time was, time will be. . . . They used to write it on sundials. And nothing really matters if you think like that, does it? Nothing at all."

Immediately I heard an echo of Madame Sosostris in my mind: "Time, time, time! Zo stupid you take me for, eh? See now, vorse it vill be——" Now I knew whose ear had been listening then, whose tones, speaking too low for me to understand them, had been answered by her, that day at Culbertson's school.

"Things change," I said gently, "but that makes no difference to actions. She was blackmailing you, wasn't she?"

"Things happen. Actions happen," he insisted obstinately.

"No."

"Yes. You kill once, you have to kill again."

"But you said you couldn't kill Culbertson——" I stopped. My heart thudded. "Before Madame Sosostris, you——"

"Yes."

"Before that——" I stared at him, stupidly, helplessly.

He swallowed. He was blinking faster than I had ever seen him blink before, and he said savagely, with the determination of a weak person to lay the blame elsewhere, "It was all your fault."

"Mine? How could it possibly be mine?"

"For making me want to marry you."

He must be mad—— "I didn't—there was Roger. There——"

"She was never difficult till then, you see. So long as I paid up quietly, it was all right."

"She. . . . Who?"

"My wife. Alice."

"But Cosway, you divorced her, you——"

"I suppose you'd better hear it all, Jane. We haven't much time." His patience was formidable, and seemed to me now inhuman. I looked at him, and he was staring out to sea—that curious, copper-streaked sea beneath the boiling sky. Our arms touched. Imperceptibly I edged away.

"She went off, you see, and the chap couldn't, or wouldn't marry her. They lived together, and I was going to divorce her, and then—— Out of the blue, she told me. She knew something about me, something fairly discreditable. She'd no intention of being divorced. So long as I paid them an allowance, and didn't try to get rid of her, she'd keep her mouth shut. So I paid. It wasn't a lot, and she was quite reasonable till I made the mistake of telling her about you. That seemed to poke her up. No divorce and a bigger allowance. She was the biggest bitch it's been my misfortune to come across."

I remembered Susie's constant complaints about how Cosway never seemed to pay his bills or have any money. I had no idea what the "discreditable" something was, but he told me:

"Embezzlement. I called it borrowing. It was the firm I was working for when I first married. We were pretty hard up—I don't know how she discovered what I'd done, because I was never caught out, and I never told her. Perhaps she knew me too well. All my weaknesses." Although the storm was quickly moving south-west his next words were almost drowned by thunder. "I wanted to marry you badly, and Roger's chances seemed to me to be fading. Besides, you know how they say it is with blackmailers, once they start raising their demands. . . . All the same, I didn't mean to do anything, Janey; I swear I didn't." He looked at me appealingly, and made as though to take my hand. Again I edged away.

"Cosway——"

"No, let me finish. I was in London, but she threatened to come to Seaminster, to the flat. I didn't let Susie know I was going to be there that night, I was hoping to head Alice off. I knew the way she might come, and I went down on the esplanade, and waited for her."

"That woman. That woman who fell down the steps into the sea——"

"It happened, Jane. I didn't mean it, I tell you. It was an odd night. Brilliant moonlight, sudden patches of fog. The sea right in, slapping at the stairs. I waited an hour—thought she'd got lost, or perhaps gone to the flat and I'd missed her. Then I saw her coming towards me. She looked old, haggard. I knew something was wrong, as she came up. She said: 'You're looking very prosperous,' and I answered something stupid like, 'Appearances don't count.' She looked me up and down, maliciously, and said: 'That's rich, your falling for this woman, whoever she is. Well, I've news for you, too. I'm coming back to you. So you won't need a second wife, will you, Cosway?' The suspicion crossed my mind that she was going to have a child. I said nothing in the world would make me take her back."

"Go on."

"Well, we quarrelled. She was adamant. It was that, or—— She made me so angry that at one moment I raised my hand as though to hit her. She must have thought I would, for she jumped back, and slipped, and caught at the rail. She was teetering there, almost saving herself, when I—— The tide was right in. She must have hit her head on the steps when she fell.

The sea sucked her under. I didn't mean to do it, Janey. It happened. Like I told you. It happened."

Poor horrible Alice, I thought. Poor Cosway. They were both the sort of people to whom it happened. Their characters had betrayed them into that ugly meeting by the sea.

"She fell silently. She didn't scream. It was late, there was no one else down there on the esplanade. I had to think fast. Perhaps someone knew she was coming to see me. If they did, I'd had it anyway. The thing was, I mustn't rouse suspicions." He moved restlessly. "I'd driven a friend's car from London, but he thought I was going to Newbury——"

"Cosway," I interrupted. "The storm's moving on a bit, and the others will wonder . . ." particularly I thought what Roger would be wondering, if Culbertson was even now pouring out her tale.

"Well, that's it, really, Janey. No one identified her, and I thought I was in the clear."

I got to my feet, and he followed. "But there was Madame Sosostris—waiting." I remembered those sinister field glasses.

"Old bitch," he said furiously. "Inquisitive as a monkey. She must have spent all her spare time spying. Profit in everything." He took a long shivering breath, and stared at me bleakly. "The whole thing began all over again. Only worse. You can demand a hell of a lot more for murder than you can for stealing. She wanted more all the time. More. And she loved every minute of it. She wasn't afraid of me, either. Only thought me weak——" He caught himself up, and looked at me sideways. "She had a charming habit of telling my cards first—a macabre joke. That evening——"

"That evening—— You said you were going back to London, and——" I swallowed—"you didn't."

"There was her sharp paperknife lying around and——" He stopped, gave a short appalling laugh which made my spine creep. "When you've done it once, it's not so hard to do again. . . ."

"And all this time you've been around with Culbertson, like someone carrying plague; and we didn't know."

191

"And I didn't know where she was found, till I read it in the paper I got in Plymouth."

So that was why he was so agitated then! And I had thought it only concern for Culbertson.

"You didn't—so you haven't had much chance to——"

"I told you, Janey, I wouldn't." His voice sounded oddly like a child's, making excuses. A dishonest, not to be trusted, child. "I wouldn't have."

"I can't stand this any more. I just can't bear to listen to it. I'm going down. Oh, Cosway, you fool—what do you think they'll do to you?"

"Nothing."

What I had learned had had a paralysing effect. For I continued to gape at him, not taking things in at all, and repeated: "Nothing? Don't be stupid, Cosway." The rain was streaming over my face. I blinked my lids, and saw jagged lights against the copper sky. A flicker of lightning across the gloom might have been the cleft in my own brain.

"Don't you be so stupid, Janey dear." It was so much his usual manner returned that I was almost convinced of my own insanity. Sudden hot gusts of wind blew my hair across my face. I couldn't speak. I was conscious only of Cosway's eyes looking into mine, of the impersonal pity on his face. Something else as well . . . pain. "You know you've lost Roger to Gabriella, don't you, Janey? Just as well, perhaps—— Come on, then. You'd better come with me."

"Come? Come where?" I said blankly, and then, as what he meant to do dawned on me, "No, Cosway—no!" I stepped backwards, but Cosway's reactions were quicker than mine, and he grabbed hold of my wrist before I could escape.

"Yes, come with me, Janey. I'm going to throw this book off the cliff. I can't think why I ever kept it, except that looking at it made me realize I wasn't living in a crazy dream." He looked so normal, and sounded so crazy. He gave my wrist a tug, and pulled me towards him, and turned to face in the direction of the cliff. His grip was effective. He stepped forward, and willy nilly I went with him. I screamed, and tried to dig my heels into the ground. The cry was pointless in this vast space as the cry of a gull. My feet slipped over the wet grass as he continued his slow, determined walk forward. He was like someone sleepwalking, calm, withdrawn, inexorable, and the pull on my wrist dragged me after him as though I were his handcuffed partner in crime. I struggled, I struck at him desperately with my left hand, but he was far stronger than I and even so I'd never suspected Cosway of such strength. The distance between us and the cliff edge slowly diminished until we reached within yards of it. I flung myself desperately on my knees, and still Cosway dragged me forward inch by inch as I struggled and pleaded and eventually wept. And then he stood still and stared down at me.

"I only said I was throwing the book over."

"You mean us to go too." The words would hardly come. I could see over the edge now, and what I saw made my spine crawl and the palms of my hands sticky with sweat. It was still raining, but the sky was lightening, and the light flooding in over the sea's surface made the distance down look even greater than it was.

"Cosway, don't. Let me go. I can't bear it. Don't, don't don't——"

"Be quiet, Janey. I've got to . . . I couldn't go to prison, I tell you. I couldn't. Oh Janey darling, do stop crying. It will be quick. You won't know anything." He dragged me forward a few inches. I scrabbled with my toes, and only slid faster. The edge was no more than a yard or two away. I could no longer speak or scream. I was soundlessly sobbing, with a dry open mouth.

"I've got to, I've got to," Cosway was saying tonelessly. "You've got to come with me, Janey. I can't go alone."

My knees were brought up sharp against a ridge of rock. It acted as a brake on our progress. Cosway strained to pull me over it, but even through my jeans the rock's edge cut into my knees, and I remained where I was, crying now with pain, finding words, "Cosway—— Let me up. Let me—— I'll come with you. I really will. I can't come like this. It's horrible. I'll shut my eyes. I'll hold your hand. If you promise I won't feel anything——"

"Janey, I promise." Cosway walked backwards a step, and slid his hand upwards from my wrist to my palm. I got up shakily, blood from my knees trickling down inside my jeans.

"My eyes are shut——" I took a careful hold on his hand. His fingers relaxed for a second as he shifted his grip and in that second I wrenched myself free, and turned, and ran. It would have been impossible if Cosway hadn't stumbled on that ridge of rock. Even so it was hopeless. He would outrun me easily. It was only the instinct for survival that made me try to escape at all. It would have been easier to go over the cliff, than be caught a second time. It would be easier to go over the cliff, than let Cosway catch up with me on the causeway above the rocks——

All the same I ran, bent double, panting, slowed by pain and terror. The rain was deceptively gentle on my face. I was following the direction of the retreating storm. There was light on the ruins mounting up before me, the grass was lit to fluorescent green, the sky ahead the colour of bitter chocolate. It was like running in one of those dreams when you're followed by something fearful that you cannot see. I dodged and twisted, and jumped over a low stone wall that defined a cell, and ran to the altar space, and jumped the other wall which was only a few inches high. I was tiring, and even that was an effort. I climbed a ridge almost at walking pace, and heard Cosway's feet scrabble up behind me, and his hand caught and held me by the waistband of my jeans as I reached the top. I was crying without sound, and he held me firmly and calmly, and wiped my face with his handkerchief. "Oh Janey dear, that was tiresome of you, wasn't it? Don't let's have any more fighting——"

"Please, please Cosway, don't——" I twisted round and stared towards the mainland. What could Culbertson be doing? Hadn't she found them? Had she trailed all the way up to the car, thinking they were there? There was no sign of help—of Roger. We had Tintagel to ourselves. And the cliffs. And the gulls now screaming like a funeral wake as the storm passed over. Cosway pulled my hands behind my back, and pushed me in front of him towards the gilded cliff edge, this time so much further off. I fought as before, but with less strength. With Cosway behind me it was hopeless. When I tried to go down on my knees he stopped me by pressing my arms upwards. We went in a straighter line than I had come, and our progress was horribly sure. Once I managed to jerk out, "But you said you loved me," and his surprised voice answered, "But of course, that's why I'm doing this," which prevented further argument with someone plainly mad. This time I couldn't even cry—I could only watch the cliff's approach, and feel that inexorable pressure against my back, edging me nearer.

For the second time we were within yards of the drop. Desperation is supposed to produce strength; in me it produced weakness. Instead of dropping steeply away the cliff rose up giddily to meet me. Black circles edged with light rolled, turning, down tunnels of sky. I felt myself sinking towards the ground, and this time even Cosway's painful jerk on my arms failed to prevent me. He had to let me fall, or break my arms. The gulls screamed very loud, almost humanly. Cosway was trying to pull me up, as my consciousness obstinately receded. I remember knowing I would sooner go over the cliff unconscious: and then Cosway had let go, and unexpectedly moved away....

A dark shape flashed between me and the receding sky. My vision cleared suddenly, brutally. Cosway stood on the cliff's very edge, his arms spread dramatically wide. He was facing an outraged Dog. And then he made a slow backwards cartwheel dive into dizzying space. The grasses waved against an empty sky. The black circles edged with light returned.

I couldn't understand what had happened. Dog snuffed at my face, and whined.

Roger, bending over me, said, "Jane—oh darling Janey—I thought we weren't going to reach you——" and realization came back, and I began to cry. I pulled myself up on to my knees and crouched staring at the empty cliff skyline. There was nothing but silence; a pale yellow sky; the slow, hypnotic movement of clifftop grasses. I believed Cosway was calling me to crawl forward by myself over the cliff. I began sobbing hysterically to Roger, "Hold me—hold me, don't let me go," and a weird hallucination swamped me, as though someone were pulling the clifftop away from underneath me, like a carpet. If ever I had a suicidal compulsion, I had one then. Only Roger's arms round me, and Dog pressing himself real, evil-smelling and slobbering against my face, curbed my insanity.

Chapter Twenty-one

Tintagel had been nightmare. The next five days were merely the sort of bad dream continually busy with disconnected incident, where people reveal themselves as more or less than lifelike, those you know speak with the voice of doom or utter words of total irrelevance, and where the depths and shallows of the mind are irrevocably confused. Through it all I was haunted by Culbertson, as the Idée Fixe haunts the Fantastic Symphony from calm to funeral march. Culbertson prattling, Culbertson saucer-eyed, Culbertson explaining the Tarot in retrospect with ruthless logic, Culbertson shedding rivers of tears for Cosway, Culbertson sleepless from the nervous terrors she had suppressed while Madame Sosostris' killer went free. And eventually Culbertson's fears drove out mine, while Roger and Gabriella and I battled with hers. The monumental force of Susie's hysterics occupied Erik to the exclusion of all else.

"The police are so thorough," wailed Nicola on the fourth day. "Imagine sending them from Seaminster right down here! When will they let us go away, Janey? I can't bear to stay any longer—even those nests of darling mice make me feel quite sick, now I know they tore up Cosway's book, selfish beasts." For Roger, searching the linen cupboard, had come across a neat ball of that deadly notebook's pages surrounding three pink wriggling babies; while a mother's round eye regarded him reproachfully from the very page which contained Cosway's name.

"Tomorrow," I said, sitting down at the kitchen table, and wondering if I looked as pale, shivery and peculiar as I felt. "They'll let us go then, I believe, now they've found——" I put a hand over my eyes, and felt sick.

"Darling Janey, you'll feel better after the funeral," said

practical Nicola. "But that won't happen till Seaminster, will it? Whatever hymns can we possibly have?"

"I may easily feel worse. Let's talk of something else. Whose car do you want to come in—Roger's or Erik's or mine?"

"Gabriella could drive yours. You'd much better go with Roger." Nicola eyed me speculatively.

"I'd sooner drive," I said lightly. "It's therapeutic. Stewart can go with Roger. They can take Culbertson—Erik's got enough with Susie, at the moment. You and Gabriella come with me."

If Roger had been temporarily overcome with emotion on Tintagel, and afterwards, I had no intention of holding him to what might have been retrospective sentiment. For if he had wanted to resume our old relationship he had had plenty of time in the last four days. He had not. He had remained grim and unapproachable, except when he and I dealt together with Culbertson's nightmares.

Nicola was uncharacteristically tactful: "What will you do about your book, Janey?"

"Anything. Nothing. I don't know—postpone it. Leave it, and do another one—or stay in Truro later on."

"Culbertson's crying again," Stewart came into the kitchen, "double strength. She says she can never, never leave Cornwall if Dog is left behind. She says he saved your life, Janey, and we've got to take him too."

"That's something I hadn't thought of, what with the police, and feeling so sick and tearful myself. Susie will be pleased."

It seemed improbable our stay in Cornwall could end in comedy.

Mr. Ross evidently neither listened to gossip nor read the papers; but I was badly parked again, and anyway did not feel strong enough to explain why we were leaving.

"I simply can't go into it, Mr. Ross. I'm afraid we have to go, that's all. There are some very nice reporters staying locally. Why don't you ask them? Look—here's my cheque for the rest of the booking——"

I felt he hadn't heard me. "Mrs. Walter Wart will be most

upset——" His fat face puckered miserably till it seemed he might cry; his coffee was cold again. "If there were any complaints, I could easily——"

"Oh none. It was perfect, thank you. Except for the mice——"

"If that was all, the Rodent Officer could——"

"It wasn't them," I said hastily. "Look, the house was fine——"

"If you could only explain. Mrs. Wart——"

"I must hurry, I'm afraid, and——"

"A reputation for broken lettings is so——" He gazed doubtfully at my cheque. "I have your address, Miss Halliford, if anything——"

"It won't bounce," I assured him.

"Drains or beds or heating or—— But I'm sure Mrs. Walter Wart dealt with all those?"

"It was fine, just fine," I said desperately.

"People sometimes hear noises at night, but not in that house, it's——"

"It's a lovely house. The moor's dead silent. There's just one more thing, Mr. Ross. I'm taking that Dog with me. Will you kindly tell Mrs. Wart I'm writing to her?"

"You can't do that," he stared at me in outrage.

"But what else can I do?" I stared back. "He'll starve if I leave him there alone. Are you going up there three times a day to open tins of Bowser for him?"

"One tin", he said automatically, "was all Mrs. Wart specified."

"You tell her to diet if she wants to, but not to starve her animals. Three tins, and often stew as well. Does your wife cook stew?"

"I can't possibly manage it. That doesn't alter the fact that what you intend to do is theft, Miss Halliford."

"Then I can't take him, after all. Unless you can somehow explain to Mrs. Wart? No, I see it won't do. Will you come and fetch him from the car? I don't suppose he'll be a lot of trouble in your office."

Mr. Ross accompanied me to the door. He looked across the road at Dog. And Dog, who was sensitive, theatrical and intuitive by nature, looked back out of the window, and gave a sensitive snarl, like an underground train.

"He's big," said Mr. Ross in a troubled voice.

"And strong. He jokes sometimes—I mean, he likes knocking people down, for fun. But if your clients——"

"I'll explain to Mrs. Walter Wart that you didn't like to leave him behind. You're badly parked, Miss Halliford, so you mustn't let me keep you——"

Mr. Ross took me by the elbow and almost lifted me across the road. I got into the car, wound down the window, and smiled at him with all that was left of my natural smile. "Goodbye, Mr. Ross. You will explain to Mrs. Wart?"

"Oh yes indeed. But I wish you would let me tell her why——" His face puckered again.

"Tell her to read the papers."

A look of indescribable anguish crossed Mr. Ross's face. "The papers!" he cried. As I drove forward the words, "Reputation—haunting?—drains?" followed us on an agonized wail, a beseeching note of interrogation doomed to go unanswered; at least, by us.

In Seaminster I yielded to Culbertson's tearful demands and Erik's wish that I should stay temporarily at The Lime Tree House. At least it was good to be further off from where Madame Sosostris had died, and I was glad not to be too alone, since Culbertson's sleeplessness had passed to me. Of course Susie had taken to her bed, alternately bemoaning her lot as a murderer's sister, Cosway's death, and the fact that I had ever taken him up Tintagel, which she seemed to put down entirely to malice aforethought.

"I wonder if Dr. Fosborough knows it's worse to blink than to cry?" speculated Nicola. "What a worry, having her in the family. Do you think she'll take to it?"

"No, no." Stewart was engaged in articulating the bones of a dead rabbit. "Susie's dottiness comes out, whereas poor old Cosway's went in. There you have it in a nutshell."

I removed the rabbit's femur from Susie's tray, and carried her tea upstairs to a semi-darkened room. A lamp shone by the bed. A strong scent of sandalwood emanated from two half-burned joss sticks in a saucer. Susie looked very pretty, delicately made-up, wrapped in layers of frills, and propped up by four pillows. She was reading a thriller which she thrust slightly under the bedclothes as I arrived. Considerations of insensitivity crossed my mind, and were rejected after a struggle as uncharitable.

"Oh Jane, you are marvellous. You're so strong. I wish I were stronger. Haven't we any fresher cake? That one's rather stale."

"Yes, there's a new one. The children have got it. I thought you and I ought to sacrifice ourselves to Erik's household good."

Perhaps there was a little something in my voice, for she looked at me uncertainly. "I'm so sorry you've had a lot to do, Janey dear. But this has been such a blow to me. I'm sure Gabriella's being a nice helpful girl, anyway. And Roger did tell you to keep busy, didn't he?"

"Roger did."

I sat down on the bed. It fascinated me to see how far she would go. "I do feel rather tired, Susie. If you're getting up later, I might go to bed myself."

The result was predictable. Tears almost dripped out of the frills. "Oh Janey, don't be so heartless. You're so tough. You don't mind the police at all, do you? If I come down, that Inspector will start getting at me."

"Getting at you? How could he? What would he possibly get at you about?"

She was twisting the bedclothes with her pretty white hands. "About Alice. About C-Cosway. He asked and asked. It made my head feel funny. How can I possibly remember if Cosway ever said anything to make me feel worried or suspicious?" She eyed me nervously. "Well, I knew he hadn't divorced her, of course—though he would never talk about it. But I needn't have told the Inspector that, need I?"

"Susie, you were pushing me to marry Cosway!"

"Yes, well, but she was dead by then, and——"

She broke off. There was a silence louder than when the

storm ceased on Tintagel. Even tears were useless now to Susie.

"You knew it," I said. "You knew it."

"Janey, don't look at me like that! Of course I didn't know it. I mean—I never knew he pushed her! I just knew that photograph was so like her, in the papers, when I saw it. At least, it wasn't really a photograph—it was a sort of drawing. But I swear I didn't know what happened." She put out a hand and clawed at me. I moved back out of reach.

"Did you ask him if he knew it was her likeness?"

"I didn't have to, did I—— He didn't mention it. And I didn't want him to get involved with anything about that woman, if it was her, again—she never brought him any good."

"Didn't you wonder if she'd come down here to see him? Had you guessed why he was always short of money?"

"Oh Janey dear!" She gave a laugh that didn't quite come off. "Why don't you go and join the police?"

"I may well go and see them soon, if you don't tell the truth."

She turned pale. "You wouldn't! You couldn't do that to me, Janey? It had nothing to do with me, what Cosway did. And I didn't know, anyway. I only sometimes wondered how he felt free to marry you if he didn't know she was dead. And if he saw that picture, why didn't he say so, to me? Of course it might have been that he couldn't bear to talk of her—— Or it might not have been her picture at all. He could have heard from his lawyers that she died some other way—in her bed, or, or anything. I—I only *wondered* about things, Janey. That's all."

"He was shorter of money after Alice died, wasn't he?"

"Was he?" She wouldn't look at me. The sheet was in a knot.

My memory was good. "You seemed worried about his staying in England. You wanted me to go to New Zealand with him."

"Now you're just getting at me too. You've always hated me." She threw back the bedclothes and struggled hysterically out of bed. I seized her arms and forced her back.

"Sit down. Now tell me the truth, Susie. Did you suspect there was a reason Madame Sosostris could have been blackmailing him? Did you ever suspect who could have killed Madame Sosostris?"

Her eyes wandered away from mine. "No."

"You really didn't?"

She shook her head. "The police said she blackmailed lots of people." It was a hesitant whisper. "You know they did."

"But you could have been nervous about Cosway?" Now she looked at me, and in spite of her I read the cowardly evasions in her eyes.

"You had Culbertson in the house. You were trying to stifle suspicions about Cosway. *Yet* you let him come to Cornwall. Even when she fell down that shaft you said nothing."

"No one ever knows anyone else, really. That was what I thought. Honestly, Jane. The police got hold of someone else. I didn't do anything," she whimpered. Her hair had fallen forward in limp strands. The delicate make-up was smudged.

"I believe you. Sins of omission. You're passive. So passive, you shouldn't have crawled out from under your stone, Susie. If I were Erik, I'd let you crawl back there." I stood up.

She let out a wail of self-commiseration, and clutched at me. "Don't be so brutal, Janey! You mustn't tell Erik I was worried—you couldn't."

"I don't need to." I stood up and turned towards the door. "He's heard it. He's here. You stop being so indolent and try to deal with Susie as she is," I told him, as I passed him on my way out. "You deal with your whole family, too; I've had more than enough. As for Susie, she can bloody well cook stew for Dog every day of her life, from now on, as a penance." I went downstairs and shut myself away from everyone, in the drawing room. Overhead I could hear the sound of Erik's voice, interspersed with an occasional wail from Susie. Then after a time there was silence, followed by the determined shutting of a door.

I was sitting on the sofa staring blankly at an empty vase, which Susie usually kept filled with flowers, when Erik came heavily into the room. He looked as though tiredness had seeped right into him. As though he would never get it out. He stood by the fireplace and looked down at me.

"I'm sorry, Jane."

"Sorry?"

"Yes, sorry: I ought never to have let you get involved with this." He was silent for a while. I stared at the vase. Then he said: "When are you going to marry Roger?"

"I'm not going to marry him."

He sounded as though I hadn't spoken. "I don't think you could say it's been my fault—— Not knowing what Cosway was like, I mean—or, or even Susie too, for that matter." He brushed his hand across his eyes. "But the rest has been my fault."

"Erik——"

"No—let me finish. You said I was indolent, and I ought to cope with my whole family. Well, I will——"

"I was in a rage. At Susie. Not at you, really. And besides, you'll need me. Think of Culbertson with Susie, now."

"Think of Culbertson between you and Susie," he said, almost brutally. "What were you meaning to do—sit by them at meals to see if poison gets in the soup?"

"But Susie's not—not *actively* bad, Erik. She's—it's just——" I found it hard, without tactlessness, to describe what Susie was.

"Passive and self-centred," he said, unconsciously using a word I'd used to Susie.

"So you see, you must let me help while Culbertson needs me—psychologically. Erik——"

"Are you sure you don't 'psychologically' need her? Aren't you perhaps thinking of using her to put off making a decision? No, Jane, as a result of my 'indolence' you almost died. You've had enough, as you said. Marry Roger. And stay out."

I was silent. I didn't want to say, even to Erik, that it might not be my decision. Although perhaps he guessed this. I saw he assumed anyway that I'd no intention of going to America.

"I want to help," I said stubbornly.

"But I don't think you quite understand what I'm saying. I won't have you here, Janey. Not after a few weeks or so. It's bad for you. It's almost ruined your life. And I'm afraid it's almost ruined Susie's. No, Jane: for the first time in her life Susie's going to cope, and she'll never do it while you're here. I've got a responsibility to Susie too. She's going to cope if I have to stand over her on one side, and Dr. Fosborough on the other. She can do a lot better, you know, but no one ever forced her to try. And again, that's partly been my fault."

"She's unbalanced," I said. "She must be. And the children will——"

"Then Fosborough will advise on treatment."

"But Nicola at least needs——"

"Neither of the older children will be at home much, except in the holidays. Stewart's going to full board anyway, while he's doing his last A levels. And Nicola might be taken as a weekly boarder, if I asked—unless she'd sooner shift."

"Then you mean——" I stared at him. He sat down opposite me in a chair, with an air of decision such as I had never seen on him before. It struck me suddenly that this must be what he was like daily, at his office; and I remembered the words I'd carelessly spoken to Gabriella, not so very long ago: "One day, when the surface breaks, we may see a different Erik emerge."

He was talking, and I hadn't heard what he was saying.

"——and I could ask old Aggie to come and help housekeep, I really think she might like to. She's unobtrusive, and she used to have a calming influence on Culbertson."

"Masterly!" I said; I was beginning to feel annoyed. "The only snag is that dear Aunt Aggie never left London in her life—she adores it."

"She won't have to leave it. You've not been listening, Jane. I've been thinking of switching my main office to London for some time, instead of just having an agent there."

I blinked. "You'll uproot completely?"

"Wouldn't it be better? Aren't there obvious moments when a clean break——"

"Sell this house?" I looked round the room, rather sadly.

"Perhaps not. I may keep a branch office here, and whoever manages it——"

"Erik," I interrupted, "I see now why your firm got rich so fast. I never *quite* understood it before. Why the hell didn't you apply all this decisiveness to Susie long ago?"

He hesitated, and I saw he was feeling a certain loyalty to her. But he overcame it.

"She's an emotional blackmailer, and you know it," he said bluntly. "It was just too exhausting, after work. But now I'm afraid I've got something on Susie, and when two can play at that game——" He stood up. Overhead I heard a sound of footsteps. Perhaps it was my imagination that they were softly apologetic.

"But Culbertson——" I said.

"I can talk to the Principal—they take a lot of boarders there—but I think she'll certainly agree with me that Culbertson should come to London; and extend her training. Particularly after these local shocks——"

"All the same, Culbertson does need me, she—what are you laughing at?" The first smile I had seen for days was on his face.

"'Man is born free, and is everywhere in chains.' Really, Jane, how strongly you're determined to chain yourself to Culbertson, aren't you? The children will always love you, be sure of that, and they can stay with you whenever you like. But you grow up, and let Culbertson grow up. It's high time you were standing on your own feet."

"Oh——" I said, leaping up, "I've never been so angry in my life—if you think I'd bloody well come back to help uninvited in this house or anywhere else. Wh-why——"

"Go on—say it: 'After all I've done for you.'" He smiled at me kindly, reassuringly, and with a certain amusement that I found inexpressibly galling. "I fully appreciate it, Jane. Just as I fully appreciate my own laziness——"

"And if you think I've never stood on my own feet I can only say——"

"I never said that. But I do think you were unconsciously using my laziness and the children as a buffer to something more——"

"You're a loss to psychiatry. You're——"

"I've had plenty of time to think, the last few days, when Susie was on sedatives, and that scene upstairs finished it. No one is going to live in blinkers any more. I'm sorry if I've additionally shocked you." His face softened.

"You begged me to come and stay. . . ."

"Of course," he was unruffled. "Still lazy, you see. I'll need you badly—for a little while, at least. After that you'll be a welcome guest, but the family troubles are no longer your concern. Marry Roger. It's going to be a cold world otherwise, isn't it? And don't be hurt, Janey. Don't think I don't realize all you've done. But if you're honest about it you'll admit that we've all been playing along nicely into each other's needs."

"How honesty has suddenly afflicted this whole family." I sounded bitter. To my surprise my knees felt almost as wobbly as when Cosway had tried to murder me.

"I never realized before that under your indolent kind manner you have your full share of male ruthlessness, Erik. That's the second time one of my nearest and dearest has tried to push me off a cliff."

"This time I should jump," he said encouragingly. I could have hit him. He got up and came over to me and put his arm round my shoulders. I shook it off.

"I know it will be a wrench," he said soothingly, "but it was your idea, wasn't it? You were thinking of it, upstairs——"

"You know I was in a temper, you know——"

"You know bloody well I'm right, or you wouldn't be so annoyed. I'm not very good at coping with women tactfully, I'm afraid. If I were I'd have dealt with Susie long ago. Now I'm going back upstairs to her."

I was thinking that it had been different when I had said it. He read my thoughts.

"I know it's always different when one says it oneself. Darling Janey, I'm undyingly grateful to you. Go and have your tea with the children—you'll enjoy it so much better now that the family troubles are no longer yours."

Chapter Twenty-two

It was not so easy to opt out of the family troubles. More were in progress when I reached the kitchen. Nicola and Stewart had Culbertson pinned across a kitchen chair, while they alternately administered a beating. Dog sat impartially by Culbertson's head, licking her face.

"Why are you bullying Culbertson?" My voice still sounded furious. Nicola looked at me consideringly.

"Just one more," said Stewart; and released Culbertson, who came howling to me for comfort. Dog, sometimes slow in the uptake, gripped my ankle. "We weren't bullying her. We were curing her of telling lies."

"I don't lie," sobbed Culbertson, rubbing her backside. "I only didn't say I had my memory back. It came back in Cornwall."

"That was as bad as lying," said Nicola severely.

"It wasn't! It was more fun pretending I might have seen someone—I might have trapped them into action, mightn't I?"

"Indeed yes," I said grimly. "What did you see—Cosway?"

"Nothing. I couldn't see. Boring old row, she was making. I was coming away, and then I thought of dancing Juliet on the end of the balcony, and I fell downstairs." She sat on the floor, gathered the attendant Dog to her bosom, and sobbed into his muzzle.

"Cosway must have guessed she took his book, anyway," said Stewart. "If he missed it, of course."

That, we should never know. "All the same, Cully, you were a perfect fool. What a lot safer you'd have been if you told. Think of that shaft!"

"But Janey, I didn't get it back till later," she said between lessening sobs. "Not till I was dancing for Mrs. Haileybury, and fell; you remember? Do you think it was Cosway? I thought it was Dog. He does snuffle so, and I thought I heard a snuffle. Oh, I do mind about poor Cosway. He wouldn't have ever killed me really, do you think, Janey?"

"I don't know. I hope not," I said dully.

"He looked awful funny when I laid out those cards on the floor, though. Do you remember?"

"The Tarot? Yes."

"They were the ones I saw that night—you know, the ones she laid out, when I was watching."

"Culbertson!" I was startled into horror. Stewart gave a muted whistle. "You laid them out . . . were you suspecting Cosway, then?"

"Oh no, not really anyone, Janey. It was just for fun. I was pretending it was one of you, you see. Roger didn't like them either, but he doesn't like the Tarot. If I'd known what that little book meant, I might not have done it."

"I should hope not!"

"Or I might." She considered. "The thing is, what would Scotland Yard have done?"

"They wouldn't use the Tarot."

"I thought that little book was odd, but I couldn't see quite how, so I hid it."

"Very Humboldt of you, and remind me to give you an aunt's lecture against stealing, when——" I broke off. It wasn't my business now, anyway. I sat down behind the teapot. Culbertson regarded me with a compassionate seal's eye.

"Poor Janey. You didn't really love Cosway more than Roger, did you? You didn't really?"

An involuntary shudder went over me. Cliff top and sea spun before my inner eye, with a different impact to Wordsworth's daffodils. "Oh Culbertson, do be quiet——"

"Here is Roger, anyway—and Gabby too," interrupted Nicola. "Hello, Roger. We haven't seen you for days. We think Jane's got morbid. Her mind needs taking off."

"Two days, only." Roger sat down at the other end of the table and regarded me. "Why does Jane's mind need taking off?"

"I fear you're insensitive, darling Roger." Nicola sat beside him, and put her arm round his neck. "She's got withdrawn, sort of. We think Dr. Fosborough, but we're not sure. Could you do something first, do you think?"

"Possibly. I'm going out after tea. For a fairly long drive. Like to come with me, Janey?"

"Yes—— Oh, I don't know. There's a lot to do here, with Susie having such a couvade. Wouldn't Gabriella like to go?"

"No," said Gabriella in her soft voice, eyeing me solicitously. (She had been all right with me again, since Tintagel. Now I noticed that she looked much happier too, and I gloomily put it down to Roger.) "I've been out all afternoon. You go and have the evening off, Jane."

"We'll start in ten minutes, then," Roger told me.

"That's right, Roger," said Stewart. "Decision. That's how Nicola and I deal with Culbertson. Janey's character and Culbertson's are more related underneath than you think."

"Curiously enough the thought had struck me too. Do you want a coat, Janey? I should get one now."

"If we're going to be out late——" I went upstairs. When I came down again Roger was standing in the hall, watching me with a thoughtful eye and a frown.

"You look disturbed. What's the matter?"

"Nothing that probably can't be put right. Come on. The car's outside."

As we left the hall Erik and Susie were coming downstairs. Susie's face bore a look of shining righteousness, and she made towards the kitchen wearing a determined smile.

Roger drove out of Seaminster in silence. We had had little or no intimate conversation since the day of Cosway's death, and I felt restricted by a lack of ease, and also by my inner turmoil. Presently I decided to clear something up. "Roger. Are you still livid with me for having slightly suspected you?"

"I like the word 'slightly'. Are you saying now that I can't be forgiving?"

"No, of course not. Oh dear, it seems impossible to get things right. Gabriella looks happier, anyway," I said tentatively.

"Doesn't she?" He was not giving anything away. Then he looked sideways at me, and relented. "She's had a letter from France."

I was at sea. "Saying what?"

Roger smiled. "Evidently a satisfactory letter. I don't think she'll be staying over here, after all. Did she tell you, Janey, that Madame S. had a try at upsetting her, too?"

"No, she didn't—although Nicola noticed something——"

"It's old history now, but Gabby's father was found to have been a prize collaborator at one period, she reluctantly told me. Madame, in her French period, had picked up some nasty rumours . . . I think Gabriella put her firmly in her place, when cash was hinted at, later. She told the police."

"Good—I know she saw them. But was that the talk Gabby was on the run from?"

He stirred uneasily. "Look here, I'm not sure how much I ought to tell you——"

"Tell me everything," I said firmly.

"There isn't much. Just that she was almost engaged, when the boy's family found out, and got rather fierce. They were a family that suffered heavily under the Occupation, you see. And Gabby, all dignity, fled."

"Leaving no address?"

"Of course not—she's very young. Anyway, he's defied his family, and tracked her down, so—I'm glad I was able to give temporary comfort," said Roger smugly.

"*Are* you?" I felt less compunction than I might have as I said: "Do you know, I thought Madame might be blackmailing you?"

He took it calmly. "Janey, I've long realized that you see my character as black and desperate as midnight. Which crime did you pick on?"

"Cosway——" my voice stumbled on the word—"hinted that you might have killed your wife."

"Did he indeed? One thought on his mind, poor fellow. Well, I didn't, though I don't undertake not to kill the next. One doesn't have to promise, in the marriage service."

The car was now climbing steeply up towards the downs. They were large and golden in the light of the westering sun, and looked placid as primeval animals stretched out for a long siesta. The sea, the distance, the downs themselves all had the faint burnished haze of high summer.

"That fog has gone at last," said Roger, "long may it stay away. It had a most haunting presence. I shall always connect it with this town. Perhaps we've all had enough of Seaminster, like Erik. Do you approve of his new London plan?" His voice was casual—too casual. I looked at him sharply.

"It's very—comprehensive. I don't know what I think of it, yet."

There was an annoyingly bland expression on his face. "Never mind. You've been sleepwalking lately, Jane. Anyway, it will be a good plan for Culbertson, I should think. She can train with greater ease. 'If it were done when 'tis done, then 'twere well it were done quickly.' "

"You mean Culbertson's training?"

"Janey, what else could I possibly mean?"

I glanced at him again, with acute suspicion. The blandness was impenetrable . . . and he hadn't seen Erik for two days; yet the telephone had gone, and Erik had answered it, just as I had been making Susie's tea. . . .

"It's wrong for people to interfere in other people's lives," I said sternly.

"Yes, of course, darling. That's why you're not going to interfere with Susie's any more, are you? She'll feel less conspicuous in London, won't she—and she can be treated there. As a matter of fact, I think she looks much calmer already."

I stared at him. He appeared concentrated on his driving.

"Roger——"

"And speaking of London," he said conversationally, "I went there myself yesterday. To get a special licence. And I looked in on Canada House—I'm mulling over the thought of a job out there. What would you think of that?"

"Are you serious?" I felt suddenly happier.

"Perfectly. It would be handy for your American novel, wouldn't it?"

Strangely enough I no longer felt a need to object that my work couldn't be combined with marriage. Of course it could: it easily could.

"I can't be married for at least a fortnight."

"Of course not," said Roger soothingly. "But before you start airing more objections, Janey, there's something else we must do first. You know where we're going now? Up Beachy Head."

"If that's a joke it's not funny, and please don't ever, ever make it again."

"It's not a joke. I've been watching you, Janey. You come downstairs hugging the wall, you creep along the esplanade practically clutching the cottages, you turn white if someone says 'sea' or 'cliff'."

"So would you."

"Of course. That wouldn't stop me doing something about it. I'm not going to have a wife who can't take the children for a clifftop picnic by the sea."

"I can't help that. Nothing would make me set foot on Beachy Head."

"Not even with me? Do you think I want to push you off? It was seeing Cosway try to push you off that made me realize how I'd miss you."

"You are harping on it, aren't you?"

"The days are past, darling, when people muttered 'spare her that'. Haven't you read Eysenck? Well, it's Eysenck or Dr. Fosborough for you, Janey, on your present form. You might just as well take your medicine with me. You'll feel so much better afterwards, and you always liked going up cliffs."

"You're being beastly cruel. What happens if I give a loud scream and jump off? I nearly did, you know, after Cosway."

"I'll catch you," said Roger comfortingly.

"I'm not coming, and I hate you. Were you thinking of proposing up there?"

"Coward. No—I'm certainly going to wait till we come down." He drove firmly on. "I've delicately waited several days already, you may have noticed, to let you calm a bit."

"It didn't calm me. I thought you were after Gabriella...."

Beachy Head was innocently sunlit, with people strolling to and fro. The voices of children were loud and gay on the air. I felt almost normal as we reached the top, breathless within twenty yards of the edge; and then I shook increasingly.

"There. You needn't go any further."

"I wasn't going to." I stared downwards, as though hypnotized. The sea was placid, almost milk white. There was distance and space, and gulls' wings sailing between us and the sea. I clenched my hands, and cold sweat broke out all over me, and I felt sick.

"Yes, isn't it a lovely evening?" I heard Roger saying to an old man who had paused to lean upon a stick.

"It's over here they goes, if they can," said the old man ghoulishly with a cordial smile. "Two last week. Lady not feeling well?"

"Run down. The doctor's ordered her fresh air."

"Ahr—lots of fresh air up here, me dearr," said the old man, as he chuckled away on his stick, "but there's no need to go looking for it over the edge. Evenin'."

And suddenly I felt perfectly well. Hundreds of times I had walked up to cliff tops with Roger, and with the children; and only once had nightmare followed. Only once had terror, and the terrible, happened. If that dizzy old man, leaning on his stick, could bear this height, then so could I.

"All right. You win. I've stopped shaking and I'm cured. Let's go. As soon as possible I'll start looking round for someone else to marry. Someone who'll pander to my every weakness."

When we at last reached the car, Roger said: "Are you going to waste this emerald I bought you yesterday?" He took it from his pocket. "Try it on, Janey, it looks just right to me."

I put out my hand. The emerald's fire made the colours of grass and sky as dull as blotting paper.

"How could you play on my weaknesses like that, darling Roger? How could I ever give this back?"

"I thought you wanted your weaknesses considered. You've given up being boldly independent, haven't you—or dependent on those children?" We kissed, oblivious of staring hot-faced strangers. "And now I'd better feed you somewhere, Janey," said Roger. "You look exhausted. Almost greener than that emerald."

"You know, it's very odd, but when you love me you always tell me something horrible. It's only when you hate me that you say I'm looking elegant."

"Ah well, the positive and the negative, how they do get mixed. Like me loving you and making you stand on that cliff. . . . Come along, my emerald-green love. Time for food."

We reached The Lime Tree House fairly late after all, but Nicola in her night things was still hovering about the hall.

"Here you are at last. Culbertson won't go to sleep till she's seen you both. She's had a clairvoyant feeling that things were coming to a head, and she's determined to have a look at you tonight. Janey, what a wonderful ring. I'm so glad about you." Nicola preceded us upstairs, kissed Roger sleepily on the neck as the provider of the ring, and went off to bed.

Culbertson was sitting upright, waiting for us. She looked us over critically as we came through the door, and her gimlet gaze settled on my ring. She gave her radiant, deceptive smile. "Oh good, it's happened. In spite of everything else being horrible, the cards were right, weren't they? Roger must be the Emperor after all, and the Sun means it will work out, although you're both so very old, by now."

I kissed her, and persuaded her down beneath the bedclothes. The gimlet gaze swivelled upwards at Roger. "Were you talking about Canada as you came up the stairs? Are you going there?"

"Perhaps. If you'll allow it. Or perhaps somewhere nearer, like Scotland, where we can keep an eye on you." He sat down on the bottom of her bed and smiled at her.

"We're going to London, and I can train—— If you go to Canada, could I stay with you and go to the Calgary Stampede?"

"If we get there. Jane's going to be very rich and successful—aren't you, Janey?—so we'll fly you out, and find a strong young man to take you. Janey and I wouldn't be quite up to it."

"I do look forward—I say, I'll dance at your wedding if you like. You'll be glad of something to take people's thoughts off, I should think. I wouldn't mind at all, Janey," she said generously, "there are at least six ballets funnier than yours and Roger's wedding's going to be, you know. But I shall miss you so." Her voice sounded tearful.

"Oh Culbertson, don't cry."

"It's hay fever," she said fiercely, blinking. "Roger, do kiss Janey just once, properly, for me to see. After all, I'll be older than you one day."

Roger bent across, turned off the light, and kissed me soundly.

"I couldn't see," said a disapproving voice muffled by bedclothes, and then it gave a deep sigh. "Still, it must be marvellous to be kissed like that in the dark, and better still in bed——"

"Thank God for dear Aunt Aggie," said Roger, carelessly betraying himself as we groped our way towards the door. "We may find ourselves starting in Scotland, Janey, but I'm taking you far far away to somewhere like British Columbia long before Culbertson's fourteen. Erik's going to have his problems, I'm afraid. Thank God for Canada, too."